STREET GIRLS

STREET GIRLS

Linda Regan

CRÈME de la CRIME

This first world edition published 2012
in Great Britain and the USA by
Crème de la Crime, an imprint of
SEVERN HOUSE PUBLISHERS LTD of
9–15 High Street, Sutton, Surrey, England, SM1 1DF.

British Library Cataloguing in Publication Data

Regan, Linda, 1959-
  Street girls.
  1. Detective and mystery stories.
  I. Title
  823.9'2-dc23

ISBN-13: 978-1-78029-021-8 (cased)

All Severn House titles are printed on acid-free paper.

Severn House Publishers support The Forest Stewardship Council [FSC],
the leading international forest certification organisation. All our titles that
are printed on Greenpeace-approved FSC-certified paper carry the FSC logo.

MIX
Paper from
responsible sources
FSC® C018575

Typeset by Palimpsest Book Production Ltd.,
Falkirk, Stirlingshire, Scotland.
Printed and bound in Great Britain by
MPG Books Ltd., Bodmin, Cornwall.

*This book is dedicated to my husband, Brian, who is kind
enough to walk the streets with our little dog Millie, dressed in
a pink woolly coat and cap, to keep out the cold.
(No, not Brian – Millie wears the coat and cap!)*

ONE

Sunday, around midnight

Bethany fought down amusement as she watched Carly tug her tiger-print shrug over her bony shoulder, then clumsily pull out her tiny tit and jiggle it up and down as an approaching car slowed and pulled into the kerb. The driver accelerated noisily and headed toward the end of the road where he indicated, turned right and disappeared out of sight.

Bethany burst out laughing.

'It's OK for you,' Carly said indignantly. 'I'm gonna get frostbite before I get a punter at this rate.' She stamped her stiletto-heeled, gold sandals on the frosty pavement and blew warm air into her cupped hands. 'Why do we have to stand around here, anyway, freezing our fucking tits off? Who in their right mind wants to get their rocks off out here tonight? It's too fucking cold.'

'We have to,' Bethany told her. ''Yo says we have to, so we have to, an' if we don't earn for 'im, we don't get no gear, do we?'

'We ain't fucking earning for 'im, though, are we?' Carly argued. 'Cos it's too fucking cold for punters to get their dicks up, so all that's getting fucking stiff out here is our fingers and toes!'

Bethany shook her head. Carly both amused and irritated her. She was edgy too. She needed to get another punter herself; she wanted to get home and smoke a rock. 'Jade's doing a punter,' she snapped.

'Yeah, but after standing around for two and a half hours! She was blue when she got in that car. With them green streaks in her hair, she could have passed for an upside-down hyacinth.'

Bethany ignored her.

Carly stretched her needle-marked arm straight and

examined it. 'I'm going blue. I swear I bloody I am, in patches.' She looked at Bethany, horrified. 'I'm patchy blue over me arms. Any punter that comes along'll mistake me for a lump of gorgonzola. I'll offer to let 'im grape me.' Bethany was hardly listening, but she carried on wittering regardless. 'If I ever see another punter, that is.'

Bethany cast a glance at Winston Mitchell, known on the streets as Scrap, a lieutenant to Yo-Yo Reilly, leader of the Brotherhood. Scrap was supposed to be their minder. He had been standing a few yards away, watching the girls, but now, either bored with Carly's incessant rabbiting or off for another noseful of crack, he had turned his back on them and was walking towards the pub. Bethany's dark red lips spread into a wide smile. She jerked her head to indicate to Carly that their minder wasn't watching them any more. 'Light a joint,' she told her.

'This job's like being a postman,' Carly said, fumbling with the frozen clasp on her shoulder bag with cold, stiff fingers. 'It's all right if the weather's good.'

'No, it ain't like being postman,' Bethany said, wrinkling her runny nose and laughing. 'Postmen get pensions.'

'Yeah, we just get herpes and worn out fannies,' Carly agreed. She wiggled her fingers until they bent enough to open the clasp and dig inside.

Bethany watched greedily as the young girl pulled out a packet of Rizla papers. She licked her lips with delight at the thought of the joint.

'I ain't thinking as far ahead as pensions.' Carly pulled a paper from the packet and held it between her teeth as she prised open the tobacco tin. 'I just want enough to pay off some of me debt, and get me gear for tomorrow, and have a bit over for nappies and milk.'

Bethany couldn't take her eyes off the grass Carly was rolling. She could almost smell it, and she could hardly wait to taste it burning in her throat. 'Someone'll come along,' she said. 'It's like we said, trade's just slow tonight.'

'If someone's gonna come along, why's Scrap fucked off to the pub?' Carly demanded. 'He's supposed to be minding us.' She lifted a bony knee and leaned both elbows on it, then bent forward and expertly licked the paper and rolled the joint. 'He knows no fucker's about, that's why. I need to get two punters, then I'm fucking off home.'

'That could take all night,' Bethany said, eyes still fixed on the joint. 'Like you said, not many sad bastards want to drop their trousers in the back of their motors in this weather. Easier to stay at home and have a wank.'

'We'll tell 'em to stick their dicks out the window,' Carly joked. 'If my fucking fingers are anything to go by, they'll be stiff in seconds.'

Carly was so busy talking and rolling the joint that she missed the approaching car. Bethany didn't. As it slowed to cruising, she stepped into the gutter. She pulled her micro-mini denim skirt above crotch level so the driver got a good flash of the black suspenders and lace-edged black stockings on her skinny brown legs.

'Wanna taste?' she shouted to the driver.

The car carried on cruising, then turned at the end of the short road. Bethany stuck her middle finger up as it went on its way and turned back to Carly. 'You're right, mate, too cold to get their dicks up,' she said. 'They'll be asking for blow jobs, I'll bet, so stick the dosh up for a blow, and don't be haggled down.'

'I'm up for whatever they want,' Carly said, looking up from her joint. 'I'm in debt for this stuff and you know how Yo-Yo is if you don't pay on time. He never used to be like that.' She shook her head naïvely and felt the joint's weight by rolling it between her fingers. 'I ain't paid for this yet, and I'll need more. Oscar needs nappies and milk too.' She opened her bag again and started ferreting for her lighter. 'So, I gotta stay until I earn a few quid. You've already done two, and Jade's doing one. No one's offered me fuck all. Is there some-fink wrong wiv me?'

Bethany shook her head. She felt sorry for Carly. The girl was only fifteen and new to the streets. She'd have to learn fast. 'Show out to them,' she told her. 'Show them what you've got. The way you're standing, all anyone's gonna offer you is a bus pass.'

Carly was hunched over her bag, the joint now between her

teeth. She was fumbling with stiff fingers, trying to get hold of her green plastic lighter. She pulled it out and started flicking it over the end of the joint, but it wouldn't ignite. She lifted the lighter up to eye-level and checked the gas. 'Fucking bollocks,' she muttered, tossing the empty lighter over her shoulder and ferreting again in her bag until she found a packet of matches. She gripped the edge of the open book between her third and little finger and used the rest of her hand to cup around the joint to prevent the biting wind from killing the flame, and used the other hand to flick match after match, dropping each on the icy pavement as its spark flickered and died.

'Daft cow,' Bethany said shaking her head and pointing to the wall at the corner of the alley. 'Go behind there, where there ain't no wind. Then bring it back out and share it.'

Carly obeyed. Bethany followed her.

The joint caught on the third go.

Carly sucked hard and swallowed down on the smoke. Bethany watched as she breathed it slowly back out through her nose, obviously enjoying the burning rush. 'Nice,' she said more to herself than to Carly as the other girl walked back out to the pavement.

She was about to hold her hand out and ask for a drag when another car drove up the short road. Bethany quickly stepped into the gutter again and went through the routine of lifting her skirt and flashing her stocking tops. This time she rubbed her flattened hand over the front of her black lace G-string knickers.

The car slowed and the driver lowered the window. Carly and Bethany both moved toward it.

'Whatever you want,' Carly said.

'It's here for the buying,' Bethany added.

'Just say what you want, and we'll do it for you,' Carly pushed.

'Both of us, or whichever you like,' Bethany added.

'You filthy whores,' the driver yelled. 'Scum of the bloody earth, that's what you are. They should clean the bloody streets up and lock you all away. You bring this neighbourhood down with your filth. No wonder we can't sell our houses. We pay taxes to keep our streets clean. Get away from here and leave us to bring our kids up in a decent place. Dirty bitches, the lot of you.'

Bethany had whipped her knickers off and turned her back to the car window before the driver stopped shouting his abuse. She lifted her skirt high in the air so he got an eyeful of bare brown bum, suspender belt and black stocking tops. She bent forward, farted loudly, then quickly turned back to face him. As the car accelerated off Bethany stuck her middle finger up. The car turned at the end of the road, mounting the pavement and nearly collecting a motorbike parked against a wall as it swerved and sped off.

Carly had been inhaling the joint, but froze as she watched an older, more experienced whore deal with the situation. She cackled with laughter and gave herself a fit of coughing.

'Scrap should be here,' she said to Bethany. 'He's supposed to mind us, as well as take our money for Yo.'

'He couldn't mind a packet of condoms. He'll be off his head by now.' Bethany stretched out her hand and jiggled her fingers impatiently for the spliff.

Carly passed it over. Bethany took a series of quick deep drags, inhaled, and swallowed hard on the burning smoke before passing it back. Within seconds both girls were in fits of giggles.

'Fuck it, let's have another,' said Bethany.

Carly opened her purse to roll another joint but the bag slipped from her hand and fell to the pavement, its contents littered around her. Still giggling, Bethany bent to help her, examining the flavoured condoms as she picked them up and threw them back in the bag. 'Christ, where d'you get curry flavoured? And mango? And what's this cherry cheesecake? Fuck me, darlin', you've got a supermarket on offer here, what with the gorgonzola arms.'

Carly was on her hands and knees picking up her possessions. 'Fat fucking good they're doing, there's no bastard in sight.' She chucked a curry-flavoured at Bethany, still giggling, 'Just in case you don't earn enough for supper.'

Bethany had opened the cherry cheesecake wrapper and was sniffing its contents. She licked it. 'Don't taste of much cheesecake,' she said.

'It does if you have to suck for long enough,' Carly joked, opening the tobacco tin and pulling out a small handful of grass. 'And you provide the cherry flavour!'

Halfway down the second joint, the girls were sitting on the icy pavement, still chucking condoms at each other. Neither noticed the light-coloured Mercedes that had turned into the road. It slowed, then stopped alongside them.

Bethany saw it first. She nudged Carly and opened her legs at the driver, then she looked at the other girl's face. Carly recognized this john. She'd done him before. Bethany was actually glad for her. The kid was finally going to make some brass tonight.

Carly closed her bag and held the end of the spliff behind her back as the passenger window slowly descended. Bethany stood back and watched her walk to the car and lean over so her little tits would look at their best in the mauve and black corset she wore over the tattered denim micro skirt. She did it just as Bethany had taught her: enticingly, but carefully in case she had to pull her head quickly out again if the punter turned out to be a nutcase,

'Can't keep away?' Carly said, breathing spliff smoke over him. She leaned further in, pulled the tiger-print shrug down her shoulder and pushed her tongue toward him. 'Are you hard for me?' She turned back to check Bethany was listening and approving.

Bethany nodded her head to let her know she was doing good.

Carly turned back to the punter. 'Full sex or a blow job? Only it's cold and you might want a bit of help.'

Bethany closed her eyes as the man said he wanted full sex. Carly held her hand out for the crisp notes, quickly snatching them away. Bethany moved forward and took the remains of the spliff out of Carly's hand.

Carly opened the passenger door and climbed in.

Bethany dragged on the spliff as the big posh car drove off. She smiled. Carly was only a kid herself, and she already had one of her own. Bethany had two, but she was nearly twenty. Sometimes with Carly around, it felt like she'd got another one. She watched the car turn right towards the alley where they serviced all their punters, then she turned back and looked down the dark, empty road. No cars, no Scrap to keep an eye on her, not even a parked car, just an old motorbike parked against a fence at the corner. She was very alone.

The heater was on full. Carly put her ice-cold feet under the hot air as she directed him to the cul-de-sac behind the high rise where the girls took the punters. She found herself almost smiling; things weren't that bad. Her toes were thawing out already, and now she could pay what she owed for her gear and not worry about getting beaten up by Yo-Yo. Then just one more punter, and she'd have nappies and milk and a happy day ahead.

She'd done this one a few times before. He was an easy bastard, no smell, no pain, and he got it off quick enough. As far as these pathetic fuckers went he was one of the *all right* ones. Not too old either, a bit wrinkly, but then he was about forty. He had a few sad ornaments stuck to his dashboard, so he was probably desperately boring at home, but like she cared – she didn't have to talk to him. As far as a full fuck went, she'd met a lot worse, even in the short time she'd been on the game. Some of them really bloody hurt you and expected you not to mind. She'd given him the choice of condom flavours. He'd smiled and chosen the cherry cheesecake, a sure sign he was an easy bugger. While he climbed into the back of the car she quickly whipped her knickers off, then climbed over after him, let him get his trousers down and his dick out, then lowered the plastic slowly over his surprisingly massive erection. Shame, she could have charged double for a blow job, then she wouldn't have needed another punter. She climbed on top of him and turned her head to look out the window at the high rise Aviary estate. He was already moaning in delight. It was gonna be a quick one, quick and easy, same as before. He started talking excitedly in her ear; she'd not a fucking clue what he was on about, and cared less. Then she felt the hard squeeze on her buttocks. He'd done that when he was near spurting before and now he was murmuring something about her being too gorgeous to get older. She'd be off him in an instant. So this wasn't turning out to be such a bad night after all. The car was spacious and comfy too, not like the

Smart car she'd serviced a fat bugger in a few days ago. That un-smart bastard had got so wound up that he'd started leaping up and down like a frog, and she'd banged her head on the bloody roof of the tiny, tinny motor forty-odd times in the minute or so before he came. She had a headache from it all the following day. Now she'd even managed to get her drawers into her bag while this one was choosing the cherry bloody cheesecake condom. Another trick she'd learned from Beth: pretend you're interested, but get your bag open and your knickers in it, and anything else you can nick while you're about it, so you're ready for the out. She was well ready, and from the way he was crushing into her bum, so was he. She thought about the crisp notes in her bag – half her night's work. She wasn't going to nick any of the bloody plastic boats in this motor; who would buy them, for fuck's sake? No, soon as he came she was out the door and on her way back to the pavement, and she'd light another spliff to celebrate.

She started counting the windows in the high rise. He was quite noisy, so she didn't hear the door on his side of the car as it slowly opened. The first she knew was when the jogging up and down and the moaning like a demented whippet came to an abrupt halt and his dick slipped from her. That's when she turned her head back and saw the black-hooded figure. It was only inches away from her, and all she could see were two eyeholes in a black full head mask. But she couldn't miss the big, sharp knife held against the punter's throat. The voice was heavily disguised, but she recognized it.

'Get in the front, get your drawers on and close your eyes.'

She didn't argue. She scrambled hastily over the small gear-knob, assuring herself that it wasn't her that was in for it, and that she had the forty notes, so she could pay her debt and get another hit, and tomorrow would be a good day.

As soon as her shaking hands had, more or less, pulled her drawers on, she closed her eyes and stayed still as a statue. Her hearing was even clearer with her eyes tight shut. First she heard a slicing sound, like Velcro when it's pulled open, then she felt the spurting of what felt like rain but she knew was blood. Then she was forced to listen to the gurgling cries as he died. That was confirmation enough that his throat had been sliced open. Then a few agonizing seconds of somebody moving about. Carly guessed the hooded figure was robbing the punter of his wallet, but then the slicing sound started again, this time more like a butcher cutting into a joint of gristly meat. Christ, the car was beginning to smell like an abattoir. She held herself together by thinking about the joint she would roll as soon as she got out of this car and back to the road.

'Get out,' the voice commanded. 'And don't look round.'

She opened her eyes and blinked twice. She tried not to look, but she couldn't miss it; it lay right beside her on the driver's seat. Even in this bad light she knew she wasn't mistaken. On the seat lay a penis: the same sodding penis that minutes ago had been up her fanny. There it lay, limp like a lone raw sausage in a butcher's window. She felt the sudden urge to giggle as she clocked it. She quickly checked herself, stifling the impulse.

'Get out of here. You never saw this, got it?' said the disguised voice.

She nodded. 'I need me bag, it's on the floor in the back.'

Black gloved hands flung the bag at her. It was soaked in blood.

She made no comment. She scrambled out, praying the notes were still clean.

As soon as her stilettos touched the pavement, she made a run for it, clomping hastily back down the road towards the spot where she had left Bethany. Her hands shook and her teeth chattered, but not because the temperature was minus zero, or because the wind was whipping around her. It was because she had a baby to protect and she was frightened, absolutely bloody terrified and she didn't know what would happen next.

TWO

It was common knowledge in the station that DI Georgia Johnson was an insomniac. This morning she had been up since five a.m. and in her office since seven. She'd eaten breakfast in the café across the road – they did the best toasted sandwiches in South London – and was now preparing for a day at her desk.

Sergeant Stephanie Green's daughter Lucy was starting her work experience in the murder department today. And Georgia was delighted. Stephanie was Georgia's closest friend on the team, and Georgia was very fond of her daughter. Only a few months back Stephanie had confided to Georgia that Lucy was drinking too much and staying out late; and without the influence of a father, and with Stephanie's own long hours and heavy responsibilities as a sergeant in a busy South London murder division, she feared that Lucy wasn't getting the attention a girl her age needed.

For a while Georgia had been apprehensive that Stephanie might give up her job. Georgia didn't make friends easily; she was a loner, and rarely socialized with her team. She had just turned thirty, young to be a DI, but she already had her sights set higher. She wanted a DCI post, and was well aware how much tougher it was for a woman, no matter what was said about equality in the force. For a brown-skinned woman like herself she felt it was tougher still. So she chose her friends carefully, and kept her personal life away from work. She had worked closely with Stephanie Green for nearly five years now, and they had formed a strong bond. Stephanie was the one person in the murder division who Georgia truly trusted, and one of the very few whose company she would seek outside of work hours, despite the sweet wrappers and chewed bubblegum Steph left all over Georgia's immaculate car.

Stephanie had a habit of eating a lot of chocolate when
she wasn't getting regular sex; then, when there was a man
in her life, or someone she was chasing, bubblegum replaced
the chocolate as a way of cutting down on calories. You didn't
need to be a detective to work out what was happening in
Stephanie's private life, but then she had never been discreet.
At many a morning meeting Steph would perch on the edge
of her chair chewing maniacally on either gum or a chocolate
bar. Georgia often found it hard to keep a straight face as
she stood at the top of the room taking the meeting.

When Lucy showed an interest in joining the force,
Georgia was over the moon. It looked as if Stephanie would
be sticking around. So Georgia was going to do everything
she could to make sure Lucy stayed interested. The only
problem she foresaw was that Stephanie's personal life, in
particular her high sex drive, would have to be moderated
with her daughter around. No more getting off her face
and shagging whoever happened to be available after a good
result on a case; Sergeant Stephanie Green would have to
learn to be circumspect. Her behaviour had never been a
great example for new young police cadets, let alone her
own daughter, but her sharp detective skills and fierce loyalty
amply compensated.

Stephanie also struggled with punctuality, so Georgia
wasn't surprised when she and Lucy rushed in at quarter
past eight. Stephanie had bits of jam stuck in her shoulder-
length flyaway mouse-coloured hair, and her clothes looked
as if she'd pressed them with a cold iron. Lucy's long blonde
hair was tied neatly in a ponytail, and her T-shirt and jeans
were pristine.

'You've had breakfast then?' Georgia teased, nodding
at Stephanie's hair. Georgia had brought them Starbucks
coffee, which Lucy refused, and a leaflet on the police dog-
training kennels, where she intended to send the girl that
afternoon.

Lucy flicked through the leaflet as Stephanie picked the jam
out of her hair and Georgia sipped her latte.

A minute later there was a knock on the door, and trainee
DC Hank Peacock poked his head in.

'Guv, a body in a car in a street near to the Aviary estate,' he said. 'Uniform phoned it in. I thought you might want to take a look. It sounds pretty horrific.'

Georgia flicked a glance at Lucy. The girl looked interested. 'In what way?' Georgia asked the young trainee.

'The penis has been cut away, from what I hear, ma'am,' the trainee detective answered. His cheeks reddened as his eyes met Lucy's.

Georgia looked at Lucy. The girl hadn't batted an eyelid. She had the makings of a good copper, Georgia decided. Stephanie was looking at Lucy too, and it was plain the same thought had occurred to her.

Hank Peacock was still hovering in the doorway, and still blushing. The tall, skinny trainee DC had been nicknamed Broom, partly because of his build and partly because he was the new boy.

'Where exactly near the Aviary?' Georgia asked him.

'On Tidal Lane, at the corner of the alley leading to the back of the Aviary estate.'

'Hooker's paradise.' Georgia nodded. 'Someone on the wrong patch, or someone didn't pay.'

'Or a trophy killing?' Stephanie suggested.

'Or whatever; but penny to the penis it'll be to do with the hookers, so the pimps will know about it.' She stood up. 'We're going to take a look at this one. You too, Peacock. That area is Stuart Reilly's patch. Remember him?' she said to Stephanie. 'Street name Yo-Yo? Runs the Brotherhood gang. And we all know sadism is his favourite pastime.'

'How could I forget?' Stephanie said, pushing her chair back and grabbing her coat.

'Can I come?' Lucy asked.

Stephanie turned to Georgia for approval.

Georgia looked thoughtful, then she nodded. 'Yes, you can. It'll be a baptism of fire, but it'll be good for you. But if you get in the way, I'll send you back here to file papers and do the coffee run for the rest of the day. So just make notes and do exactly as you're told, got it?'

Lucy saluted smartly. 'Yes, ma'am,' she said.

*　*　*

The street was already cordoned off with blue and white crime scene tape as they drew up and parked near the entrance. Two uniformed constables, a male and a female, stood beside the cordon to keep the public away.

'Get forensics to show you how to cover yourself properly so you don't contaminate the scene,' Georgia told Lucy. She signed the book that the male officer handed her and took a blue plastic forensic overall from another officer and started to climb into it. 'And stay on the perimeter. You're an observer. Got it?'

'Got it.'

The grey Mercedes in which the body had been found was crawling with forensic officers all dressed in the same blue plastic overalls, with matching hoods and shoe-covers, and white mouth masks.

Phoebe Aston, the head of the forensics team, was kneeling on the pavement, her hands and head inside the rear passenger side of the car, her plastic overalls sticking against the coagulated blood. The team around her were gathering everything they could find from the blood-soaked scene: an odd hair or piece of tissue, skin particles from the back seat, a discarded condom. Everything was placed in see-through evidence bags, which were passed to a waiting assistant to take to the Lambeth lab for testing. The shapeless, forensic outfits made it hard to tell one forensic officer from the other, but these days Phoebe was easy to spot; at every murder scene or post-mortem that Georgia attended, Phoebe's baby bump seemed to get bigger.

The dead man lay across the back seat, eyes wide and staring, face twisted in pain and thick with blood. There was a jagged, uneven cut across his throat where the skin hung back like a flap at the corner of a sealed envelope, as if the knife had jarred as it entered, or perhaps he had put his hand up to stop the knife ripping into his neck. There were many cuts and much congealed blood on his stiffened hands. His windpipe was severed, which accounted for the white mucous mingled with the blood sliding from his throat. Streams of blood bespattered the car. Rigor mortis had set in, so it was difficult for the Phoebe to manoeuvre herself over frozen outstretched arms and legs that had splayed into a V-shape.

Georgia moved in closer. 'Was this the cause of death?' she asked, pointing to the cut across the throat. 'The penis wasn't cut off before he died, surely?'

'Where is it?' Stephanie asked.

Phoebe turned to look at her and burst out laughing. 'Listen, I'm six months pregnant, I'm still feeling sick, and regretting ever having sex, and true to form, all you want to see is a man's sexual organ.' She reversed slowly out of the car and lifted an evidence bag from the forensic cooler box standing beside the back wheel. Inside the transparent plastic bag was a squashed and shrivelled lump of flesh, barely recognizable as a penis. She held it in front of Stephanie's face. 'Only you could ask to see this,' she joshed. 'And if that sight isn't enough to put you off, you are totally beyond hope.'

'It isn't,' Georgia said dryly. 'Nothing will ever put her off sex, I swear to God.'

Georgia bent to examine the driving mirror; she looked toward the alley where the mirror was angled. It had been knocked, but when and by who? 'Make sure this gets gone over in detail, will you?' she said to another forensic officer.

'Incidentally,' she added to Phoebe, 'Lucy, Stephanie's daughter, is over there, on work experience. Might be a good idea to keep the sex jokes to a minimum.'

Stephanie and Phoebe looked at each other and raised their eyebrows. With a pang Georgia realized she had spoken without thinking. What did someone like her, a woman of over thirty, who would never have children of her own, know about the way a teenager's mind worked? In future she'd keep her thoughts on that subject to herself.

The black mortician's van was parked at the end of the road. Georgia checked with Phoebe, then authorized the technicians to take the body out of the car. She told Phoebe she'd await the post-mortem, and walked over to join Lucy.

The girl was standing by the cordon with a pen and spiral notebook in her hand.

'How are you doing?' Georgia asked.

'Yeah, yeah, good. It's cool,' Lucy said. Her notebook was open and she had been taking notes. Georgia was impressed.

'DC Peacock is looking for residents whose houses overlook

this lane,' she told Georgia, 'and any late-night drinkers in the pub opposite the end of the road. And he's rung in to find out who the car belongs to. I heard Mum give instructions for a door-to-door in the area, and some of the forensic officers have found a green plastic lighter and a book of matches.'

'Good girl. We'll have you in CID in no time.' Georgia smiled. 'Do you want another coffee before we head back to the station for a briefing?'

Lucy shook her head. 'No thanks. I don't do coffee. I'd like to see the body, though . . . I think.'

Georgia thought of the blood-smeared corpse, in full rigor and minus its shrivelled penis. She shook her head. 'Not this time,' she told her with a small shake of her head. She didn't want to put Lucy off sex before her life started.

'OK. Can I just see the penis then?'

Georgia was taken aback. She shook her head again. 'No. Sorry.'

'Why not?'

Georgia put her arm around Lucy's shoulder. 'Because I don't want to put you off something that everyone says is great. Sex should be something very special, for you and whoever you are in a relationship with.' She tilted her head and met Lucy's gaze. 'Trust me, you really don't want to see it.'

Lucy nodded and shrugged. 'OK, if you say so. You're the boss. But you know, sex isn't all it's cracked up to be. I've slept with loads of blokes. It's just something to do.'

Desks and tables were untidily spread with half-eaten sandwiches, cardboard cups of hot drinks and coffee-stained notebooks. Computers whirred into life and telephones rang constantly as the murder squad took the calls, ate their lunch and waited for the first meeting of the new murder investigation to start.

Georgia had given Lucy permission to attend the briefing, but told her to sit at the back of the room, ask no questions, and just listen and learn. Lucy obeyed.

Stephanie sat at her own desk at the front of the room and Georgia stood by the whiteboard pinning photos to it: the dead man, the car he was killed in, the road and its access points. There was a picture of the green lighter too, and of the book of matches with the name *Holster Club* on the front. The final photo was of the penis in an exhibits bag. This caused no end of amusement amongst the team, who seemed happy to carry on eating their lunch as they made various jokes. One older detective dared one of the younger squad members to get his out on the table to prove it was as large as he claimed.

Stephanie was eating a Twix bar. Martin, the young detective, made a remark about the way she fitted the chocolate bar into her mouth.

'It's a better fit than that specimen of yours,' she retorted, loudly enough for the whole room to hear. 'The sad fact is it's about the size of that one in the photo – and I should know, I've seen it enough times.' A gale of laughter swept the room; Stephanie's reputation went before her. 'No, in his dreams!' she scoffed. 'He's so desperate he gets it out and flashes it at anyone who might be interested. Not that anyone ever is.'

Georgia was still at the whiteboard with her back to them, writing with the thick felt pen and listening to everything that was going on. She never joined in the smutty talk, but she always kept tabs on what went on in her team. She turned around and flicked a glance at Lucy to see her reaction to her mother's banter. Lucy was too busy writing in her notebook to take any notice. Young Hank Peacock, on the other hand, had clearly made a point of sitting himself next to Lucy, and was blushing like a Belisha beacon. Georgia quelled the urge to smile.

DCI Banham walked in and the room fell silent. He walked to the front and stood beside Georgia. Georgia respected Banham as her senior officer, but privately found him slightly chauvinistic. She hadn't been a detective inspector for long, but this wasn't the first time Banham had made her senior investigating officer on a case. Each time, though, he attended her daily meetings and couldn't resist the temptation to take over. Irritating though this was, Georgia said nothing.

The rumour was that Banham had an on-off relationship with another female DI, and when things were not going well with this Alison Grainger, Banham took it out on other female officers. Only a few minutes earlier, they had been discussing this case in his office. He had told her he was making her SIO because she had recently headed up another murder enquiry around the crime-ridden Aviary estate; her familiarity with the troubled territory and its resentment to police interference would be an asset – as would the fact that she was dark-skinned and female. She hadn't quite known what to make of that last comment, but she took his confidence in her as a compliment.

But now, here he was again, standing right beside her and claiming everybody's attention.

Women had to fight hard against chauvinism in the police force, but Georgia was prepared to deal with it. She acknowledged him with a smile and addressed the room.

'We've got a nasty one here,' she began. 'Tidal Lane is a cut-through from the back of the Aviary estate, and it's where the estate toms work. It's Brotherhood gang territory, and that means Stuart Reilly again. We all know Stuart by his street name, Yo-Yo, and we also know he's a sadist. If only we could prove it.' She pointed to the photo of the dead man. 'Rigor had set in, so we estimate that this murder happened in the very early hours of this morning.' She paused, waiting for questions. No one spoke, so she carried on. 'First off we need to bring in the toms who were working the area in the early hours. That's a job for all of you. We'll be working flat out for a while, probably well into the night.'

Everyone nodded agreement, and Georgia continued. 'The street where the victim was found leads to an alley at the back of the Aviary. There was a condom in the car, so clearly he went to this location to pick up a tom. High chance she'll have a record, so once forensics get DNA from the condom and runs it through the database we'll bring her in.' She looked at Hank Peacock, who was still sitting next to Lucy. 'Have we ID'd the victim yet?'

'Yes, ma'am. His name is Tom Solden and he lives over the water in Wandsworth. He has a wife and daughter.'

'Good work. Sergeant Green and I will pay her a visit, after uniform have broken the news and appointed a family liaison officer. Likelihood is it wasn't his first tom. Maybe the wife can tell us more about him. Maybe he went regularly to pick up toms, and maybe the wife found out.'

'Or maybe this is a turf war, maybe another pimp is trying to move in,' Banham interrupted. 'That turf is pimped by Yo-Yo Reilly. Perhaps someone is trying to imitate Reilly's work, to send us down the wrong trail so that another pimp can move in. Or it could be Reilly's handiwork; it's right up his street. He's famous for his use of knives and cutting.' He turned to Georgia. 'We'll pay him a visit too. And keep our eyes on the pimps in the neighbouring areas.'

'What about the toms? Georgia suggested. 'Does anyone have an in, or a snout among the ones who work the Aviary area?'

No one put their hand up.

'It would be good to talk to any other toms who know our victim,' Georgia concluded.

'We've got a lighter, and a book of matches. They're with forensics at the moment,' Peacock told them. 'The matches are from a bar in Brixton – the Holster. We could pay that a visit, see if that turns anything up?'

Georgia opened her mouth to agree, but Banham got in before her. 'Wait for forensics on it first,' he said. 'We know that place well.'

'What about Alysha Achter?' Stephanie suggested. 'Her sister was a tom, pimped by Yo-Yo Reilly; she committed suicide a while back, after her friend was murdered. Alysha still lives on the Aviary estate and knows a lot of the toms. She's only thirteen, but I think she might be worth talking to.'

'Good thinking,' Georgia agreed.

'You go, Stephanie,' Banham said. 'Take Lucy with you. It will help Alysha to feel more comfortable, and she might open up with someone younger there.'

'No!' said Georgia.

Banham stared at her.

'It's the most violent estate in South London.' Georgia knew it wasn't a good idea to disagree with a senior officer in front of the team, but this was Lucy he was talking about, Stephanie's daughter. 'It's run by one of the most notorious gangs on our patch. You've said that yourself,' she added. 'We can't risk putting Lucy in any danger.'

Stephanie looked at Georgia, but said nothing.

After a few silent seconds Banham gave a quick nod. 'Yes, you're right. It is gang territory – things can get violent. I think I'll give Dave Dawes a call. He's a gang expert; I think we should use his expertise on this one.'

Banham was undermining her, but Georgia said nothing.

He turned to face the room. 'Some of you will have already met DI David Dawes. He helped us on a previous gang-war case on the Aviary. He's first class; there isn't a thing he doesn't know about territorial warfare. I'll give him a call, and get him on board if I can.'

Georgia caught Stephanie's eye. Last time Dawes had been on attachment with them, Stephanie had been all over him like a rash. Georgia had encouraged it; she had even made a bet with Stephanie that she couldn't bed him, as a way of finding out more about him. He lived in North London, yet he had an almost unhealthy interest in gangs this side of the water, as well as a lot of expertise; Georgia had wanted to find out why. So she had made the bet, hoping that if Stephanie seduced him and got him talking, she'd find out. But Stephanie had lost the bet; they had solved the case before she could do the business. It was all history now, but she noticed that Stephanie put her chocolate bar down at the mention of his name.

Lucy was perched on the edge of Hank's desk, making notes. Georgia was pleased with her. The girl had behaved very well all morning. She hadn't even argued when Georgia had disagreed with Banham about letting her go with her mother to interview a young girl on the estate. This was a real baptism of fire for her, and she was taking to it like a duck to water. Georgia wondered how she would react if she saw her mother chasing DI David Dawes.

She became aware that Banham was waiting for her to carry on.

'Right,' she said, 'Sergeant Green and I are going to see the widow, then we'll pay a visit to young Alysha Achter. We'll be out a while, but as ever, at the end of our phones. Peacock, I'm going to leave Lucy in your capable hands. You can both wait here for the forensics report on the matches and lighter – let me know as soon as you get something. Meanwhile chase up the victim's phone and bank records – find out what floats his boat. The rest of you, trawl the streets around the estate, talk to hookers, find out who might have been down that cut last night, and what they are talking about down there. Any news, get back to me pronto.'

Stuart Reilly, known to his Brotherhood gang, and to anyone else who hung around the streets of South London, as Yo-Yo, was pacing up and down his ground floor flat on the Aviary estate.

Dwaine Ripley, whose street name was Boot, sat on the edge of a grubby tan armchair holding his two pitbull terriers with gilded leads clipped to their spiked collars. Both dogs bore cuts, gouge marks and scars, souvenirs of the many fights their owner had put them in to win money.

Winston Mitchell, known as Scrap on the streets, leaned against the open door into the hallway. He was, as usual, away with the fairies. It was only early afternoon, but he had sniffed a nose full of cocaine and swallowed a cocktail of pills.

Yo-Yo Reilly was over twenty stone, with short black hair, cropped and gelled to stand erect on his large head. He was famous for his volatile temper, and much feared around the surrounding estates. His dark eyes narrowed and his mouth twisted as he listened to Boot recounting last night's happenings.

'So you're saying the word's out that I had the punter clipped?' Yo-Yo shouted, stabbing a finger hard in his own chest.

'As I heard it,' Boot nodded.

'Have you told Alysha I want her?'

'I told her half an hour ago, Yo. She said she'll come down.'

Reilly looked at Scrap. His pupils were dilated and resembled a child's kaleidoscope. Scrap was a Brotherhood lieutenant, but he was becoming more of a liability with every passing day. The drugs Yo fed him used to keep him subservient, but the boy was now losing the plot, and Reilly wouldn't put anything past him when he was this loaded. Scrap was keen on cutting too, Reilly reminded himself.

'You were watching that territory last night,' Reilly said to him.

'Three girls were working there last night,' Scrap told him indifferently. 'Two were around when I went for a piss. I never saw nothing going up. Jade had gone off somewhere with a punter, and Bethany and Carly were touting trade. When I came back it was deserted. And fucking freezing. I reckoned they'd taken off.'

'They're supposed to take their orders from you!' Yo-Yo shouted. 'Which means me. I said they don't go till they've made some money. They fucking know that. Lazy cows.' Reilly clicked his fingers at Boot. 'Talk to them, will ya, find out what they know and report back. Someone's after our territory. They've fucking set us up.'

Boot and Scrap exchanged a glance.

Yo-Yo raised his voice again. 'I'll find the bastard that crapped on my turf, and when I do I'll cut his nuts off. You can tell that to anyone who asks.'

'I think Michael Delahaye is after your patch, Yo,' Scrap said. 'He ain't forgiven you for sticking him. He's gonna get even somehow, innit? I reckon this is his doing. I heard he was threatening – gonna be coming down with something.'

The veins on Reilly's neck stood out and he breathed more heavily. He pierced Scrap with a dark look. 'If you hear another peep that he's trying to muscle in on our territory, you are gonna kill him right there and then. Have you got that, bro?'

Scrap stretched his mouth into a smile. 'I have got that, Yo. Yes, mate, I've got that good and clear.'

Reilly wondered which of them was the bigger problem: Scrap, or Michael Delahaye. He decided to keep his own ears to the ground. If Scrap wasn't coming up to Brotherhood lieutenant standard, it wouldn't be long before the fucker was found in some gutter with an overdose in his vein. And who would miss him? Nobody!

When Alysha knocked two minutes later, the front door wasn't properly closed, so she sauntered in without waiting to be invited.

Alysha knew more about life than was good for any thirteen-year-old girl. She had things well sussed. Officially her father lived with her, in the flat, but he was an alcoholic and the only time he ever came home was to borrow money. She pleased herself, sleeping most of the day and using her body all night to make money for dope. She had never been happier. She was earning good around these streets; lots of punters liked them young and black, and she was making hay while that sun shone. Officially she worked for Reilly, and she made him a good wad. Reilly specialized in very young but very experienced hookers. When he got good offers in from up west, he always took her along to service the party of perverts. She happily did anything they asked of her without blinking, as long as a lot of money changed hands.

Yo-Yo had had her himself, many times. He too had a penchant for very young girls, and he liked them brown-skinned. What he didn't like was that Alysha had got under his skin; he now couldn't get enough of her. He normally used them, tired of them, and moved on to the next, but Alysha was different; he couldn't stop wanting her. He had surprised himself a little while back; hiring her out to a party of rich perverts had given him a sick feeling in his gut. He nearly changed his mind, but she had caught on and had quickly persuaded him it was OK. She wasn't giving up on the wad she'd get for doing all the tricks they asked for. Reilly waited while she did her stuff, then drove her home: something he had never done for any other whore, no matter how young she was, or what state she was in after entertaining his perverted clients all evening.

Alysha was streetwise, and had sussed Yo-Yo right away. She had made her mind up that she would wind him around her little finger, tighter and tighter, then one day she'd take the territory and all his money, and he would be history.

She carried a torch for Michael Delahaye, the ex-Brotherhood lieutenant Reilly had stabbed and nearly killed. Alysha had stepped in and saved his life, and Michael, whose street name was Mince, said he loved her, and he always would, for doing it. She dreamed of taking Yo-Yo's territory and sharing it with Mince one day.

She was clever, but not quite as clever as Reilly. He hadn't become leader of the most notorious and terrifying gang in

South London by being stupid. The man's brain was as sharp as the razors he used to keep enemies away from his territory, and he made it his business to seek out the weakness of everyone who worked with him. Alysha was no exception. He knew only too well that she fancied Mince Delahaye rotten, and always had. Her secret was no secret to him. He also knew that if anyone knew what was going on in Delahaye's head, it would be Alysha. He gave her enough rope so she could hang around Delahaye, because it suited his purpose. But if he ever found out that she was having sex with the bastard, Yo-Yo would kill Mince himself, and Alysha too. That was a cert if ever there was one. Alysha Achter was his property. He said who she fucked.

Delahaye had been one of Reilly's top lieutenants, because he was handy with a knife, and knives were the main tool of the Brotherhood. So Delahaye had been a top man until he had broken Brotherhood rules and disobeyed an order: to take Alysha's virginity. Yo-Yo had stabbed him, and nearly killed him. The two had been arch-enemies ever since. Reilly had taken Alysha's cherry himself, and now he feared he couldn't get enough of her. She was like a drug to him, and he knew she had the power to make him weak.

'What d'you want, Yo?' she asked, wiggling her little butt into the room and pinning her big brown eyes on him.

She wore a tiny, fitted, pink T-shirt embellished with a large strawberry, and black leggings, with trainers that lit up and flashed pink lights as she walked.

'I need to know what went down last night in the lane.'

'I went down on a few punters last night in the lane,' she teased, giving him a cheeky come-on look.

'Behave yourself, will you,' he said sharply. 'You weren't working Tidal Lane last night. I want you to ask around. See who saw what. Got it?'

'Is this about the punter without a prick?'

'How d'you know?'

'All the girls know. Someone told me this morning.'

'Who?'

'Jade, I think, or maybe Bethany.' She laughed. 'No it wasn't, it was Carly. He was her punter.'

'Don't fuck me about. Which one was it?'

'Carly.'

'What did she see?'

She put a hand defiantly on her hip. 'She says she saw nothing, but she's scared for her life. Shall I tell her you wanna talk to her?'

Reilly narrowed his eyes thoughtfully, then shook his head. 'No. She won't say fuck all to me, she'll be too scared. Get her to tell you what she saw. Everything. Got it? I wanna know every fucking detail.'

'She says she ain't working for a few nights, she wants to keep a low profile.'

'Tell her to spill everything – tell her I wanna know, cos I'm gonna sort it.'

'OK.'

'And tell her if she don't talk to you, her baby's in danger. That'll make her spill.'

Alysha snorted. 'That'll get her on the first fucking train out of town. You've no idea, Yo, you really ain't. I'll find out, but I'll do it my way.'

Scrap and Boot looked on with interest. Reilly took a breath. No one else would dare speak to him like that. He was the leader of the Brotherhood, and couldn't be seen to take disrespect from a tom. He pulled his flick-knife from his pocket and held it to the side of her eye. 'You're getting too big for your fucking mouth, do you know that?' He pressed the point of the knife into her skin. 'The message is, I wanna know what she saw. It's my territory, and I wanna know what happens on it. Tell her that, or else her kid's in danger.'

Alysha pulled her head back. If he had frightened her, then she wasn't letting on. She gave a little smile. 'OK.'

'You'd do well to remember what happened to Mince Delahaye, when he disobeyed my orders.'

'Yeah.' She grinned, pushing his hand away. 'But he don't give you blow jobs.'

Reilly flicked a glance at Scrap and Boot. They both looked away, but they were sniggering. Reilly was now furious. Not only was Scrap being a pain in the arse, but now Alysha was getting out of hand too. This was Brotherhood of Blades territory, and he ruled; and that was how it was going to stay. He earned too well out of it to let anyone take his stake.

He narrowed his eyes, keeping them pinned on her face. 'OK. You tell her I ain't cross and she ain't done nothing wrong, but I wanna talk to her. Got that? Say I'm gonna give her some good gear, and a wad, and she can have a couple of days off.' His mean eyes narrowed until they were tiny slits in his head. 'And then you tell her if I find out she's double-crossing me, her kid's for it. Got that, have you?'

THREE

Steph indicated left and turned her car into an unmade-up private road. Her car began to bounce on the uneven surface, and stones flew around the base of her car.

'I suppose if you can afford to live in this sort of a road you can afford to keep replacing your exhaust,' she said to Georgia as the car jolted in and out of a pothole with a screech of stone scraping metal.

'Amazing houses,' Georgia said.

'And amazing prices,' Steph answered. 'I only live two miles down the road and any of these would cost five times as much as mine. How the other half live!'

'It's your own fault,' Georgia teased her. 'A: for wanting to join the police force and B: for having such terrible taste in husbands.'

'I've only had one husband,' Steph protested. 'He was more than enough.'

'He gave you beautiful children,' Georgia said.

A proud smile spread across her friend's mouth. 'And that's something I wouldn't change,' Stephanie said, 'no matter how untidy they are.'

Georgia was speechless. No one in the whole world was as untidy or disorganized as Stephanie Green, and the woman didn't seem to know it.

Georgia put her mind back into work mode as they turned into the driveway of the victim's house. 'Uniform have already informed the widow. You play the sympathy role. You know how bad I am at that sort of thing.'

'I wondered why you were being nice to me.'

'I'm always nice to you.'

Stephanie locked her car, and they made their way up the

long drive. At the top Stephanie removed the bubblegum from her mouth and fixed it to the base of her shoe.

As Georgia rang the doorbell, she said to Stephanie, 'As you only live round the corner we could pop back to yours after this if you want.'

'What for?'

'DI Dawes is expected later. I thought you might want to change your clothes. Maybe find something without coffee down the front.'

Stephanie's plump cheeks dimpled.

'The bet's back on, if you want,' Georgia told her. 'Twenty, wasn't it, that you wouldn't bed him by the end of the case? I'm up for it, if you still fancy him?'

'I could certainly do with a night of lust,' Stephanie said, flicking her hair behind her ears and pulling an impish expression. 'Especially with him. He's got big hands. OK, you're on.'

'Not everyone with big hands has a . . .'

She stopped in mid-sentence as the front door opened.

Mrs Kate Solden was well dressed, well preserved and devastated. In the large sitting room of the Wandsworth house that she had shared with her husband, daughter and two cats, the widow sobbed into her floral handkerchief and Georgia took the opportunity to study her surroundings. It was down to Stephanie to give Mrs Solden the full details of her husband's murder. Georgia passed on that job whenever possible.

While Steph talked quietly to Kate Solden, Georgia took a look at the photos on the sideboard. There was a wedding picture; Kate had been a young, beautiful, happy bride. Another showed a little girl, with beautiful, and very long, blonde hair, presumably the daughter, looking innocent and sweet in school uniform. A third was of Tom Solden and the same girl on a beach; the girl wore a bikini and was almost as tall as he was. The rest were of cats.

Kate Solden blew her nose and looked at Stephanie, shaking her glossy, expertly highlighted dark hair. 'Sorry. I'm finding it hard to take in.'

The woman's complexion was white with shock, and the make-up smudged around her eyes made her look like Alice Cooper.

'That's understandable,' Stephanie said gently. She always managed to sound genuinely involved, even though she had done this a hundred times or more; Georgia was always impressed with her sincerity. Maybe that was why men enjoyed sex with Stephanie, Georgia thought. She was overweight and hardly a looker, but she was clearly tactile, and had no problem expressing emotion.

Georgia needed sex more than she liked it. It eased her tension, and she couldn't go without it for long, but she didn't enjoy it like Stephanie did. If Steph had been born a rabbit, the countryside would be overpopulated, but there would have been some very happy bunnies around. Sometimes Georgia wished she was more like her friend. Perhaps she'd feel more complete. She had never been good at anything to do with feelings or sympathy. She cared all right, especially about injustice and killings; and she desperately wanted to solve crimes, find the perpetrators and make them answerable to the courts. But showing how she felt simply wasn't in her make-up. She hadn't been brought up to it. She was the daughter of two highly driven doctors, both trained to keep their personal feelings hidden when dealing with patients, and they forgot to expose them to their own children.

Georgia had been raped on Clapham Common when she was fifteen. She didn't tell a soul about it, or about the degrading, heartbreaking backstreet abortion that followed. Afterwards she learned that she would never bear children; the pain of that was always going to be too great to talk about, so she kept it hidden and got on with her life. Consequently she found people who expressed their feelings not only hard to deal with, but frankly embarrassing. She told herself it was better for the job if she showed nothing, even to victims. While someone else broke bad news, Georgia used the time to study the people and their behaviour: always a big plus in solving a case.

Here, a variety of bottles were lined up on the sideboard. There was a half-empty gin bottle with the cap lying beside it, clearly used recently. There were also unopened bottles of wine, champagne, vodka, brandy, port and another bottle of gin. The Soldens either drank a lot or entertained frequently. She already knew money was no object.

'What did your husband do for a living?' she asked Kate.

The woman turned her pinched face towards Georgia. 'He owned a chain of bakery shops.'

'I'm sorry to have to ask you this, but did you know your husband visited prostitutes?' Georgia asked.

Kate lowered her head, and Georgia noticed how well-kept her hair was: professionally blow-dried as well as the highlights. One of her hands gripped the other; she had neutral-coloured nail extensions, and a large diamond on her third finger. She shook her head. 'Not till today. I'm disgusted. Devastated.'

'You had no idea at all?'

'None.'

'Did he go out at regular times? Or on certain evenings? Did he ever leave you wondering where he was?'

Kate lifted her manicured hands defensively. 'My husband owned bakery shops. The bakery works all night. He often did the same.'

'I'll need the addresses of all the shops and all the staff who work with him. Can you get that for me?'

She nodded. 'I can give you the number of his manager. He'll let you have lists of the shops and the staff. I don't know any of that.'

'Did you get involved in his work at all?'

'No. That's Tom's preserve. I look after the home.'

'Does your husband have a study or a work room here, with a computer, perhaps?' Georgia persisted.

'There is a home computer, but Tom never used it, it's for Alice. She's studying for her GCSEs. All the work computers are at the shops. He doesn't have a study here either. All his personal things are in the bedroom.'

'Can I see it, please.'

Kate looked hesitant. 'You want me to show you our bedroom?'

'Please.'

'Well, I suppose if it's absolutely necessary . . .'

'It is if we're to find your husband's killer, Mrs Solden.'

Kate led the way up the long Victorian staircase. 'We'll need to talk to Alice too,' Georgia told her.

'She isn't here at the moment,' Kate said. 'I can't get hold of her on her mobile either. You know what teenagers are like.' She opened a door and led them into a twin-bedded room. Everything was immaculate.

'She'll be back later,' Kate said. 'I expect so, anyway.' Her eyes darted from Georgia to Stephanie. 'I'll have to break the news to her when she gets home. Better than on the phone.' She looked back at Georgia. 'I don't want her to hear it from anyone else, I really don't.' Tears tumbled from her eyes again. 'I'm sorry, I'm having trouble taking all this in.'

'We understand,' Stephanie said gently.

Kate pulled her handkerchief from her sleeve and held it to her eyes. She moved to the window and stared out over a large, well-tended garden. She folded her lips. 'Would you let me . . . let me . . . know,' she began haltingly, 'how long this . . . visiting of prostitutes had been going on? If you find out, of course.'

'Yes, of course,' Stephanie said. Then she took a breath and added, 'Mrs Solden, I'm sorry to be heavy-footed here, but were you and your husband having sex?'

Kate turned her head quickly. 'Yes.' She nodded. 'Yes, we were, as it happens.'

'Regularly?'

'Yes. Regularly.' She looked at Steph as if she had forgotten her table manners.

'Did he ever ask . . .'

Georgia saw Stephanie's hesitation. 'Did he ever ask you to do something, anything . . . unusual?' she asked. 'Something you preferred not to do?'

'Never,' Kate snapped.

'You might want to get yourself checked out,' Stephanie said quietly.

Kate Solden stared at Stephanie. 'Dear God,' she said.

'I'm sorry.'

'Can you tell me where you were last night and in the early hours of this morning?' Georgia asked.

Again the look of disbelief. 'Are you suggesting that I . . . ?'

There was a pause, and she and Georgia locked eyes. 'I didn't kill my husband,' she said.

'I'm sorry. I have to ask. It's routine.'

'I was here, in bed, asleep.'

As Georgia opened her mouth to ask the next question, Kate continued: 'Alice was here. In the next room. Fast asleep, I grant you, but so was I. I assure you I wouldn't leave my daughter alone to go and murder my husband. She's only fifteen.'

Georgia decided that was their cue to leave. They made their way downstairs, and she handed Kate her card. 'We've got your husband's mobile phone, but if I could take the number of his business manager?'

Kate opened a drawer and took out pen and paper. While she scribbled a number on the paper, Georgia said, 'We have a few belongings of your husband's which we'll need to hang on to for now. And I'm afraid we will have to ask you to make an official identification of the body. Tomorrow will be fine. In the meantime, if you think of anything, you will call me, won't you?'

Kate handed the number to Stephanie.

'Anyone he might have upset, or crossed swords with,' Georgia persisted.

Kate was barely listening.

'Do you have help in the house?' Georgia asked.

'Yes, I do. Edna has been with us for years. I trust her implicitly.'

'I'll need her details,' Georgia said, 'And a gardener? Does someone help you with the garden?'

'Yes.' She closed her eyes and her jaw tensed.

'We're trying to build up a picture of your husband's life. I'd like a list of everyone that works for you, no matter how infrequently.'

Kate pulled open the drawer again and took out an address book. She opened it, scribbled a couple of numbers on the pad and handed them to Georgia. 'I'm having trouble taking all this in,' she said again.

''Course.' Georgia smiled as sympathetically as she could. 'We'll leave you alone for now. But we will be in touch again, very soon. An officer will be along shortly to see if you need anything. And I'd like to talk to Alice as soon as possible. Can you please ring us as soon as she gets back?'

Kate nodded. It was plain she was fighting to not break down again.

As she opened the front door to let them out, she said, 'I wonder if you could keep the full details of his murder from Alice when you talk to her. She doesn't need to know . . . well, not everything, does she?'

'For the moment,' Georgia agreed.

Stephanie was quiet as they walked back to the car. Georgia knew she was thinking about Lucy, and how she might feel herself in Kate Solden's position. Georgia sympathized, but her job was to catch this killer, and if that meant asking a fifteen-year-old girl if she had any idea who might have cut her father's penis off, that was exactly what she was going to do.

Carly puffed greedily on the joint Yo-Yo had given her. It was good stuff and she was surprised that Yo-Yo had gifted it to her, and she didn't have to do nothing for it. He hadn't done that since she first met him. Back then he'd given her free gear, good pills, even the odd pipe of heroin. Now she knew him better, and he scared her witless. Any time she stepped out of line, or didn't pay on time, she'd get a good thumping.

But she told herself if she was up for a belting, he'd hardly give her some top-class grass first. And after what she'd seen last night, she was more scared someone else was going to come after her. She was keeping well buttoned. Whatever she knew or didn't know, she was saying nothing.

She took a long draw, swallowed hard, tried to pretend she hadn't noticed the way Reilly was looking at her. She leaned back in the front seat of his black Porsche and looked straight ahead through the black-tinted window. Then the strength of the weed hit her brain, and she leaned back against the headrest and closed her eyes. It felt good.

'Better?'

'Yeah.'

'Correct me if I'm wrong, but you're saying some punter picks you up, and before you can do the business you're told to fuck off by someone else. You've no idea who it is, but you do as you're told – you get out and do a runner.'

She nodded, taking another deep drag on the joint. 'I didn't want no trouble.'

'Why would you get trouble if you don't know who either of them were?'

'I did know him.' Her head felt light and her brain was scrabbling.

'The punter?'

She nodded. 'Yeah. I done 'im before. I done 'im lots. I don't know his name, but he's picked me up a few times, and booked me over at his place. He likes me and always asks when I'm gonna be around. He asked me how old I am, an' I just said however old he wants me to be. I never told 'im I'm underage or nothing. He could be the fuzz, so I never said. He said he likes what I do to him, like.'

She stopped, suddenly aware that Yo-Yo was watching her even more closely. 'It was freezing out there,' she pleaded. 'Jade had gone off with someone and we hadn't seen her for a bit. Me and Beth had been standing around. Beth had done two punters and I hadn't done no one, so I was well glad to see that one. He has the full story and pays OK, and he's got a big, comfy car. That's all I care about. An' it was cold . . .'

'I asked what you know about the bloke in the car. I don't need to know who you sucked off or what the fucking temperature is at three o'clock in the fucking morning.' Yo-Yo's voice grew harder. 'I want to know who got in the car with you. Anyone you recognized, I want to know everything about what you remember. This is my territory, I run the Aviary, and if some fucker is trying to have one over on me, I'm gonna find out, and when I do, they are gonna really fucking regret it. Now tell me everything you remember. Was it a bloke or a bird? Were they tall or short? What did they say?'

Carly's eyes met Reilly's. She was frightened and the gear was making her gab; she knew she had to keep a lid on it.

She looked away. 'There's nuffin',' she said. 'It just happened so quick. They told me to get out and fuck off, so that's what I did.'

'Has there been any more bother down there of late?'

'I've only been working a couple of months, Yo-Yo. I just do as I'm told. I need the money, and I'm a good girl . . .'

'Don't fucking bleat on, all right. If you don't even know if it was a bloke or a bird, just fuck off.'

She reached for the door with shaking hands. Yo-Yo leaned over and grabbed her shoulder. 'Don't talk to no one about it. D'you hear? I mean no one. If someone is after my territory, you could be in trouble yourself. You take a few nights off work. I'll keep you in gear, OK?'

She had the door open to leave before she answered. 'Thanks,' she said. 'I don't want no trouble.'

Georgia and Stephanie dropped by Stephanie's house for a bite to eat and a chance for Stephanie to change her coffee-stained top before returning to the station. A message from DCI Banham was waiting for them.

'Dawes has arrived,' Georgia said, lowering her voice. 'I hope DCI Banham remembers I'm SIO on this case. I find all the testosterone very hard to swallow.'

'Hey, chill.' Stephanie grinned. 'Dawes is after putting away Yo-Yo Reilly, that's all. And we all want him off the streets. Word is Banham's got the hots for that DI, Alison Grainger. She's been on compassionate leave for months – a fellow officer was killed during a case she was on. That's why he's being grumpy with us. He's a pussycat really.'

'Perhaps you should bed him too, that might solve all our problems.'

'I wish!'

Georgia closed her eyes. 'Don't tell me you fancy him. Oh, please!'

'Don't tell me you don't. I thought everyone did. He's gorgeous.'

'Not in a million years.' Georgia shook her head.

'Oh, well, one less,' Stephanie teased. 'But Dawes'll do nicely for starters.'

They approached Banham's door. Georgia straightened her shoulders. 'OK, mind back on the job.'

Georgia and Stephanie shook hands politely with DI Dawes, and settled in the two corner seats while Banham updated him. Georgia took the opportunity to study Dawes. He wasn't a tall man: just average height. In fact, there was nothing out of the ordinary about him: brown hair, grey eyes, not at all special. She couldn't work out what Steph saw in him, unless it was the challenge. At least DCI Banham had a pleasant face, even though his fair hair was thinning on top.

Georgia didn't like Dawes. She had found him difficult to work with last time. He had been arrogant, and blinkered, whereas Georgia considered everything from every angle. She found his self-confidence irritating, but she was very keen to find out what made him tick. She had already discovered that his sister had died of an overdose, and he believed the bad heroin that killed her came from the Aviary estate, so he was determined to bring down Yo-Yo Reilly, who ran the drug business over half of South London as well as the Aviary. Reilly deserved to be locked up; no question, the streets would be a lot safer when he was. As well as the drugs, they knew he was behind unsolved shootings and stabbings on the Aviary, but so far no one could prove it.

She watched Dawes as Banham brought him up to speed on the case.

'Yo-Yo Reilly,' he said right away.

Banham nodded agreement. Georgia clenched her teeth. She wanted Reilly as much as they did, but fair and square, not fitted up. And she wanted the right killer brought to justice for this murder. On the previous murder investigation on the Aviary, Dawes had caused more problems than he solved. He laid every crime at Reilly's door, without looking for evidence. But there was no point trying to tell Banham; he and Dawes went back a long way. This time, though, if Dawes got in the way, she would fight to have him thrown off the case.

Maybe if Stephanie could seduce him, it would help to keep him in his place. Stephanie would be more than happy to oblige, and would be off the chocolate for a while – another bonus for Georgia in the form of a wrapper-free car. But right now her main problem was that Dawes and Banham were old pals. Add the fact that Banham's girlfriend was on leave, and she foresaw a lot of flak coming her way. Being a woman in the police force was never going to be easy, but she was determined to be in Banham's position one day, so she would deal with whatever she had to. Including DI David Dawes.

'Nice to see you again,' Stephanie said to Dawes as he handed her a cup of freshly brewed coffee from Banham's filter machine, a present from the missing DI Grainger, or so rumour had it. Much better coffee than the stuff from the new contraption in the corridor by investigation room, Georgia thought. That was another good thing about being DCI: you picked your own team, got your own office and a decent cup of coffee. She was aware that Stephanie was staring into Dawes's eyes. She had changed into a blue floral shirt over her jeans, and had brushed her hair and added a little lip-gloss and mascara. She looked very presentable.

Georgia opened her black leather holdall and got her papers out. 'We've got another briefing in an hour,' she told Dawes. 'And Sergeant Green and I have a contact on the Aviary; we'll be paying her a visit later. We've got officers doing door-to-door around the estate as we speak, and . . .'

'That's a waste of manpower. No one around that estate will talk to us,' Dawes interrupted. 'They're too afraid of repercussions from the Brotherhood. It would be better to put the uniform help further out, on the other side of the estate. That's not Brotherhood territory, and you might get the odd person over there might say something.'

Georgia opened her mouth to argue, but Dawes carried on. 'We're in the golden hours; we need to move the enquiry along. First twenty-four hours are vital.'

Georgia just managed to refrain from reminding him that she had been senior investigating officer on several cases during the year she had been a DI, but she decided against it.

'We need to talk to as many street toms as we can,' she said.

'They won't talk to us. They're all pimped by Reilly, so

they're too frightened. I suggest we find a reason to bring him in. Once he's away from the estate, some of them just might talk to us.'

'We're waiting on some forensic tests,' Stephanie put in. 'We picked up a lighter at the scene, and an empty book of matches from a club in Brixton.'

'Is that the Holster?' Dawes asked sharply. 'Reilly provides the protection there.'

'Yes, it is,' Stephanie said, flicking a glance at Georgia. 'I was about to say there's a connection to Reilly.'

'There's your link then,' Dawes said. 'He puts the muscle into that club. You can bring him in for questioning.'

'He'll deny he has anything to do with it,' Georgia argued. 'And no one at the club will admit to paying him to beat up other dealers who try to sell in there. I think we need more than that. His solicitor is red hot . . .'

'I'll talk to him,' Dawes cut in. He sipped his coffee and stared back at her. 'I'll trip him up, then arrest him.'

Banham leaned back in his chair, obviously listening, but making no comment. Georgia's irritation stirred, but there was no sense in antagonizing Dawes this early.

'OK,' she agreed. 'We've also got the victim's business contacts and domestic staff to interview.'

'We're going to talk to Alysha Achter on the Aviary,' Stephanie told him. 'You remember – her sister jumped off the roof of the high rise.'

Dawes gave a sharp nod.

'She is only thirteen, so . . .'

'Definitely needs a woman's touch,' Banham said.

Georgia glanced at Stephanie.

'What if you and Sergeant Green go to the estate?' she said to Dawes. 'Stephanie could talk to Alysha, she knows her socially, and you could look out Reilly.'

'Yes, I think that's a good idea,' Banham said.

'After the briefing will be a good time,' Georgia added. 'I'm going to speak to the victim's business manager. I'll meet you at the Aviary afterwards. If you haven't seen Alysha by then, we could pay her a social call.'

'I'll be at the briefing,' Banham said to Georgia. 'The press are going to be all over this one if the details get out, so we need to make sure everyone keeps shtum about how the victim was killed. We'll refer to it as Operation . . . what? What shall we call it? Any ideas?'

Georgia looked Dawes full in the face. 'How about Operation Prick?'

FOUR

Monday, late afternoon

Computers clicked, telephones rang, and most of the team sipped from polystyrene Starbucks cups and ate a hurried sandwich between answering the calls or making notes. Their adrenalin was flowing, and they were all anxiously aware how vital the first twenty-four hours were. They needed to sort the evidence while it was fresh, and talk to potential witnesses while their minds weren't clouded with time; they were used to settling for a couple of snatched hours' sleep. They were like greyhounds after the rabbit. There was a killer out there and they were running against the clock to hunt them out.

The new drinks machine was proving a huge success, and had already been replenished three times. It had been DCI Banham's idea; Georgia was delighted when he pushed for the funding at a departmental finance meeting. It was good budgeting, he argued to the board. Coffee kept the detectives on their toes, and if they didn't need to leave the building to get it, they stayed focused. Georgia had warmed to Banham after that.

Banham and Dawes walked ahead of Georgia and Stephanie into the squad room to start the meeting, Dawes still holding his china mug of coffee from the machine in the DCI's office. They took up a position in front of the whiteboard at the top of the room. The photos on the board were grim and the mood in the room was sombre. A close-up photo of the victim showed his throat cut from ear to ear and his eyes only half open; the agony he had endured as his life left him was clear. Another photo showed his lower body, pants and trousers hanging pathetically around one of his ankles and his groin covered in congealed blood; beside that was a picture of the severed penis

in its exhibits bag. All the photos were secured to the board
with Blu-Tack.

Stephanie moved to her desk and Georgia joined Banham
and Dawes. Lucy sat in the same place as before, at the back
with trainee DC Peacock. She had a notebook in one hand
and a pen in the other, and like her mother she was chewing
gum. She seemed to be hanging on Hank Peacock's every
word as he explained the protocol to her. The lad had only
been in the force himself a few months and here he was
instructing someone even newer than himself. Georgia warmed
to him at that moment. She had recently met his mother. The
woman was as proud of her son, the detective, as Stephanie
was of Lucy.

Banham introduced Dawes to the team, some of whom had
worked with him before, then stepped aside and handed the
meeting over to Georgia. Georgia told the team how delighted
she was that DI Dawes had been brought in to help.

'DI Dawes's knowledge of London gangs is second to none,
and could be very useful,' she said. 'This murder could well
be the start of a gang turf war over prostitution territory.'

Dawes nodded vigorously.

'Of course, we still need to explore all possible avenues,'
Georgia added firmly. She agreed wholeheartedly that Reilly
was the biggest and most dangerous drug baron in their area;
he used underage girls for his prostitution racket, dealt in
firearms, and had a passion for knife torture. Like Dawes, she
wanted him put away for the longest possible time. He was
on her patch, and locking him up would be a big coup for her
station, but she wanted to do it right, and to nail him for the
crimes he had actually committed. If she found the first hint
of evidence that he had murdered Tom Solden, she would go
after him, and not stop until she had him behind bars, but until
then her job as SIO was to keep all options open and the
team's minds alert.

She updated them on the interview with Kate Solden, and
sketched out the plan for the rest of the day.

'Alysha Achter could be very useful to us,' she told them.
'She's only thirteen, but she's very clued up about what goes
on in and around that estate, and she does talk to us. We

befriended her on another case and she seems to like and trust Sergeant Green, so we are keeping that contact up.' She glanced at Dawes; his face was impassive. 'We all know how hard it is to get anyone on the Aviary to talk to us. Let's make use of something we have.'

She selected a couple of officers to go with her to the bakery, and gave Stan and Morris, two older detectives, the job of interviewing the Soldens' cleaner and gardener. 'We need to make the jigsaw come to life,' she concluded.

Dawes jumped in to remind the team that the prostitutes around the Aviary were all pimped by Stuart Reilly. 'No one has managed to get a conviction against Reilly for running an underage prostitution racket, or for any of the dealing or stabbings. We know he's behind it all, but we can't prove it. Yet.'

Georgia watched the faces of her experienced team as Dawes, still holding his china cup, told them that everything – *everything*, he repeated the word again, around the Aviary estate went back to Reilly, as this would too. She interrupted quickly, before someone pointed out that this was their own home patch, and they knew what went on.

'I agree,' she said as politely as she could. 'It's highly possible Reilly is involved, and he's a major suspect, but at this stage we keep our options open. Let's not forget that eighty per cent of all murders are committed by someone close to the victim.'

She noticed Stephanie was staring at Dawes. Christ, what did the woman see in the little squirt? 'We haven't found the weapon yet,' she pointed out. 'Sergeant Green, will you keep in close contact with uniform over that, please?'

'Ma'am.'

'Peacock, as soon as you get anything back from forensics on the knife, can you make sure you get straight on to Sergeant Green.'

'Yes, ma'am.'

Dawes jumped in again. 'The victim's injuries point to Reilly. Cutting is his trademark – this is his doing. He's a sadistic bastard and he relishes it. You'll all remember the recent incident with one of his own lieutenants, Michael

Delahaye, street name Mince, who was brutally stabbed in the stomach, nearly fatally. As ever, there wasn't enough evidence to charge Reilly, and no witnesses, so we couldn't get a conviction. Michael Delahaye lived, but he swore he didn't know his attacker.'

Georgia nodded. 'OK, he's all yours for the moment,' she told him. 'See if you can find a reason to arrest him and bring him in for questioning.' She leaned a little on the word *reason*. 'The removal of a man's penis is Reilly's style, one hundred per cent.'

'So prove it,' Georgia said. It was a struggle not to sound confrontational.

'The question is why,' Dawes said. 'Find the answer to that and we have the bastard.'

Stephanie stood up. 'We need to get down there, then,' she said. 'See if anyone might drop a hint as to what's going on.'

'There's no doubt in my mind,' Dawes said. 'This is a gang killing. We know Solden used prostitutes on Reilly's patch. Did he do drugs too? Did he owe money, perhaps? His penis was cut off as a message – so what was the message? That is what we are looking for.'

'We need to find out everything we can about Solden's personal life then,' Georgia said. 'Maybe someone didn't like him using prostitutes, let's not rule out that one. The man had a wife and fifteen-year-old daughter.'

'I have absolutely no doubt that Reilly is behind this,' Dawes insisted. 'Although of course he might not have done the actual cutting. Let's work from there.'

Georgia was growing furious. Dawes had just dismissed her advice about keeping all options open and given the team just one line of enquiry to follow. She looked over at Banham; he was listening to everything, but made no comment.

Stephanie caught Georgia's eye and shook her head almost imperceptibly. 'The weapon will tell us a lot,' she said, 'just as DI Johnson suggests. If only we could find it. Shall I talk to uniform and get the weapon search widened, ma'am? We could search the adjoining estate as well as the Aviary. It may well have been dumped further afield whether or not it was Reilly.'

'It'll be in a river the other end of the country by now,' Dawes said patronizingly.

'Do that,' Georgia told Stephanie. She looked out over the room. 'What else have we got?'

Hank Peacock raised his hand. 'We're still waiting for forensics, ma'am. No clue so far about the size or shape of the knife. Must have been a sharp one, though.'

Everyone laughed, the tense atmosphere relaxed and Peacock blushed.

Lucy was clearly unable to resist the urge to jump to Peacock's defence. She spoke up loudly and confidently over the laughter. 'I don't see what's funny about that. There are loads of stabbings with blunt knives. In my school plenty of people carry, for protection. Girls, as well as fellas. Fruit knives, nail scissors, penknives – anything they can conceal.'

Georgia looked at Stephanie, eyes wide. Steph beamed with pride; obviously she knew about this.

Banham interrupted. 'Can we move on? Until we know the rough size and shape of the knife, or find the bastard that used it, we're wasting time. This is golden hour; let's make the most of it.'

Dawes nodded agreement. 'If we use all our manpower hunting for a knife, we'll find at least a hundred buried on that estate, none of them the one we are looking for.' He looked at Georgia. 'Best to wait for forensics and hope they'll be able to give us a clearer picture of the weapon, and use our resources on something more productive.'

Georgia took a deep breath to quell her annoyance. 'OK. The victim's bank accounts, phone records, everything that's available. Let's look for prostitutes, drugs, gambling debts, anything that might link him to Reilly. And I want all the available CCTV of the area brought in.'

'How about that camera that records all car registrations that enter Brixton?' Stephanie suggested.

'Good thinking. We'll check out every car that entered Brixton during the evening – interview drivers and passengers and find out what they were doing there.'

A few eyebrows were raised but no one argued about the manpower that would use up.

'We need to find the hooker he picked up,' Stephanie said.
She looked over to Peacock. 'Any leads from the car?'

Peacock's face flushed again as he updated the team.
'Forensic has reported three different DNAs on the condom
found in the car. Separating them will take another day.'

'Three?' queried one of the detectives.

'The victim and the tom, obviously. The third – who knows?
Maybe the murderer,' Peacock said. 'Or maybe he had two
hookers in there with him.' He blushed again. 'Hopefully we'll
have names by tomorrow, possibly even later today. They're
sure to have a record.'

'If it is another tom,' Stan added.

'Good work,' Banham praised him. 'Well done.'

'The book of matches came from the Holster club,' Peacock
then told them. 'That's . . .'

'A hundred yards from the Aviary estate,' Dawes finished.
'And Yo-Yo Reilly has the protection contract on it, yes we
know. And a lot of his girls work there too.'

'I think we should keep trying to talk to the toms around
the area,' Stephanie said. 'We know most of them won't give
us the time of day, but there's a chance this may have frightened one of them enough to say something.'

'There certainly is,' Georgia agreed. 'Looks like you and
I are pulling an all-nighter, Sergeant. Uniform are all over
the estate, so we'll need to stay in close touch with the
operation sergeant. We all know how dangerous it is. You
can start approaching the toms on your own, while Dawes
talks to Reilly. I'll meet you there later and we'll look up
Alysha Achter.' She turned to Banham. 'I don't want anyone
other than Sergeant Green or me talking to Alysha Achter.
She may well not want to cooperate, but at least she knows
us, and Stephanie came close to winning her trust last time
we were there. I think she may be susceptible to a bit of
bribery too.'

Banham nodded his agreement. 'Fine. We'll be very
stretched tonight.' He looked round the room. 'DI Dawes
and Sergeant Green are going to need serious back-up, and
more on stand-by. All available uniform will be used on
that. I want as many eyes as possible on the CCTV.' That

raised a few groans; no one wanted to spend golden hour scrolling through grainy tapes. He turned back to Georgia. 'I'll accompany you to the bakery, and help you interview the staff and managers to see what we can dig up on the victim.'

'Thank you, sir.' Georgia wasn't sure if she was pleased to be working with him or not. She turned back to the room. 'OK, now everyone knows what they're doing, let's get out there. Any questions?'

Lucy's hand went up. 'Can I help?' she asked.

Before Georgia could reply Stephanie jumped in. 'Yes, you can take charge of coffee and tea for the detectives working in here. It's going to be a long night.'

Lucy glared at her mother for a second, but nodded obediently. Georgia gave her a reassuring wink.

At eighteen years old Michael Delahaye had grown to six feet six inches. He sat on a low, grubby, graffiti-stained wall in a small side road close to the corner of Tidal Lane, gangly legs splayed to allow his black trainers to park comfortably on the ground. He wore a black tracksuit with the hood of the zipped nylon jacket over his head, so only his dark face was visible. He always wore black; along with his dark African skin it let him blend with the shadows.

That was the way he liked things. Since the stabbing that nearly robbed him of his life he had taken to looking over his shoulder every time he went about his business: selling drugs on the neighbouring estate to the Aviary. Not quite on Reilly's patch, but near enough to cause competition. Delahaye liked that too.

Alysha Achter stood facing him. She had changed her clothes and was now wearing a denim micro skirt and a tan bolero in suede and sheepskin, over a low-cut bright orange T-shirt which advertised the lacy edges of the vivid scarlet bra underneath. Her long, thin legs modelled black leggings and on her feet were suede, shin-length tan Ugg boots. Her brown face was heavily made up, with black eyeliner and too much shiny cerise lipstick. Her arms were folded across her chest.

Alysha had spent most of her thirteen years learning how
to survive on this dangerous estate. She let some people think
she enjoyed being Yo-Yo's personal whore, or his woman as
he now referred to her. It suited her very well, though in truth
she was the one using him. She was crazily in love with
Delahaye, and was playing Yo-Yo in order to help Michael
– Mince, as he was known on the street – to build his own
drug business and start a competitive prostitute racket. The
plan was that one day he would take over the whole territory
and get his own back on Yo-Yo for nearly killing him. Yo-Yo
would be dead, of course, and Alysha would get what she had
always wanted – Michael Delahaye.

First, though, she had to play the dangerous game of being
Yo's woman and Mince's ear. If she got it wrong, Yo-Yo
would happily cut her throat and move on to the next young
brown bitch. But Alysha was clever. She already had Yo-Yo
wound around her little finger. He couldn't get enough of
her; he had even stopped her whoring for anyone else and
earning for him. She was his property, he said, and he didn't
want no one else touching her. She was delighted; her
plan was working, and the net was closing around him. And
Mince was loving her for it. He had been her one true
friend through all the shit when her sister was killed, and he
said he loved her and one day they would have sex – but not
till she was old enough. She had three years to wait. The
fact that she had already done it with hundreds of men
didn't sway him; at sixteen it would be legal, and he wouldn't
change his mind.

Alysha had done a lot of living in her short years. She had
escaped any system she should be in. Social workers believed
her father lived with her, so they left her alone. They had no
idea that her father's appearances in Alysha's council flat were
less than occasional; that he only came home to sleep off a
hangover and get money from her, and was fully aware how
she earned it. Alysha was happy to give him the money; she
had plenty of it, and it made him go away.

Her school, too, had forgotten about her existence since she
had been granted time out for compassionate reasons when
her sister died. She had never returned, and no one bothered

to remind her. She was a loner who knew exactly how to survive on the street, and she cared for no one except Michael Delahaye.

'We've got problems brewing, you hear what I'm saying?' Michael told her, fixing a searching brown gaze on her.

'What are you saying?' she asked, arms still crossed over her chest.

'You know what I'm saying, babe, innit?'

'You saying I cut that punter? Is that it? Are you asking me if I cut that punter up?' She tilted her young head and held his eyes. 'I thought it was you that done it. Was it? Did you cut him?'

Mince shrugged and shook his head.

'Are you accusing me of doing something like that without telling you's?' Her plaited cornrows swung as her temper started to bubble. 'You keep telling me we're in this together and we work together to get Yo's territory. Then you ask if I stuck the punter?'

Michael turned to check no one was around, and lifted a hand to hush her. She ignored it. 'Yo nearly killed you, man. I told you, I'm gonna get him for that. I've made him crazy for me. I'm doing all that for you's. He gives me money so I don't have to whore for him, that's how crazy he is. But you won't even make love with me, and I'm offering it to you for free.' She shook her cornrows again. 'You ain't got a clue. I'm good, baby, I'm really good, you should taste my honey, man, you . . .'

Michael's hand flew up. 'Stop that.' He jumped down from the wall and loomed over the front of her. 'Don't do all that talk. I don't like it. You're too young and that's a fact.' He shuffled his feet on the pavement. 'I don't sleep with you because I'm your real friend, innit? I hate that bastard for doing all this to you. But this isn't about Yo, it's about that punter, ain't it? I care for you, really care for you, that's why I don't want you doing stupid stuff. Yo-Yo's dangerous. Trust me, and don't ask too many questions. You're only thirteen and you can still do stupid things.'

'Like what?' she demanded defiantly.

'You don't know the difference between having honey-time

and making a quick buck,' he snapped. 'One day I'm gonna show you, but things are starting to happen now and we've got to be ready.'

'What's that supposed to mean?'

'You're gonna find out. The new army is building, so you just be careful, that's what I'm saying.'

'You're gonna lead the Brotherhood, aren't you? You should, you's fair and tough enough, they all respect you.'

'I'm working on it. His days are numbered. The brothers are coming round, you know it and I know it – not long and he'll be paying, innit?' He let his eyes roll over Alysha. 'You look so sweet, babe. Don't let him ruin you like this. You could make some corn helping me sell my grass.'

She rubbed her thumb along her knuckles. 'I like having lots and lots of brass. Yo gives it me, and you need me in there with him. I'm doing it cos I love you, man.'

'You ain't doing that fat bastard because you love me.' His teeth flashed white in a smile. 'You truly don't know.'

'Yeah, I do. I want us to be together. We can run this empire. After we kill Yo-Yo.'

'Dream on, lady.' He shook his head. 'You gotta be careful, too much ambition will get you nothing but trouble.'

'I'm gonna get him. He cut you cos of me.'

'No,' Michael shook his head again. 'He cut me cos I wouldn't do as he said, that's a whole different thing, babe. He wants to be top dog whatever, but that's a dangerous place to be. He's losing it; no one wants to be in his Brotherhood no more, you'll see. It's working out slowly, but it's working out. I'm doing it my way, and you don't have to put yourself in danger for me. I don't want you taking these risks.'

Alysha pulled a small bag of white powder from the top of her boot and handed it to him. 'This is good stuff. Yo gave it to me when I done him yesterday. It makes me do mad things, so I don't mind. Here, try it, it's good.'

Michael took it and then got back on the wall, leaning a hand on the top of his leg. 'When you are a bit older, I'll show you what making honey really means,' he said. 'That's if Yo ain't killed you first, for trying to double-cross him.'

'He wouldn't hurt me, apart from the odd slap. He's mad for me.'

'Did you cut that guy's nuts off?'

'I think you did.'

'Why would I ask you, if I done it?'

She shrugged. 'I know what you're capable of. Anyway, like I said, what you don't know you can't tell.'

'I'm gonna have to hope you're bluffing or you are going down for a very long time.'

She laughed. 'I go down every day.'

They took a blue Toyota from the car pool, and Banham asked Georgia if she wanted to drive.

'I'm happy to,' she said. 'Though I expected you'd want to do the driving.'

'Are you suggesting I'm chauvinistic?'

Georgia gave him a speculative look. 'Yes. Yes, I think you are, a bit.'

Banham was taken aback. She had worked in his department for several years, but he hadn't been DCI for long, and she had been on no other cases with him. He had always worked with Alison Grainger, and while she was on compassionate leave he always chose to work with one of the male DIs. The rumours were rife that he and Alison had had a brief love affair and she had let him down; because of that, he got on much better with the male detectives.

'I'm not the least bit chauvinistic,' he said. 'You've obviously never been in a car with DI Grainger. She's the worst driver in motoring history, and I still let her drive.' The corners of his mouth curved. He said half to himself, 'I still bear the scars.'

'Emotional or physical?'

'I beg your pardon?'

Georgia gunned the gas and took off. 'Sorry. None of my business.'

'No, it's not,' he agreed. 'That's how rumours start.'

'You brought it up.' She took a deep breath. Was this how it was going to be for the rest of the evening? She hoped Stephanie was having an easier time with Dawes.

They drove in silence for a little while, then Banham said, 'What about you? No one knows much about you. You're good at your job and never step out of line. How come there's no office gossip about you?'

'Sergeant Green grabs the headlines.' Georgia smiled. 'She likes to have fun.'

'You mean she takes the flak, and you get to keep your private life private.'

'Something like that.'

A few more minutes of silence followed. Georgia turned the radio on. Banham switched it off. 'What made you want to join CID?' he asked.

She blinked. No one but Stephanie asked her personal questions these days. In this situation she was usually the senior officer, and probably no one would dare. She slowed as the lights turned red. 'I want to catch criminals,' she said, taking care to look straight ahead. 'You?'

He took a deep breath. 'Something . . . happened a long time ago. When I was in uniform.'

'Oh, yes?'

He didn't continue. They sat in silence until the lights turned green. Then as she pulled away he said quietly, 'I'd stayed late at the station, filling in reports. When I got home my wife Diane and Elizabeth, my eleven-month-old daughter, had been murdered.' His voice became barely audible. 'Hacked to death with an axe by some madman.' He paused before adding, 'He was never caught.'

Georgia turned to look at him. What a thing to carry around with you.

'Watch the road,' he shouted.

She was impressed; it was brave to be that upfront. Braver than she was; she could never admit her own secret, that she decided to join the force because she was raped at fifteen. The rapist had never been brought to justice either, but then she hadn't told a soul about it. No point, she hadn't seen his face, but she remembered his voice, and she always would, just as she would always remember the smell of the dirt mixed with stale garlic, as his hands squeezed her mouth and nose to stop her screaming for help.

'I'm sorry,' she said sincerely, 'but glad for the force. You're an excellent DCI.' She flicked a glance and a brief smile at him; his blue eyes bored into her.

They were at their destination. She indicated and turned left into the road where the bakery stood, and parked the car carefully. As they unbuckled their belts, Banham said quietly, 'I miss her, very much.'

Georgia wasn't sure if he meant his murdered wife or Alison Grainger. She decided not to ask. 'Of course you do,' she murmured, hoping she sounded suitably sympathetic. She had made such a good job of blocking out her feelings that it was a struggle to find them when they were needed.

Stephanie Green was determined to win the bet to seduce Dawes this time round. She didn't like losing when it came to sexual conquests. She had combed her hair and put lipstick on when she knew she was partnering Dawes on to the Aviary, but now realized she had seriously overdone the perfume. It was a cold March evening, windy and wet, yet Dawes had wound his window more than halfway down. Every time she asked him a question about himself, or the Islington station where he was based, he kept his answers to a minimum and never asked anything in return. He was going to be a challenge, she thought, but she would get round him. Her two teenage children had taught her a lot about getting through to people who didn't want to talk to you.

She decided to get him talking about South London gangs. 'The Brotherhood still run the Aviary,' she said. 'But any contacts we had down there have moved on. Or died. Mostly died. Alysha Achter is a good contact, we need to keep in with her. I'm hoping she'll talk to us tonight. We managed to creep into her confidence on that last case down there; here's hoping we can do it again.'

That seemed to open the floodgates; suddenly Dawes wanted to talk to her. 'You know no other gang has tried taking territory from the Brotherhood since the last murder we investigated there?'

She nodded.

'The Brotherhood are infamous, and Reilly puts the fear of God into people. He still has all his pitbulls, and he's widening his drug territory, as well as his underage prostitution racket.'

She nodded again.

'Well, now there is a weakness in the Brotherhood's standing, and his name is Michael Delahaye.'

'I remember him,' Steph said, turning briefly to him. 'He was one of Reilly's top boys. Reilly stabbed him, but we couldn't prove it. Delahaye was hospitalized with about twenty stitches in his stomach. He said he was attacked in the street and wouldn't give evidence, so Reilly got away again.'

It was Dawes's turn to nod agreement. 'Rumour has it Delahaye is building up a crew, and plans to take Reilly out. They both live on the Aviary. It could go up any day.'

'I know how badly you want Reilly,' she told him. 'I would too, if he had fed my little sister heroin.'

He turned towards her, and she had the impression he was listening now – but then he turned to the window and inhaled a lungful of air. She really regretted the perfume.

'I'm sorry for your loss,' she continued. 'What was she like?'

'She was very, very pretty,' he said, almost to himself. 'She wanted to be a model. Reilly got her on drugs, and then into prostitution – you know the pattern. Then he left her to die of an overdose of dodgy heroin.'

Stephanie gave him an encouraging look.

'My father was a superintendent at Scotland Yard at the time, and way too strict with her. I let her stay in my flat and gave her time and space to go out and have fun and pursue her modelling dream. I was too busy building my own career to notice what she was doing. By the time I did, she was on heroin. I tried to get help for her, but then . . .' He suddenly became angry. 'He's ruined so many young lives that way. He's an animal. I won't let up until he's off the streets for good.' He shook his head adamantly. 'I will pursue him until he is behind bars.'

Stephanie reached her hand out and touched his. 'I'll help you,' she said. 'I have a daughter, Lucy. You've seen her, she's on work experience back at the station. I'd feel exactly the same if it was her.' She squeezed his hand.

Dawes turned to answer her, but was overtaken by a thunderous sneeze.

FIVE

The night manager of the Wandsworth branch had kindly gathered the staff from all Tom Solden's shops, and made staggered appointments with them, so they could give their statements in the same place and save Georgia and Banham the trouble of journeying around.

Three hours had gone by, and they were approaching the end of nearly forty interviews. So far nothing had come to light; everyone could account for their moves the night before, and no one had struck Georgia as having a possible motive, or being in any way a suspect.

It was getting on for eight o'clock when Harry Turpin came in. He was a middle-aged man, and had been working in the firm since he was a boy. He told Georgia much the same as the other staff. The Solden family came across as normal, middle class, and nothing out of the ordinary. They had a teenage daughter, Alice, who was a bit wild, but then most fifteen-year-olds were, weren't they?

Georgia bent over the table to write down what he was saying. She felt him lean in a little, and he cleared his throat. She looked up.

'I feel disloyal mentioning this,' he said, lowering his voice, 'because Mr Solden was a good and fair boss. In fact, I sort of feel I shouldn't mention it, but then, I sort of feel that I should, under the circumstances, as it were.'

Georgia was tired. 'This is a murder investigation, Mr Turpin,' she snapped. 'Can we stop going round in circles and just spit it out?'

Harry nodded. 'Which is why I think I should say.' He paused again. 'This wasn't common knowledge, of course, but Tom Solden had a bit of a thing with one of the shop managers. Jean Eden, her name is. It probably isn't even relevant, but

I thought someone should mention it, just in case. Maybe someone already has, but . . .'

'By a *thing*, I assume you mean an affair?'

'Yes.' Harry nodded vigorously again. 'Jean and Tom had had a secret affair for about ten years. All in the past now, of course. Even if he . . .'

Georgia sat up. 'I think you'd better tell me everything you know.'

Harry obliged. There wasn't a great deal to tell, he said. Jean Eden had come to work at the bakery shop in Clapham as a Saturday girl, and joined the full-time staff as soon as she left school. She and Tom Solden had begun a relationship which ended a while ago, and Jean was now engaged to another bakery manager, a man called Nigel Jones.

Georgia quizzed him for more details, but nothing else was forthcoming. That was it, that was all he knew. She thanked him, dismissed him and went into the next room where Banham was still taking a statement. She waited for him to finish, then passed on the new information.

'I interviewed this Jean Eden myself, about an hour ago,' she told him. 'She's worked at the Clapham shop for twelve years, said Solden was a good boss, but she didn't know much about him on a personal level. She did say what happened was dreadful, though I hadn't mentioned the full details.'

'Get her back,' Banham said.

Georgia already had the statement in one hand and her mobile in the other.

Jean Eden arrived back within a few minutes. She was a peroxide blonde with a round face, ruddy complexion and piercing blue eyes. She was quite short, and about a stone overweight. When Georgia had interviewed her less than an hour earlier she had come across as cool and in control; now she was nervous.

'You told us that you knew nothing about Mr Solden's personal life,' Georgia said fixing her astute brown eyes on the woman.

Jean bit her bottom lip, then lowered her head and shook it.

'We have reason to believe you've lied to us in the course

of a murder enquiry,' Georgia told her, showing no sign of sympathy.

Jean looked up. Her cheeks were glowing. 'I suppose I should have known someone would say something. You're talking about my affair with Tom.'

Georgia nodded.

'His wife never knew, and I didn't see any point in hurting her any more, so I didn't mention it.' She blinked. 'The affair has been over for a long while. I realize now that I should have said something. I'm very sorry.'

'It's called perverting the course of justice,' Banham said sternly. 'It can carry a custodial offence.'

Jean's eyes opened wide. 'I haven't lied to you,' she protested, tears beginning to welling up. 'I just didn't think it was relevant. I wanted to save Kate's feelings.'

'Who broke it off?' Georgia asked.

'He did.'

'When?'

'Over a year ago.' She lifted her hand and flashed her ring. 'I'm engaged to someone else. Life has moved on.'

'Why did he break it off?' Banham asked her.

She shrugged. 'It should never have happened. It went on too long because neither of us had the courage to stop. Eventually he had.' She blinked again. 'I was relieved, to tell you the truth.'

'Really?' Georgia said. The woman was gazing at the floor. She didn't seem able to look Georgia in the face.

'Where were you last night?' Georgia asked.

Her head shot up, and she looked at Georgia. 'Am I a suspect?'

'Answer the question,' Banham snapped.

'At home in bed.'

'Before that?'

'Working.'

'Till what time?'

'Ten p.m.'

'Then where did you go?'

'Home. Straight home.'

'Anyone with you?'

'No.'

'Not your fiancé?'

She shook her head. 'He manages the main bakery, in Twickenham. He was working all last night.' She looked at Georgia again. 'Does he have to know about my affair with Tom?'

Georgia gave a sharp nod. 'Probably. So there's no one to corroborate your alibi?'

'You may not have a very high opinion of me,' Jean said crisply, 'and I'm not proud of what happened, but I assure you I am not sleeping with anyone other than my fiancé. So, no, I have no alibi. No one was with me when I went to bed last night.'

'We have no opinion of you,' Banham said dismissively. 'Our job is to catch a killer. And, yes, until proved otherwise you are a suspect. Since you lied to us.'

The woman's eyes were hard, Georgia thought. She had met her type many times: one of life's takers.

'I wouldn't kill him,' she said.

'Did you still get on?'

'Yes. I work for him, don't I? There were no grudges; we outgrew each other, that's all. I'd had a crush on him, and he was infatuated with me. We both grew out of it and moved on. He trusted me to run a shop for him, and I have never said a word to his wife. I would still prefer she didn't have to know.' When neither Banham nor Georgia answered she added, 'This could break up my relationship.'

Georgia flicked a glance at Banham.

'Perhaps you should have thought of that before,' she said flatly.

It was another hour before they headed for a quiet pub and sat at a corner table, both sipping St Clements: Georgia because she was driving, Banham because he wanted to keep his wits about him.

'I could come to the Aviary with you if you want,' he offered. 'I'm in no hurry.'

Georgia shook her head. 'That's not a good idea. Alysha Achter is very young, and nervous of police. She won't say anything in front of anyone she doesn't know. I'm sure of that.'

'Fair enough.'

He seemed disappointed.

'Don't you have a home to go to?'

He half smiled. 'I do, but I don't feel like going there.'

'When is DI Grainger coming back to work?'

'Not soon enough. And you are very perceptive, Detective Inspector Johnson.' Georgia raised her eyebrows. 'Isn't that my job?'

Banham sipped his drink.

'Well, I think this case is going to be messy and tricky,' she said, 'and I'm glad you want to be hands-on, whatever the reason.'

'Have faith,' he said, putting his DCI face back on. 'It's still the first twenty-four hours, and we are moving forward. When we get some forensics back we should know who was in the car with him. And if we find the weapon, we'll sew it up in no time.'

'Yes,' she agreed. 'But there are still a lot of layers. As well as gang warfare brewing on the Aviary, there are things going on in Solden's private life. So where do we start digging? The wife didn't know about the toms he visited, or about the jilted mistress, or so we're told. Dawes thinks everything on the Aviary is down to Yo-Yo Reilly, and he won't entertain anything else.' She studied Banham's face; he gave nothing away, but he was paying attention. 'That in itself could make this complicated. If forensics throw up a result so much the better, but until that happens my gut says we should dig further into Solden's personal life.'

Momentarily unsure she should be speaking out, she looked at him again; he still said nothing, so she brushed her fears to the back of her mind and carried on. 'I think people are afraid to disagree with Dawes. We all know his father was high up at Scotland Yard, but that doesn't mean he's always right, even though he thinks he is.' She paused again. Banham leaned back in his chair, still listening. 'You made me SIO on this. I want you to know I won't tiptoe around him, and I certainly won't kow-tow. I'm spending time on the victim's personal life and leaving no stone unturned.'

Banham lifted his glass. 'Which is why I'm being hands-on.

Not just that I miss Alison and want to fill the hours.' He paused for a second. 'You and Dawes are quite different. I believe he'll be an asset on this. When it comes to South London gangs, he's the top man – but at the end of the day it's your case. Don't dismiss Dawes, though; he has a sharp mind and a good eye, and he wants the right killer behind bars as much as you do.'

'I think he just wants Yo-Yo Reilly.'

'And he may have the opportunity to put him away this time. Reilly is a strong suspect no matter how many other avenues there are. I know you'll cover every one of them because you're very good at your job, Georgia.' He sipped his St Clements. 'Ambitious too.'

She didn't answer. He went on, 'If you want my opinion, I think it could go either way at the moment. It may go back to gang warfare on the Aviary, or there may be something happening a lot closer to home.' He leaned towards her. 'There's no one better than Dawes on gang crime, and no one puts anything past you.' He smiled. 'You certainly saw that I'm missing DI Grainger.'

Georgia changed the subject. The last thing she wanted was a heart-to-heart about Banham's dysfunctional love life; she was a detective, not a Samaritans helpline. 'What do you think of Solden's girlfriend?' she asked him. 'She's engaged to Nigel Jones, the manager of the Twickenham bakery. He said in his statement that he was working there last night, on his own. He did say he was engaged to someone who had worked for Solden for ten years, but he didn't mention that his fiancée had known the victim well.'

'What did he think of Solden?'

She glanced at the statement. 'Same as nearly everyone else: quiet, respectable, a very private person, good to work for. That doesn't sound as if he knows the woman he's marrying was once his boss's mistress.'

'Unless he's lying, like she was. Do you want to talk to him again?'

Georgia nodded. 'Not tonight, though. We've got a car registration for Jean Eden. I'll get Peacock and Lucy Green on to the CCTV footage between Twickenham and Brixton.

If she was in the area last night, at least one camera should have picked her up. I'll get them to check out Oyster cards for night buses too. If she was there, something will come up.'

'Do the same with the boyfriend. If he was working alone he could have slipped out for a couple of hours.'

Georgia stabbed numbers into her mobile and gave the order. 'I'm meeting Stephanie at the Aviary. I'll drop you on the way.' She drained her glass and placed it back on the table. 'Thanks for letting us take a pool car. I've lost count of the slashed tyres I've had parking near that estate. Word always goes round that it's a fed car.'

They walked back to the car in silence. As she opened the driver's door he gave a little embarrassed cough. 'Um, about our conversation earlier . . . Just between us, OK?'

'Of course.'

'No point feeding the rumours.'

He gave a little smile, and Georgia nodded. She had seen a different side of him tonight. The chauvinism was only a front; underneath he was as vulnerable as she was, and had learned to hide his feelings. Suddenly she realized they had something in common, although she would never say as much to him. She wondered if DI Grainger knew how deeply Banham felt about her, or indeed if she felt the same. The rumours around the office claimed they'd had a brief fling, but his feelings clearly ran a lot deeper. He had opened up to her a lot tonight, something she could never do. She admired him for it.

Her mind returned to Stephanie Green and Dawes. How were they getting on? she wondered.

'Oi, Reilly!' Dawes yelled, sticking his head out of the passenger window.

Yo-Yo was sauntering along the pavement with three ugly, bad-tempered pitbulls on the end of gilded choke-collars. A tall, spotty youth walked beside him, holding another; all the dogs huffed and puffed breathlessly.

Reilly stopped and looked round. Dawes opened the car door and sprang out, his ID in his hand. The dogs started snarling, and one attempted to leap at Dawes. He remained unperturbed; he knew Reilly wouldn't risk getting them confiscated yet again.

'Shut them up,' he snapped at Reilly. 'Or I'll have the dog patrol down.'

The dogs carried on snarling.

'Now. Do it.' Dawes raised his voice to a shout. Reilly sniffed condescendingly.

Reilly rolled his eyes and pulled on the leads until they half choked the animals. Reilly and Dawes had crossed swords many times in the past but Dawes was confident that Reilly didn't know that Philly Dawes, the young hooker to whom he had fed dodgy heroin, was his sister. To Yo-Yo, Dawes was an irritating cop who was hell-bent on putting him away. But no matter how many times the police arrested him, Reilly's bent solicitor always proved him to be squeaky clean. As for the dogs, neither Dawes nor any one else had ever proved they were illegal purebred pitbulls; the so-called dog experts in the area were on the payroll of the Brotherhood. The police had given up trying on that score.

Dawes was pleased to see Reilly tug the dogs back and muzzle them. Round one to him.

'What is it this time?' Reilly asked. 'I ain't carrying, no weapons, no drugs. I'm just walking my pets. This smells like harassment to me.'

Dawes ignored him. Instead he spoke to the other boy, Dwaine 'Boot' Ripley; the police knew him as one the most violent of the Brotherhood lieutenants. 'Take his dogs home for him,' Dawes told him. Without waiting for Boot to answer, he turned back to Reilly. 'Get in the car. I want to talk to you.'

There was a beat, then Reilly handed his dogs over to Boot and made his way to Stephanie's car.

'What do you want this time, then?' he asked, settling his twenty-stone bulk into the back seat and smoothing down his top-of-the range leather jacket.

Dawes slid into the front passenger seat and turned to face Reilly. Stephanie decided to lead the questioning. She didn't trust Dawes not to lose it.

'We know you run the street trade on Tidal Lane,' she said to Reilly.

He laughed. 'Who told you that pack of porkies?'

'We aren't interested in that at the moment. We want to know about the punter that got killed there last night.'

Reilly shrugged. 'I don't know nothing about it.'

'Nothing? You must have heard. So who told you?'

Reilly gazed out of the window. 'I don't know nothing about nothing. Are you accusing me of something here? Do I need my solicitor?'

Reilly's solicitor was even more bent than the low-life he represented.

'This is an off the record chat,' she said to Reilly with as much charm as she could muster: not a great deal, she had to admit. 'We know everything about you, Reilly, you know we do. We know you run that corner, and this makes you look as if you can't handle things. It won't be good for business, will it? That must make you very angry.' She paused, and held his eyes. 'Unless you were involved in the murder.'

He lifted his chin defiantly, but said nothing.

'A man was killed last night, and his genitals were severed,' Stephanie went on.

'Is that so?'

'Don't play fucking cat and mouse with us,' Dawes suddenly snapped. Steph thought he looked like he might leap across the car and land one on Reilly.

Stephanie was used to playing good cop, bad cop with Georgia; fortunately her role was always the gentle one, so she immediately jumped in to cool the situation. 'Come on, Reilly. What happened? What did he do?' she coaxed. 'Tell us who to go after. It'll work in your favour. What we've heard is someone's trying to elbow in on your patch.'

His eyes narrowed. 'Don't know what you're talking about.'

'Are you after the killer?'

He eyed her. 'I told you, I don't know nothing. I'm just walking my pets.'

'Who was in the car with him?'

'Wouldn't know.'

'Yes, you do,' Dawes cut in again. 'You know who was working the street last night. Who owed you big-time for the drugs you get them.'

66 Linda Regan

'This is all *off the record*,' Steph reminded him.

'*Off the record* then, this chat is over,' Reilly said, feeling for the door handle. He turned back, his temper flaring. 'Unlock the fucking door, or I'll have you for holding an innocent man against his will.'

Stephanie released the door and as Reilly struggled to get his bulk through the door, Dawes shouted, 'Your card is marked, Reilly.'

'I'm shitting myself,' Reilly laughed as he walked off.

Stephanie put her hand on Dawes arm. 'Cool it,' she said. 'We'll get him for something.'

'I want him for more than *something*,' Dawes snapped back. 'I want him to rot in prison. I can't bear to look at him.'

'I know. But you need to keep calm. Look, I've got to go and meet Georgia. We'll be talking to that girl we know on the estate. She might just tell us something. Do you want to meet for a late night drink, and I'll bring you up to speed?'

'Sure, give me a bell when you're through. Tell you what, I'll drop you off, then drive around a bit and wait for you.'

'I've got a better idea.' Stephanie rummaged in her bag. 'That's my house key. Lucy would love to talk to you. She's desperate to follow me into the force, and as you come from a police family, you'll get on like a house on fire. She's still at the station and she needs a lift home. If you take her home, I'll meet you both there with a takeaway and some beers, and bring you up to speed.'

'That works for me.' Dawes took the key, and held her eyes for a second. 'Thanks,' he said with the hint of a smile.

Somehow Stephanie managed to keep the smile off her own face. The excess perfume must have worn off. She made a mental note to pick up condoms when she got the takeaways and beer.

SIX

Carly didn't want to work tonight. She wanted to fill a pipe with the top-grade rock Yo-Yo had given her, inhale the lot and just chill. She had been looking forward to it all day after Yo had told her to take some time out, enjoy the free gear and forget what had happened. Then he had changed his mind. Scrap had turned up at her door in the afternoon, and told her that Yo-Yo had decided it was best to carry on as if nothing had happened. That meant working the lane tonight.

The thought terrified her. Scrap was stoned out of his head, as usual, but he assured her he would be there to look out for her, and she'd have nothing to fear. She had thrown a proper wobbler, really kicked off, told him she wouldn't do it. She even pleaded, told him she was really scared, but he insisted that it was the best thing to do. She said if she had to work, she'd work another street. Scrap got angry at that and slapped her. She took the slap and still said she wouldn't bloody do it.

That was when Scrap reminded her that Yo-Yo didn't take kindly to his whores disobeying him, and she'd get a real beating for her disobedience, and no more gear. If she just got on with it and worked, the Brotherhood would guarantee her safety, and she'd get loads of good gear.

She finally gave in when he told her Bethany would work with her. Beth was scared too, but had said she'd work if Carly would. Beth was her mate; she had looked out for her when Yo-Yo first put her on the streets to pay a heavy drug debt she had run up. Bethany was a laugh, they had fun together even when they were standing around in next to nothing, toes and tits blue and numb. Bethany was nearly twenty, quite old really – she'd been on the game for years. She was hard and streetwise. She had told Carly that whoring was easy money, if you knew how. Carly trusted her; she felt safer with Bethany than she did with any of the minders. As for that Jade, the other tom who worked Tidal Lane, Carly didn't want to work with her, not ever again. Jade was young too, and lots of punters liked the thrill of jail-bait, so Jade was hot competition.

As for Alysha, the one she used to do the private parties with, she knew her game, though she wasn't letting on. Carly still did well at the private parties with the special clients who liked the perverted stuff. She had blonde hair and blue eyes and could do the innocent look. Jade was tall, with lots of green streaks in her waist-length dark hair, and Alysha had brown skin and dark eyes. The punters preferred the angelic look, so Yo told her, so she made money at parties, providing she did as asked. She didn't care what she did; she just wanted the money.

It was at one of those parties she originally met the saddo that got his nuts done last night. He liked the underage school-girl stuff, booked her to dress up in a nappy for him and they did it in a cot. He tipped her really well. She told him which street she worked, and he often came looking for her. Sometimes for a bit extra she even agreed to meet him during the day, for a shag in his car near one of the bakery shops he had. She had to pretend she was customer; once his wife had come up when she was walking from the shop to the car with him, and another time she'd been given a grilling by the manageress in the shop about why she wanted to see Mr Solden. He told her she'd handled it well, cos she never let on who she was, but after that he stopped chancing it. He used to drive to Tidal Lane when she was working instead. He was a good regular. She'd miss his extra tips, and the warm car, even though he was a sad weirdo.

She asked Scrap if Jade was working that night, but he'd said he didn't know where she was. She didn't live on the estate, he said; she only came down for gear, then worked a couple of punters to pay Yo-Yo for it. Sometimes Yo-Yo gave her gear for a fuck himself. Carly liked that; it meant she didn't have to do him. He was a sadistic, perverted bastard who only got off if he was hurting you. Sometimes he whipped her arse raw. These days he only wanted Alysha, though. He was obsessed with her.

Alysha was an underhand scheming cow. She was a clever whore, though, and knew how to get all the punters for herself. She'd been asking around all day about what happened last night, finding out how much everyone knew. Carly said nothing, not even that the punter was a regular of hers. She reckoned if she said nothing to no one, especially the feds, it would eventually just blow away.

So she had agreed to work with Bethany tonight. She'd earn enough for another rock or two and some bits for Oscar, then she'd take a couple of nights off, smoke the rocks and slide off into another world. When she came round it would all be forgotten.

It had been a good night so far: only two o'clock and she'd done two punters. The second one stank, and wanted her to suck him off. His limp, rancid cock was nearly impossible to get moving, but the thought of that pipe of top-class rock kept her going, and she managed the job. She scrambled out of the car and into her drawers, and was wiping her mouth with a wet-wipe as she hurried back to the end of the dark alley where she'd left Beth. Then she heard the footsteps behind her.

She didn't dare turn round. She decided to run, but before she'd gone a few steps the rope was over her head and round her throat and she was struggling for breath. Her hands clawed at it, but it tightened across her windpipe and her fingers weren't strong enough to get a grip on it. Panic consumed her. She had to get air. She had to breathe and run. Oscar needed her. He was waiting at home for her. She started to fight like a tiger, legs kicking and fingers pulling, but all in vain. Her knees buckled and she toppled forward. A pain shot through her head like a rocket, and she hit the ground hard. As her whole world went dark, little Oscar's face flashed through her mind. He would be crying for her.

Three youths stood at the corner of the walkway, watching Georgia and Stephanie make their way to the flat where Alysha Achter lived with her father.

The flat was in darkness. 'It's a bit early for either of them to be in bed,' Georgia remarked, glowering at the youths then checking her watch.

Stephanie took a few steps towards the boys. Hooded sweatshirts and bandannas concealed most of their faces. 'Do you know Alysha Achter?' she asked them pleasantly.

'Who wants to know?' one answered.

Stephanie flashed her warrant card. 'No one is under arrest. This is just a social call.'

The three looked at each other, shook their heads in turn like a rehearsed routine, then turned away and disappeared down the steps.

'I'm surprised they even spoke,' Georgia said, knocking again.

'Let's hope they don't arrive back mobhanded,' Stephanie said. 'I don't want a brawl – I'm trying to keep myself reasonably tidy. Hot date later.'

Georgia's face broke into a wide smile. 'You've pulled him!'

Stephanie winked. 'Just make sure you go to a cashpoint on the way in tomorrow. Fifty quid, wasn't it? I'm looking forward to treating myself.'

Georgia was delighted, even if Stephanie had upped the odds from twenty. 'Fifty quid it is,' she agreed. 'But you have to get lots of gossip. We know about his sister. I want to know about his influential father in the Met, and anything else about his personal life.'

'I'm on it,' Steph told her. 'His father was George Farrah, assistant chief constable in the Met. Dawes took his mother's maiden name so he wouldn't get promoted for the wrong reason. His sister was a bit younger than Lucy is now.' She turned to face Georgia. 'We know about Reilly feeding her the rough smack that killed her. It left the family in pieces. Remember when ACC Farrah retired, about two years back?'

'Yes. It surprised a lot of people.'

Stephanie nodded. 'That was why. The mother will never be the same either. She lives on tranquillizers. Now you know why Dawes wants to put Reilly away more than he wants anything, and who can blame him?'

'Who indeed?' Georgia pursed her lips. 'I just hope his personal vendetta doesn't cloud his judgement.'

'He's a pro. He'll be an asset on this case.'

Georgia looked at Steph. At the moment she was struck with Dawes, but Georgia knew the pattern only too well. Once she'd had sex with him the novelty would wear off. Before she had time to answer, Alysha Achter appeared on the walkway, coming from the back stairs. She was out of breath, and a bead of perspiration ran down her temple.

'Are you looking for me?' she asked.

The group on the walkway a few minutes ago had obviously known exactly where to find Alysha.

The girl looked nervous. Georgia was aware that word went round the estate very quickly when the feds were around. She also knew the boys who had just tipped her off were Brotherhood members. She tried for a sympathetic smile. 'Hi, Alysha. Remember us? We said we'd keep an eye out for you after you lost your sister. We thought we'd call to see how you are.'

'That's nice,' Alysha said sweetly.

'And we wanted a chat, run a few things past you,' Stephanie added.

'I don't know nothing about the punter got strung last night,' Alysha answered warily. 'That's what you're after, ain't it?'

'Among other things,' Georgia said. 'Can we come in?'

'Yeah. Yeah.' She opened the door. 'My dad'll be asleep in his room. He goes to bed early these days.'

Georgia and Stephanie said nothing. They both knew the father probably wasn't even home, and hadn't been for days. Georgia liked Alysha, but had soon realized girls like her didn't accept help from feds. The girl was a survivor.

A flash of maternal instinct stirred in Georgia, taking her by surprise. Alysha could have been her daughter; she was thirteen and Georgia was just over thirty. She pushed away the feeling, remembering DCI Banham's warning after the previous case: she was a detective, not a social worker. Her job was tracking down killers.

They sat down on a worn, lumpy sofa that smelled of cheap perfume. Georgia noticed that Alysha's T-shirt was on back to front and her tiny ra-ra skirt wasn't properly fastened. Her cornrows were tangled and ragged, and her brown legs were bare.

'How's your dad, Alysha?' Stephanie asked.

'He's not too well,' the girl answered quickly. 'He's in bed.' There was a pause.

'You know we're not here to judge you,' Georgia said. 'If you need us, you know where we are.'

Alysha nodded carelessly. 'It's nice to know . . .'

'. . . that we care?' Georgia finished the sentence. 'Yes, believe it or not, we do. We told you we'd look out for you, and we will. So care about us back. Tell us what the gossip is. You know that a man was murdered last night, in Tidal Lane?'

Alysha nodded cautiously. 'Everyone's heard. This is an estate, word travels.'

'What's the word? Did someone cross Yo-Yo Reilly? Or is someone after taking his patch or bringing his gang down?'

Alysha looked down at the grubby carpet. 'I've not heard nothing about no one trying to take Yo-Yo's patch,' she said. 'But this didn't come from me, OK?'

'Of course.' Georgia watched her carefully.

'I don't think nothing's going off down here,' Alysha said. 'If it was, something would have leaked, and it hasn't. I think you'll find it's personal to the punter. He might have been followed here, that's what I have heard. The girls' minder wasn't there, so someone got the opportunity they were waiting for, and done him.'

'Who was the minder?'

'Oh, I don't know that much.'

'It's between you and us, this conversation,' Georgia assured her. Her fingers closed around her shoulder bag. 'We could help you with a little money if you needed it.'

'I don't know who the minder was,' Alysha said calmly. 'I've already told you stuff I shouldn't. If anyone knows I said that, you know what would happen to me. That's already worth money.'

'OK.' Georgia opened her bag and handed her a twenty-pound note. 'Will you keep your ears open for me?'

Alysha shrugged. 'I'll do my best.'

'I know we're the enemy,' Georgia said carefully. 'But we really are your friends, do you know that?'

'It ain't for me to know,' Alysha said. She stood up. 'I think you should go now, case my dad wakes an' gives me grief.'

Georgia pulled a card from her pocket and held it out. 'Just in case,' she said, leaving it on the arm of the dilapidated sofa when Alysha made no effort to accept it. 'You never know, you might need me.'

It was well past midnight by the time Georgia got home. She went straight to the bathroom and took a long shower, washed her body three times and stepped out of the shower. Then she stepped back in and washed herself once more before drying off and climbing into striped jersey pyjamas and wrapping herself in a thick towelling dressing gown. She heated a bowl of soup and toasted a slice of bread that had lain in the bread bin for nearly a week: there had hardly been time to eat since this enquiry started, let alone shop for groceries.

She pulled out her reports, read and re-read them as she blew over a spoonful of soup to cool it. The toast tasted stale, but she was too hungry to discard it. She kept her notebook by her side and made notes, flicking toast crumbs off the page as she ate and scribbled. There was something dodgy about the ex-girlfriend, Jean Eden, and they were going to check the boyfriend out again too; she'd run his name through the PNC first thing in the morning. She sighed; a difficult day loomed. The wife and daughter of the victim were going to do the formal ID; she hoped beyond everything that no one would mention the missing penis.

She had to remember to get to the cash machine on her way in. It looked as if Steph had actually pulled David Dawes; he was picking Lucy up, and they were all having takeaways at Steph's house. Now she had managed to get him to her house, Georgia was more than confident that Steph would bed him; she was like an octopus when she had her sights on a man. Georgia was looking forward to the gossip on him.

She had worked closely with Steph for five years and was intrigued that she actually enjoyed being known as the office bike. She didn't want a relationship, she had told Georgia, but she couldn't live without regular sex. Georgia's own affairs were far more discreet, and she made a point of keeping them out of the office; but she was no keener than Steph to get involved.

David Dawes was quite ordinary by Steph's standards, but there was an intensity about him that had its attractions. She hadn't noticed a sensitive side, though she hoped for Steph's sake that he had one, and that it came out during sex.

Steph had felt a little embarrassed because she hadn't had time to do any laundry and didn't even have a clean tablecloth. Reliable as ever, Lucy had set the table with raffia mats. Ben was still up when she got back; he wasn't going to miss out on Indian takeaway. The four of them sat round the table, talking about Lucy's career possibilities in the force.

'CID for me,' she announced. 'Like Mum.'

Stephanie beamed with pride.

'Good,' Dawes said. 'We need bright young officers.'

'It'll be ages before I can get on to murder investigations,' Lucy went on, dipping her naan bread into the pot of raita, then forking curry over it. 'I could have to wait years to get into the team.' She bit off a large mouthful.

'You'll have to take your exams and start as a trainee like everyone else,' Dawes told her. 'But the work experience you're doing will help. So will the fact that your mother is a highly respected sergeant.' He looked at Stephanie, who nodded and smiled.

'No preferential treatment,' she said. 'You'll make the tea and help out with filing when you are asked.'

'There are ways I can get involved, though,' Lucy said. 'I might be a big asset.'

'How's that, then?' Dawes grinned.

'I could go undercover as a hooker.'

Stephanie's jaw dropped. 'I don't think that will be necessary,' Dawes said quickly.

'Well, I'm offering,' Lucy said, giving Dawes an innocent-as-a-kitten smile. 'As long as I knew you wouldn't be far away, I'd be happy to do it.'

'We'll bear it in mind,' he said with a smile.

Stephanie cut in. 'Don't push it, Luce. Be grateful for the experience you're getting.'

Lucy and Dawes were bonding quite well. A little too well. Lucy was a good girl, but she was at a vulnerable age, and had been looking for a father figure most of her life. She particularly enjoyed talking to other detectives, which was fine, as long as she didn't get clingy with one in particular. Permanent relationships were out of the question.

Steph wasn't looking for a dad for her daughter; she was after a night of lust with Dave Dawes. They'd had a long day; she needed a good shag and a full night's sleep, then she could face tomorrow. She just wanted the kids to clear off to bed so she could invite Dawes into hers.

She tried to bring the subject to a close. 'You'll make a good detective, Luce, but you need to get your exams first. We'll talk more in the morning.'

Lucy immediately took the hint. She picked up her plate and Ben's and headed for the dishwasher. 'Night,' she shouted as she made her way up the stairs.

'Night, darling.'

Dawes yawned and stood up.

'Time I made tracks. I'll see you at the morning meeting.' He hovered by the table.

'You live in Islington?' Stephanie asked.

'Yes, I do.'

'Then, for heaven's sake, stay. We've had a drink, you don't want to be driving. You're welcome to the couch.' She turned away and started to stack the empty curry containers. 'You're also very welcome to share my bed.'

She turned back and looked him straight in the eyes.

He stared at her for what seemed like an age. Then he blinked, and half smiled.

'Is that a yes or a no?'

Before he could answer her mobile burst into a rendition of the Can-Can. She looked at the display. 'It's the station,' she said. 'It'll be urgent.' As she picked up the phone, Dawes's mobile sounded. It was the urgent ringtone he had programmed for emergency call-outs.

'Whereabouts is the body?' Steph asked.

Dawes pressed his phone to his ear with his shoulder and picked the car keys up from the table with one hand, slipping the other into his jacket sleeve.

Georgia was already at the scene, on all fours on the cold stone pavement in an alley between the Aviary estate and Tidal Lane, scene of crime officers milling around her. She looked up and threw Steph a smile. Dawes had stopped at the entrance to the alley, his mobile to his ear.

Georgia pulled her mouth mask down as Stephanie squatted beside her. 'I haven't had time to hit the cashpoint,' she whispered to her. 'I hope you've got gossip.'

'I think we're all going to be too tired for sex after we get through here,' Stephanie told her resignedly. She looked over at the body. 'What's the damage?'

'Strangulation.'

'Do we know who she is?'

'Judging by her attire and the location, and the fact that she has a bagful of flavoured condoms, I think we can safely asume she's a tom.'

Stephanie lowered her voice. 'If they weren't evidence, I might ask to borrow them,' she whispered. 'I didn't get a chance to buy any. There's only the one left in the bedroom drawer. I was getting quite panicky.'

'Behave yourself,' Georgia snorted.

'What's funny?' They hadn't heard Dawes creep up and squat beside them.

'Phoebe said to be careful – keep your forensic shoes covers on. There are lots of different foot marks,' Georgia said. 'Forensics are trying to lift as many as possible before it starts to rain.'

'What about cars? Any traces?'

'There are tyre tracks by the alley.' Georgia pointed. 'And a few used condoms, so we're hopeful. There are used tissues too, lots of gum, and dog ends, and fast food containers. Plenty to go on.'

Dawes nodded. 'A lot of draining on budget too,' he said.

'At the least we'll know which toms were working here tonight,' Georgia said. 'We can start with them. Of course it'll take a few days to get any results back.'

'I've just spoken to Banham,' Dawes told them. 'He said briefing six a.m. sharp, meanwhile get some sleep.'

Georgia looked Dawes in the eye for a few seconds. 'Fine.' She scrambled to her feet and started to walk back to her car. An extra ten minutes' sleep was time better spent than reminding Dawes that it was the senior investigating officer's job to call the time of the morning meeting, and that it was also the senior investigating officer's job to keep the DCI up to speed. Dawes had crossed her before, she reminded herself as she watched him follow Stephanie and open the passenger door of his car for her, but Georgia hadn't got to where she was by letting people walk over her.

SEVEN

Tuesday, three a.m.

Yo-Yo Reilly stood in the front room in his ground-floor flat with two of his pitbulls cowering beside him. Boot, Scrap, Bethany, Alysha and another hooker, Orla, were there too, confused and afraid.

'Someone thinks they can get away with pissing on my patch, do they?' Yo-Yo snarled, lashing out with his boot at the grubby moss-green wall. The next vicious kick landed on the backside of one of the dogs; the animal leapt in the air and cried out in pain, then growled and strained at its lead, spoiling for a fight. The girls all took a step back.

Yo-Yo continued ranting. 'I'll find the fucker and I'll kill them myself! Someone's murdered one of ours, and on our own territory. They think they can get away with pissing on our patch, do they?' He looked at Scrap, whose pupils were like saucers. 'You were told to watch the girls carefully, not to take your fucking eyes off them. I told you to keep every fucking car in sight even if it was bouncing up and down for hours.' He took a step towards his lieutenant. 'I told you to watch every punter.' He flew at Scrap, picking him up by the front of his T-shirt and throwing him against the wall. 'You're a fucking disgrace. Call yourself a fucking lieutenant, do you?' His voice reached screaming pitch. 'Someone out there's pissing on us. And you fucking let it happen.' He grabbed Scrap again and bounced him back into the wall. Scrap wheezed and fought for breath, but said nothing. All the pitbulls growled menacingly.

'Is that it? Is it? Yo-Yo shouted into his face. 'You want everyone to think we're a load of wimpish cunts? Is that what you want? Fucking answer me.'

'No, Yo.'

'No, Yo?' His voice rose further. 'Well you've let the fuckers think that it's yes, Yo.' Yo-Yo let him go, then turned and yelled at the rest of the gang. 'Most people both sides of the fucking river know not to mess with us, and now they think they can do exactly that.'

No one replied.

'No one makes us out to be cunts and gets away with it. Got it?'

They all muttered agreement.

'I own this fucking patch and anyone who knows what's happening and doesn't speak up will answer to me. Got it?'

Everyone nodded.

'I'll cut them up inch by fucking inch.' He turned back to Scrap. 'Tell me again – how did it happen?'

Scrap was heavily stoned and utterly terrified. His speech slurred as he told his story again. Carly had been missing for about an hour or so, or so he thought, but he had to admit he wasn't exactly sure how long.

'I ain't working, Yo,' Bethany blurted out, folding her arms defiantly. 'Not till all this is sorted. He's fucking useless at minding us.'

'I ain't either,' Orla agreed. 'I'm fucking terrified now.'

Alysha threw them both an angry glare and shook her head by way of a warning. Reilly ignored them. He leaned over Scrap, who was flat against the wall. Reilly crossed his arms over his chest. Alysha knew that he crossed his arms when he didn't trust himself not to stab the person in front of him. She moved a little nearer to him in case it all went up and she had to stop him.

'Go on,' Reilly said to Scrap, attempting to hold on to his temper. 'What then?'

It was about ten o'clock, Scrap told them, when Carly took her last punter. 'I think so, anyway,' he said. 'She hadn't come back by about eleven – that's when I went looking for her. Bethany was doing another punter round about then.'

Bethany nodded confirmation.

'So it was at least an hour before either of you realized Carly wasn't back,' Yo-Yo said.

Bethany sucked in air through clenched teeth and opened her mouth to say something, but stopped as she caught Alysha's warning glance.

'Yeah. Yeah, I think so. About that, anyway.' Scrap closed his eyes, desperately trying to get his brain working. 'So what did you do when you saw Carly was dead?' Yo-Yo asked with exaggerated patience. 'What do you think? I scarpered, and got on the blower to you pronto.'

Someone else had found her body and alerted the feds only a few minutes later; that's all it took for the racket to start – women shrieking, people shouting, and not long after the sirens screaming.

Boot had said nothing up to now. He sat on the arm of the sofa, a stick in one hand and his pitbull's lead in the other, listening keenly, his spotty rat-like face turning from Reilly to Scrap as if he was at a tennis match.

Now he spoke. 'It's a fucking disgrace.' He narrowed his eyes. 'We're the Brotherhood and we're gonna be a laughing stock.' He looked straight at Yo-Yo. 'Is someone trying to take us on, d'you think? Is that what this is about?' He glanced at Bethany and Orla. 'No one messes with Brotherhood goods. Everyone knows that. Someone's taking the piss big time.'

'I'll find out,' Reilly assured him. He eyed Alysha. 'Seems to me someone needs to pass that message on to our old friend Michael. See, I reckon Mince never took too well to being shanked and dumped out of the Brotherhood.' He stared coldly at Alysha. 'The way I see it, perhaps he's thinking he can get one over on us.' He drew breath through gritted teeth and shook his head threateningly. 'Big mistake. Someone should tell him that.'

Alysha held his eyes but didn't answer.

He kept his eyes pinned to Alysha's. 'Man's got a fucking death wish the way I see it,' he added.

''E ain't got the back-up,' Alysha said defensively. Reilly's face reddened with anger, and she realized that she should have kept quiet. But now she'd begun, she decided to go on. ''E just wants a bit of peace these days,' she said, waving a hand dismissively through the air. 'He sells weed, that's all, and not on your territory, cos he don't want no more trouble. He wouldn't do this, for definite.'

'Seen him, have you?' Reilly's jealous eyes flared.

''Course I've seen him.' She raised her hands. 'He lives on
the Wren block. Everyone's seen 'im.' She threw her big round
brown eyes to heaven. 'I aint sweet on him no more, I swear
to God, if that's what you's thinking. He paid the price for
disobeying, that's all I'm saying. You've scarred him badly
and he wants an easy life. She shook her head. 'It ain't him
doing this, and I ain't heard nothing around from no one. I
reckon it's to do with the punter that got done and Carly being
in the car with him.'

'Who phoned in the killing?' Reilly asked quickly.

'Someone walking home down the alley to the estate,'
Alysha told him. 'They stumbled over the body – woke that
whole side of the Sparrow block with their shrieking. I dunno
know who it was.'

Reilly looked at her appraisingly. 'You've had that punter
that got his nuts done, haven't you?'

Alysha shrugged. 'I don't know. I don't look at their faces,
and I don't ask them for nothing except their money. And I
don't remember none of them.'

'You have had him.' Reilly raised his voice again at her.
'Don't start fucking lying to me. You know full fucking well
you've had him. You've had him a lot. What d'you know about
him?'

'Nothing.' She put a hand on her hip. 'If I have had him
loads, it's cos you gave me to him loads. I've had millions of
fucking punters and I don't know nothing about none of them.
I told you, I don't look at 'em. You're the only one I look at
when I'm fucking, and you're the only one I enjoy fucking,
so don't start getting all jealous on me.'

Bethany and Orla giggled. Boot stuck his finger in his throat.

'I ain't getting jealous,' Reilly argued. 'I'm working on
who's doing our territory and why.' He pointed a menacing
finger at her. 'Don't you ever, ever lie to me.'

Alysha sighed. 'This ain't getting us nowhere,' she said.
She caught Bethany's eye. The other girl seemed nervous for
her. She made a mental note to take good care when she saw
Mince in the future.

'You ain't gonna make us work for a bit, are you?' Bethany
asked Reilly. 'We ain't safe. I'm fucking scared witless out

there.' She jerked her head at Scrap. 'He's a fucking waste of space as far as minding us goes.'

Reilly rubbed his hand across his mouth thoughtfully. 'Who else's seen Mince Delahaye lately?'

Alysha tutted.

'You think he's out to pay us back cos you cut him,' Boot said. 'Him and who else?'

'Boot's right,' Alysha agreed. 'Where's his gang? He can't do it on his jacks.'

Scrap suddenly came back to life. 'I heard he was only selling a bit of skunk here and there. You scarred him up, Yo, and he knows you'd do it again.'

'Perhaps we've got some turncoats in the Brotherhood,' Boot said flatly.

'Perhaps we have,' Reilly agreed. 'Perhaps Mince's building his own crew, and this is his way of letting us know there's a war brewing.'

Alysha shook her head. 'He ain't interested in gangs and fighting no more. He ain't got over the shanking you gave him. If he weren't afraid he wouldn't sell his weed well away from your patch.' She paused. 'I'm telling you, it ain't 'im.'

Reilly's eyes flared. 'You've talked to him a lot, have you?'

'I told you . . .'

Reilly butted in with a pointed finger. 'I say who you see, who you talk to and who you fuck. Have you got that? You are my property. You don't talk to fucking Delahaye, got it?'

Alysha returned his stare. 'Oh, yes, I got it, but it ain't no big deal. I bump into him sometimes, that's all. But I do know that he's learned not to mess wiv you, cos he told me as much, an' I'm telling you now. I'm your girl, and I don't do no one unless you say I do. Mince don't want trouble, so leave him be. I still think someone from outside wanted that punter done, and Carly got in the way.'

'This ain't getting us nowhere, Yo,' Bethany interrupted. 'My mate's just been killed, and her kid's gonna be crying for a long time. I got two kids to feed, so I need brass. But you gotta make sure it's safe for us to work, or I won't do it. I'm shit-scared and I definitely ain't gonna chance my luck if there's a murderer loose. Till you promise we'll be OK, I ain't going nowhere near Tidal.'

'Where's Jade?' Reilly said to her. 'I told you all to be here.'

'No one's seen her,' Bethany said. 'She don't live on the estate, and she ain't come back since the punter got done. She ain't answering her phone either. She'll be scared witless too, and I don't blame her, poor cow. She's only young too.'

'OK, here's what happening,' Reilly said. 'Tonight you girls go back out on the streets.' There was an outcry, but he raised his hand and went on. 'Not to Tidal, none of you are gonna be working there, it's swarming with feds. You'll be in Hill Street, just round the corner. I'll be at the end of the road in my car, and I won't take my eyes off you. You'll be safe, I'll guarantee. My Mac10 says no one messes with Brotherhood property. The first sniff of trouble and I'll use it. I'm gonna find out who's taking a piss on my patch, and make them wish they hadn't.' He looked at Alysha. 'You'll be in the car with me, so when punters drive up they'll think we're doing business.'

Alysha smiled. 'And you'll pay me?' she said.

'Maybe. If you do as you're told.'

'Pleasure's all mine, I'm sure.'

Georgia was woken by the phone at around four thirty a.m. Kate Solden had rung in to the station at about half past three; Alice hadn't returned home. She was three weeks from her sixteenth birthday so officially she was still a minor.

Georgia scrambled into the shower and stood under a cool spray for a few minutes until she felt awake. She dressed quickly in jeans and her usual clean white T-shirt with a black roll-neck sweater to keep out the biting wind, then she grabbed her long, black leather coat and her car keys and headed for the station.

Kate Solden was at the station by the time Georgia got there. She was sitting in Georgia's office, her eyes red and puffy with dark circles under them. She had originally arranged to be at the mortuary later that morning, to identify her husband's body.

Georgia sat down in the chair opposite her. 'Has Alice

done this before?' she asked. 'Stayed out all night without contacting you?'

Kate stared at her dumbly.

'OK. Start at the beginning and tell me everything you can remember. When did you last see her?'

Kate sighed heavily. 'When she came home yesterday, I sat her down and told her what had happened. She was shocked, of course. She just said that she wanted time alone. I let her be.' Kate bit her lip, and tears ran down her face.

Georgia wouldn't have had time for sympathy, even if she was any good at it. 'What exactly did you tell her?' she asked. 'Did you tell her where he was found? What her father had been doing? And how he was murdered?'

Kate shook her head vigorously. 'No, no, of course not. I told her he'd left the house and gone for a drive at night, and that he'd been murdered. That's all.' Kate's voice broke. 'She's only fifteen, Inspector . . .'

'Georgia.'

A look of desperation crept over Kate's face. 'She shouted and called me a frigid cow, and said everything was my fault and she hated me. Then she said she was going out too.' Kate swallowed, and tears continued to run down her face unchecked. 'How was I to know she'd go off like that?'

'And this is the first time she's stayed out all night?'

Kate bit her lip. 'No, it's not,' she said. 'We're always fighting, she and me. She's a handful. Tom said she was having a wild phase. She certainly is.' She looked at Georgia with fear in her eyes. 'But she's always come home eventually.'

Georgia looked at her watch. 'It's not six yet. She still could. Do you know where she goes or who she's with when she stays out?'

Kate crammed her fist in her mouth. 'I'm a terrible mother.'

'Why?'

Kate looked blankly at Georgia. 'Do you have children?'

Georgia wished Stephanie was here. Steph would handle this so much better. 'No, I don't,' she said. 'Why do you think you're a terrible mother?'

Kate looked down into her lap but didn't reply.

'I'll need a list of her friends,' Georgia told her.

'She has friends at school but I don't really know them.'

'You must know who they are? Does she never bring any friends home?'

Kate shook her head. 'Don't judge me,' she said quietly. 'If you haven't got kids, how could you possibly know what it's like?'

Stung, Georgia stood up. 'I'll get an officer to come and take some details,' she said curtly. 'I'll be back in a while. I'm afraid I still have to ask you to identify your husband's body.'

'I need to go home. I want to be there when Alice comes back.'

Georgia took a deep breath. 'All right. I'll get an officer to take you home and stay with you, then bring you back in time for our appointment at the mortuary.'

'Thank you,' Kate said. 'Do you think . . . Could it be someone in plain clothes? I don't want to frighten her into running off again if she sees police in the house.'

'Why would she do that?'

Kate shrugged, but didn't answer.

Georgia looked at her for a long moment. It was almost as if the woman didn't want to be helpful. She tried another tack. 'Which school does Alice go to?'

'Dartwood High.'

Georgia wondered for a second why the name was familiar. Then she remembered: it was the one Lucy Green attended.

Not for the first time, she was glad Lucy was here on work experience.

Alysha decided to take the long route back to her home on Sparrow block. It was nearly five a.m.; if she went via the Wren block, she might find Mince still up, unwinding and having a smoke. His mum worked nights in a massage parlour in North London, so if the lights were on, he'd be there alone. She was confident Reilly wasn't following her. She'd stayed after the meeting and had sex with him; he was being more possessive than ever, and was prone to flying into a temper if Mince's name was mentioned.

She needed to update Mince on what was going on in the Brotherhood, so she'd made sure Reilly was tired out before she left. It hadn't taken much: a few bounces on his great, blubbery body wearing her stilettos, with her hands handcuffed behind her back, and his sperm shot high in the air; then she'd sucked him off, very slowly, fighting back the urge to sink her teeth into the fat bastard's cock and draw blood. He was asleep now, snoring like a pig. It'd be quite safe to knock on Mince's window.

Yo had given her some good grass; they could smoke it together while she told him about the meeting. Mince needed to keep his head down; best not to come face-to-face with Reilly in the next day or so.

She turned the last corner of the alleys heading toward the Wren block. Mince lived in a ground-floor flat; it was easy to knock on the window. But her heart sank. The flat was in complete darkness.

If she tapped on his window and woke him, he might not be pleased. But she wanted so much to be with him. It was safe now, no one was around; she could spend an hour or so, just hanging out with him. One of these days she'd wear his resistance down and then he'd never stop wanting her. She'd learned a lot about what men wanted, and she was going to use it all to please Mince. Life was going to change big time when they were together.

The dog in the flat next door suddenly started barking. Alysha was across the road so it wasn't her that had disturbed the animal. Then Mince's front door opened; she stepped behind the drainpipe just in time. A second later, a dishevelled Bethany walked out. Alysha was shocked and furious. Bethany must have gone to Mince's while Alysha was fucking Reilly.

Her temper rose again, but she kept still and watched. She needed to find out what was going on. Bethany was supposedly a Brotherhood whore; she had to be here on the sly. There was no kissing going on, but Bethany was standing close to Mince, and they seemed to be talking intimately. Mince had never mentioned a close friendship with Bethany to Alysha, and Bethany wasn't whoring when Mince was a Brotherhood lieutenant. She didn't live on this estate, either; she came from the Random, the next one along. So what was going on here? Bethany was all teeth and mouth, friendly and jokey with everyone, but inside she was made of steel. The girl would shoot her own grandmother for a fix. Alysha carefully stepped back into the dark pathway. It was going to be very much to her advantage not to let either Bethany or Mince know she was watching.

The morning meeting had started when Georgia arrived in the squad room. Dawes was standing at the front of the room by the whiteboard, where the photo of a young, pretty blonde girl, lying dead in the dark alleyway leading to the Aviary estate, had joined the others. The girl's eyes were wide with terror. Underneath the photo in large blue letters were the words *Carly MacIntosh. Age fifteen years.*

Georgia walked through the room to join Banham, who stood beside Dawes.

'Sorry I'm late, sir,' she said. 'I've been talking to Kate Solden.'

Banham gave her a reassuring smile. 'Are you OK?' he asked.

Dawes was telling the room they were treating the two murders as connected.

'I'm not up to speed,' Georgia said. 'Do we have any solid reason to connect them apart from the location?'

'Forensics are in from the Tom Solden murder scene,' DC Hank Peacock told her. 'As well as his, there were two sets of DNA lifted from the condom found in the car. One of them belonged to the dead girl. She was in the car with him.'

'Who does the second set belong to?' Georgia asked quickly.

'A Bethany Field. She's a known class-A drug user and has form for soliciting, shoplifting, and causing an affray. It's likely they were both in the car with him,' Peacock said confidently. 'Perhaps he liked doubles.'

A rumble of amusement went round the room. Peacock went scarlet.

Banham brought the team back quickly to the matter in hand. 'We need to find this Bethany Field and bring her in,' he told them. 'No need to remind ourselves the danger she might be in.'

'I've got an address for her,' Peacock said, his blush fading.

'And now Tom Solden's daughter has gone missing,' Georgia told them. 'She ran off when her mother broke the news and hasn't been seen since.'

'Has she gone missing before?' Banham asked.

Georgia nodded. 'Kate Solden said she comes back but never says where she's been.'

'How long has she been gone?' Banham asked.

'Since yesterday evening.'

Banham looked around for Stephanie. 'Go and pick Bethany Field up.'

'Guv.'

'If she's not there, leave a uniform car outside her address, and tell them to bring her in as soon as she turns up.'

'Alice Solden goes to the same school as Lucy,' Georgia said. 'Peacock, can you check if she has form?'

Lucy was sitting near the front of the room, close to DI Dawes. 'Alice Solden?' she piped up. 'Yes, I think I know her. She's in Year Eleven.'

'What's she like?' Stephanie asked. 'Would you say she's the type to run away?'

Lucy shrugged. 'To be honest, I hardly know her. She's younger than me, and she's in with a dodgy crowd. They go to parties and hang out at places I wouldn't go.'

'What kind of places?'

'Clubs, mainly. Places you're supposed to be eighteen to get in.'

Dawes beamed at Lucy. 'Excellent. Do you know any of these places?'

'I have an idea,' Lucy said eagerly.

'How about we take you out in an unmarked car on a tour of them?'

Georgia was furious. What right had he to suggest that?

Dawes must have read her thoughts. 'Lucy will be a strong asset,' he said. 'I think we all agree that finding Alice is a priority.'

Lucy smiled delightedly. 'Awesome,' she said.

Georgia looked at Stephanie hoping for some support, but none was forthcoming. Banham wasn't against the idea either. It was clear Georgia was in the minority, and she had no wish to throw a wet blanket on Lucy's dreams. After all, who was she to mind if an untrained, inexperienced girl went out on a dangerous murder investigation? Only the senior investigating officer, or had anyone noticed?

Alysha waited until Bethany walked away and Mince went back inside, then she headed for her own flat. She was wide awake when she got in. She had the grass that Yo had given her, so she started to roll a joint. She was angry and jealous, and needed to think things through before she decided how to react. Was Bethany fucking Mince, or feeding him Brotherhood information? Bethany did crystal meth and heroin, and Yo-Yo was the sole supplier around here; why would she chance Yo-Yo finding out she was sneaking round to Mince's unless they were fucking? Unless Mince had lied to her; perhaps he was dealing other stuff as well as grass. And if that was so, perhaps he was lying about other things too – like gathering an army to take Yo-Yo out and take over the estate, and her being part of that plan.

Alysha had learned to trust no one, but she came close with Mince. She finished rolling the joint and licked the Rizla paper angrily. She flicked the gold lighter Yo had given her, and lit the end and dragged hard on it. The hit felt great; she swallowed the hot smoke and let it burn her throat and up into her nose. This was good stuff, she would chill on it.

Bethany hadn't looked too cosied up with Mince when she came out his door; they weren't kissing or putting their arms round each other like you do if you're having sex. What *was* going down with those two?

Her phone bleeped loudly. She checked her screen and closed her eyes. It was Yo-Yo. She clicked the green button.

'What you want now, Yo?'

'I want you to find Jade. Today.'

The chill from the weed quickly disappeared. 'Where? I know fuck all about her. She's only been working for a couple of weeks. Ask that bloke at the Holster; he introduced you.'

'No, its best you look for her,' he told her. 'She's underage and she's frightened. She'll trust you more.'

'What are you so worried about her for?'

'I think someone might be targeting my underage girls.'

'What about me then? Shouldn't you be worried about me?'

He laughed. 'I ain't worried about you.'

'If someone's targeting your underage girls, maybe you should be.'

'No, you're well safe. I've made it known that you ain't one of my working girls, you're my personal property. I own you, right?'

'If you say so.'

'If anyone tries anything with you, I will slice them up inch by fucking inch, make no fucking mistake, darling. No one fucks with my property.'

'They already are. And you ain't got eyes in the back of your head.'

'You'd better believe I have.'

'What, you know what I am doing every second of the day? All the time, is that right?'

'Don't ask so many fucking questions. Save your mouth for my cock. Now go and find Jade.'

EIGHT

Tuesday morning

Press conferences were always stressful, but this one took the biscuit. DCI Banham loathed these calls at the best of times, but knew only too well how much the police relied on them to move a case forward. The media did more than anything else to push memory buttons in the public's brains. Banham didn't trust them, but he kept that thought to himself as cameras whirred and flashed and microphones were pointing in his direction.

Alison Grainger was good at dealing with the press. She had been an amateur actress before joining the police force and knew how to put on the right kind of front. Banham had done numerous training days, but he knew he was pretty useless at it. He missed Alison even more than usual this morning, as he sat beside Thalia Wood, the police PR officer, and faced a room full of hungry reporters.

His face gave nothing away, but behind the mask he was furious. Despite his strict instructions, intimate details of Tom Solden's murder had got out. The press bombarded him with questions about the victim's missing genitals, and asked if the prostitute found strangled in the alleyway was linked to the same enquiry. Banham struggled to stay calm. Thalia Wood didn't utter a word. He began to wonder why she was there; it was her job to help him out, yet all she did was sit there. How he missed Alison.

He held up a hand for silence. 'I'm sorry,' he said, 'this is all speculation and I'm unable to comment. I can confirm that the victim's name is Tom Solden, and he was attacked with a knife; and also that a sex worker, Carly MacIntosh, has been found strangled. Until we have evidence to link them, the two murders will be treated as separate enquiries.'

He went on to make the usual appeal for witnesses, and

recited the phone number the public could call. Then he politely thanked everyone, and stood up to indicate that the press conference was over.

Walking back to the investigation room, thoughts whirred round his mind. The Aviary estate was back in the headlines, and the media knew exactly how Solden had been killed. Those leaked details would make the public more nervous and spread further unease. But could relations between the police and the residents of the estate get any worse?

Thalia Wood hurried up the corridor to join him. 'Sir? Were you happy with that? Is there anything else I can do for you?'

She walked along beside him, looking earnestly into his face, her hand touching his arm confidentially. His mind was on the strangled sex worker; Carly's DNA had already confirmed that she was in the car with Solden, either when he was cut up or shortly before. The murders were clearly linked, and what little evidence they had was starting to point to a gang-retribution war, as Dawes suggested, rather than the domestic murder line that Georgia Johnson was pursuing. Not that they had anything solid either way. All they knew for sure was that someone had opened their mouth to the press. Whether one of the team had made a stupid remark in the wrong place, or something more ominous was going on, was something he needed to find out.

It took him a few moments to cotton on that Thalia was coming on to him.

'Would you like me to get you some coffee?' she asked.

'I've got a machine in my office. That's where I'm heading, to do some work in peace.'

She paused, and her tone changed. 'Right. Fine. I'll see you later, sir.'

He opened his office door and stared at the coffee maker. Alison Grainger had bought it for him, after their one night together. That now seemed an age away. He spooned fresh coffee into the machine, wondering if she would ever come back.

She had fended him off for months before that night. Now there were rumours that she was planning to quit the murder division. He hadn't been in touch with her since she went on leave. What was the point? She clearly didn't feel the same. He had offered to take her to Venice after the case that upset her so much. All she said was that she wanted to be left alone.

Georgia's morning hadn't exactly been easy. She had accompanied a tearful Kate Solden to identify her husband's body, then sent her home in a police car with a promise that they were doing all they could to find her daughter. Afterwards she had to attend Tom Solden's post-mortem, and her teeth felt raw and tetchy from crunching peppermints throughout the procedure. The stench of bleach fluid mixed with body parts as they were dissected always threatened to bring her breakfast back. Crunching on strong mints was her only weapon against her erupting stomach. Phoebe Aston, the pathologist, had the constitution of an ox despite being heavily pregnant; she had flicked irritated glances at Georgia's crunching as she made verbal notes into her dictaphone over the dismembered cadaver. Georgia had apologized afterwards, but Phoebe had laughed it off, saying it was far preferable to Stephanie Green's bubblegum popping. Phoebe wasn't without sympathy; she understood not everyone could stomach the procedure, and murder detectives weren't exactly there by choice.

It had all been worth it, though; it had turned up some interesting finds. The first was a description of the weapon. The knife had entered Solden's body on the right, the side of the liver, leaving a stencil imprint of its shape. If they found the weapon, they could match it up with the imprint, and if there was DNA on it as well, they could well have their culprit. The unusual shape of the knife was a bonus too. The end was curved and forked, like a large cheese knife. The Aviary estate was littered with dumped knives and weapons, but now they knew the exact shape of the one they were looking for, the search would be a lot easier. And if the weapon turned up in the vicinity of Solden's house, or one of his bakeries, that would really narrow the field of suspects.

David Dawes, as usual, was determined that this crime would revert back to Yo-Yo Reilly, but to Georgia too many other questions needed answers. What was going on in Alice

Solden's mind, and where had she gone? Was it the marriage breakdown that had made Kate Solden turn to alcohol? Who would inherit in Tom Solden's will? Why had Solden's ex-mistress withheld information? Georgia was especially interested in the ex-mistress, who still held a responsible position in Solden's business.

And she wasn't at all happy about Lucy's close involvement in the case. Dawes knew as well as Georgia did that things could quickly turn nasty on the Aviary. The real surprise was that Stephanie seemed happy for Lucy to go along with them. Georgia was concerned that Stephanie's attraction to Dawes had influenced that decision. Lucy was Georgia's responsibility while she was with the team, and she didn't want the girl's safety jeopardized, but she was Stephanie's daughter after all. Best to keep her opinion to herself, for the time being.

She had doubts about whether Dawes should be on the case. He knew as well as she did that most murders were committed by someone close to the victim, but this bee in his bonnet about Reilly, understandable though it was given the personal circumstances, meant he wouldn't listen to other evidence. Dawes argued that the case had Reilly's stamp all over it, but Carly MacIntosh's murder now cast a whole new light on the case. Carly had been strangled; Reilly was a knife man. DNA tests had proved that Carly had been in that car when Solden was killed, so it looked as if she had been silenced. That meant Bethany Field's life was in danger – unless Bethany was the killer herself. That was possible too; her DNA was on the condom. They needed to find her, and bring her in.

Georgia was regretting her bet with Stephanie. Her judgement was usually clear, but this might cloud it. Stephanie had nearly seduced him, so as soon as she did, Georgia could breath a sigh of relief; Stephanie would be moving on to the next, and Dawes would be history.

Georgia walked into the ladies' and cupped her hands under the cold tap. After throwing the water over her face, she felt thoroughly awake. She patted her face dry with a paper towel, applied a little mascara, smoothed her wiry black hair behind her ears and secured it in a ponytail with the help of black scrunchy. She had probably had less than half a dozen hours sleep in three days. Tiredness she could cope with, but looking grubby or dishevelled appalled her. She washed her hands again and checked her white T-shirt at the back and front. She lifted the T-shirt and sprayed herself liberally with deodorant, then dotted some perfume behind her ears before returning to the office to pick up her coat and find one of the team. She wanted another detective with her when she re-interviewed Tom Solden's ex-mistress and her fiancé.

Banham was in his office with the door open. He stood by the window, a china mug of coffee in one hand and a pile of papers in the other.

'How's it going?' he asked.

'A small breakthrough,' she said. 'The weapon left an imprint on the victim's liver. I'd like to up the search near the Soldens' house, if you're OK with that. And I'm on my way to re-interview the mistress now. If Ivan's free, I'll take him with me.'

'Ivan's following up banks and collecting phone records and paper work.' Banham drained his coffee. 'I'll come with you.'

'OK,' she said, trying to ignore a sinking feeling. He had shown himself to be less of a chauvinist than she thought, but she still felt weighed down by all the male energy that surrounded her. Still, if the DCI said he was going with her, she could hardly argue with that. So much for being the SIO.

As they made their way to the car park she asked if he preferred to drive or be driven. He told her that he liked being driven. 'As long as it's not by Alison Grainger,' he added with a wry grin.

Georgia lowered her eyes. This man was so in love with this Alison Grainger that he never passed up an opportunity to mention her name. His feelings clearly weren't reciprocated; and now she would probably have to listen to him banging on about her all day. Not for the first time, Georgia felt grateful for her independence.

'Do you know any of Alice's friends?' Dawes asked Lucy as he turned the car down the long hill that led to the Holster club.

Lucy shook her head. 'Not personally. I told you, they're quite a bit younger than me. Besides, you have to be a Goth to be in with her crowd. Not my thing, I find all that stuff pathetic.'

'But you know who they are, do you? If not their names, at least what they look like? You'd recognize them if you bumped into them?'

'They look like Goths,' Lucy replied. 'Dyed black hair with pink or green streaks, an overload of black make-up, eyes, lipstick, nails, the lot.'

'We'll go and visit her school if she doesn't come home by this afternoon,' Steph said to Dawes. 'I know the teachers. I can get names and addresses.'

'The Holster is a hang-out for Goths,' Dawes said. 'The book of matches found near Solden's murder scene could be a coincidence, but we'll make that our first port of call. It's got a dreadful reputation for shootings and stabbings. And did you know Yo-Yo Reilly has the protection contract on the place?'

'I believe you mentioned it,' Stephanie said dryly. She turned back to Lucy. 'Alice had lovely blonde hair,' she said. 'What did her parents think when she dyed it black? I can't say I'd be pleased if you turned up with grim black hair with pink and green streaks. I bet that caused one hell of a row.'

Lucy laughed. 'I told you, Goths aren't my thing. All very childish.' She shrugged. 'I don't know what her relationship was like with the parents. I told you, I hardly know her. We don't mix with the younger kids, and none of our lot are into Gothing anyway. We'd rather get good exam results.'

'And a good thing too,' Dawes said, flicking a glance at Stephanie. 'We'll park in the next street,' he continued. 'Lucy, you can go in and ask if they've seen her.'

Lucy's eyes widened, and Stephanie opened her mouth to protest.

'Don't worry,' he said. 'We'll be close by, and we won't let you out of our sight.'

'Cool.' Lucy grinned.

'Open a line to my mobile and keep yours in your hand,' he told Lucy. 'Then we'll hear everything. Any problem and we'll be there in seconds.'

'And don't take any risks,' Stephanie added. 'If anything happens, just get out.'

Lucy nodded.

'Good girl,' Dawes said encouragingly. 'You are looking for your friend,' he reminded her, 'and you know she hangs out there. They'll be suspicious of anyone they don't know, so don't worry if they're not very talkative. Play naïve, then ask about scoring some grass.' He handed her some money. 'Ask for a Henry.'

'A Henry,' Lucy repeated.

'It's slang for an eighth of grass,' Stephanie told her. 'Henry the Eighth.'

Lucy decided it might be best not to tell her mother that she knew what a Henry was. Even if she hadn't, it was pretty obvious. 'No probs.' She nodded.

The club door was open and inside was in darkness. Lucy walked straight in. A black guy in his late twenties with sunken cheeks and dreadlocks was in the DJ box at the back of the club. He wore head-cans which bobbed up and down as he listened to his music. He saw her come in, but ignored her.

She noticed a CCTV camera in the corner pointing in her direction.

Within moments a thin white man of around thirty came through a door at the back of the club. He had shoulder-length hair and a gold ring in his left earlobe, and he wore an expensive leather coat. 'Can I help you?' he asked, eyeing her suspiciously.

'Yeah, sorry.' Lucy was enjoying this. How many other girls on work experience would get to play undercover detective? 'I'm looking for my friend. She hangs round here. Her name is Alice.'

The guy shook his head and opened his hands. 'No one's here. We're closed.'

Lucy stood there, unsure what to do for a moment.

He gave her a speculative look. 'Not from round here, darling?'

'No. I got the bus over. Just looking for my mate.'

'Where you from, then?'

Lucy hadn't expected questions, and wanted to do well. She played the game. 'I live in Wandsworth, but we come over here, Alice and me, so our mums can't find us. Everyone knows everyone's business in our little part of London. Alice is a Goth, so she likes it here. Now she's gone missing, and I'm a bit worried.'

'I don't know no one called Alice,' he said, studying her. He pointed towards the door.

Lucy didn't move. She pretended to be embarrassed. 'I . . . er . . . There's something else,' she said nervously. 'Can you help me? I need a Henry. I've got some money, look.' She dug in her jeans pocket and held out the note Dawes had given her.

'Who told you I could help you?' His eyes narrowed.

Lucy shrugged. 'Alice said. Everyone in our crowd knows to come here. I only want a Henry.'

The man continued to stare at her; she felt uneasy, her phone was on. Then he clicked his fingers at the disc jockey, who jumped to attention and came over. 'The lady wants a Henry,' the man told him.

The disc jockey pulled a packet out of his pocket and took out a little stash of weed. He opened his palm; Lucy handed him the note, and he gave her the grass.

She muttered a nervous thank you and turned to go.

'What does your friend Alice look like?' leather-man asked her.

'She's quite tall, nearly six feet, with long black hair down to her waist. It's got green and pink streaks either side, and she often wears earrings like skulls, and a green stud in the side of her nose.'

He seemed to recognize the description.

'She likes Lady Gaga.' This was the one thing Lucy did know about Alice; she'd been playing Lady Gaga on her iPod one morning during school assembly, and the head had confiscated her iPod. The incident nearly started a revolt; it was a talking point for weeks.

'That sounds like Jade,' the disc-jockey said.

'No, her name's Alice.' A thought struck Lucy. She tried

for a naïve smile. 'But I think she has other names when she goes out on her . . . adventures.'

'Well, there ain't many six-foot Goths who like Lady Gaga,' said leather-man. 'Specially not with waist-length black hair and green and pink streaks.' He pulled his mouth into a twisted smile. 'She's got a tattoo of a butterfly on the inside of her left thigh.'

Lucy knew that was true, too; something else that had been the talk of the school when she'd had it done. Her heart started hammering in her chest. Had he slept with Alice? Or perhaps she was on the game. Either way, this man knew her.

'Yes, that's her. Do you know where she is?'

He shook his head. 'A few people have been looking for her. My security officer said something earlier on. If you see her, you might want to tell her that.'

'Yes, I'll tell her. Who shall I say wants to see her?'

'Reilly.'

A shiver of excitement ran down Lucy's spine, and she had to work hard not show it. 'OK,' she said neutrally, turning to leave.

Leather-man shouted after her. 'Nice arse,' he said. 'And you're young and pretty too. I reckon if you were clever, like your mate Jade, you might want to get your next Henry for free.'

Lucy looked at him over her shoulder, suddenly nervous. 'No, no, I'm not heavily into it. I just like an odd puff,' she said nervously. 'I can pay for that.'

'Shame,' he told her, pulling the crooked smile. 'Being that you're nice looking and so young, you could be a good earner. How old are you?'

She thought quickly. People were always saying she looked young for her age; it was a bit of a pain sometimes, especially in pubs. But it could be useful now. 'Nearly fifteen,' she lied.

His eyes seemed to dance. 'Well, if you ever need a bit extra, or guaranteed good-time stuff, come and see me. I might be able to help you out.'

She turned to face him. 'OK,' she said carefully. 'What did you have in mind?'

The look he gave her made her pounding heart accelerate.

She told herself it was something she'd need to get used to; this kind of an adrenalin rush would be part of the job.

'Interested, are you?' he asked.

'I'll give it some thought,' she said, smiling with an effort.

'Don't leave it too long. You'll be all grown up,' he shouted after her.

Perverted bastard, she thought angrily.

'If I see Jade, who shall I say is looking for her?'

Lucy thought quickly. 'Best say nothing. She may be avoiding me too.'

'So what's your name?'

She took a gamble. 'Lucy.' No harm done, she thought; it's a dead common name.

Dawes and Stephanie were waiting in the car.

'Did you hear all that?' she asked.

'Certainly did,' Dawes said. 'Well done you.'

'Alice's mother is going to go ballistic.'

Stephanie said nothing.

'Throws new light on the father's murder,' said Dawes thoughtfully.

'Doesn't it just?' Stephanie said. 'Good work, Lucy.'

Alysha looked around to check no one was watching. When she was sure, she banged on Michael Delahaye's front door.

He quickly ushered her inside. 'You look well shagged,' he said with an air of distaste. 'Carry on like that and you'll be all used up before you're sixteen.'

'Jealous, are you?' She looked at him defiantly.

'Your life, babe, innit. I just hate to see you throw it away.'

'Don't suppose you're going without,' she said pointedly.

He turned away.

'You don't know what you're missing.' She moved in and slid her arms around him. He quickly pushed her back.

'Babe, you're gorgeous, but you're not old enough. 'Sides, you smell of Yo-Yo Reilly.'

'Yeah? Who d'you smell of, then? Who are you doing it wiv?'

'Don't ask me them personal questions, innit?'

'It's Bethany, ain't it?'

He looked shocked, and shook his head.

'You're lying.' Alysha raised her voice. 'I know you're doing it wiv Bethany.'

He didn't answer.

'You wanna watch yourself,' she said angrily. 'She's Brotherhood property. If Yo finds out you could get yourself shanked again.'

Mince chewed his lip. 'What have you heard?' he asked, raising his eyes to meet hers.

'I saw you, didn't I? After the meeting at Yo's. She was here – I saw you both.'

He didn't reply.

'You're asking for more trouble, Mince. Yo-Yo done you up bad enough before. If he knows you're hooting one of his hookers, he'll shank you again. Am I suppose to save your sorry arse while you're hooting hers?' She put her hand on her hip, and swallowed hard. 'You're my only proper friend. I don't wanna lose you.'

Delahaye took a deep breath. 'OK, babe. This weren't for your ears, but looks like you know stuff, so I'm gonna tell you. Only, it goes no further, innit?'

She nodded.

'The Block Bois, over on the Random Estate. I'm hanging with them and we're muscling together and we're gonna take Reilly out real soon and take over the territory.'

Alysha's eyes widened. 'Is that why you took that punter out?'

He gave her an appraising look. 'Babe, I know how you operate. I ain't saying no more about that.'

'Why d'you kill Carly?'

He sighed loudly. 'Babe, c'mon?'

'Is Scrap in wiv you on this?'

Mince nodded his head. 'He's had it with Reilly. He's in.'

'Did Scrap do the punter, then? And Carly?'

'Are you trying to pretend to me that you didn't?'

'I didn't. Why would I?'

'Because I know you, and you want to be running that territory.'

She tilted her head and stared at him, then shrugged. 'Yeah, right.'

'Here's what's gonna happen then. When we take Reilly, I'm gonna put you in charge of running the girls. I won't let you do any ho-ing, just the running of them, and when you're a little older, you'll be my girl.'

'Are you telling me the truth about Bethany? Is she in on this? Did you tell her before you told me?'

'She's really frightened. She don't know what's going down, nor who she can trust. She was Carly's mate and all she wanted was to ask if I knew why Carly got done.'

'What d'you tell her?'

'I said, I don't know nothing.'

'Do you?'

'C'mon, babe.'

'What about Jade and the others, what do they know?'

'Jade ain't part of this,' Mince told her. 'I ain't having no underage ho's. She's done a runner anyway. I ain't seen her since the punter was done.'

Alysha shook her head. 'No, nor me. She was around when it happened, though – she's running scared.'

'How d'you know she was around when he was done? You told me you weren't there.'

Alysha tossed her head. 'Bethany told Yo.'

Michael pulled tobacco from his pocket and expertly rolled a spliff. He dragged hard on it a few times and passed it to her.

She inhaled, letting the smoke roll down her throat. 'I don't care who's dead,' she said. 'As long as you're really going to kill Yo-Yo.'

'His days are numbered – that's a promise, innit.'

She inhaled again. 'I don't get you, Mince. You don't care if I smoke, or drink, but you won't have no honey with me.'

'You know why. I'm your real friend. You saved my life when Yo-Yo shanked me, and I'm looking out for you. A lot of changes are gonna happen. Yo-Yo and the Brotherhood are all gonna be history.'

'And Beth knows?'

'Yeah. She's with us.'

'I still don't trust her.'

*   *   *

Dawes parked on the corner of the Random estate, two streets away from the Aviary, and gave Lucy the keys.

'Stay in the car,' he told her firmly. 'You don't come anywhere near the Aviary, understood? It's far too dangerous, especially now you have an acquaintance in common with Reilly.'

'It's important you're not seen with us,' Stephanie added. 'It's for your own safety, Luce. Keep your phone on, and ring us if you need to.'

The barking of Reilly's dogs was enough to wake the dead, but no one answered the door. Stephanie banged on it again, and Dawes yelled, 'Police! Open up, or I'll be back with the RSPCA.'

That did the trick. Within seconds the door opened a crack and Reilly shouted through it. 'You've tested the dogs at least seven times this year. You know they ain't pitbulls. You ain't got fuck on me. What do you want this time?'

'We can't *prove* their pedigree, you mean.' Dawes was clearly intent on winding Reilly up. Stephanie stepped in quickly.

'We're not here about the dogs,' she said. 'Can you make sure they are locked away, please? We need to ask you some questions – here or at the station, whichever is more convenient.'

'I ain't done nothing,' Reilly snapped, but he kicked the door open. 'Go in that room,' he said, shoving the dogs through another door.

Dawes refused to sit down, but Stephanie made herself comfortable on an enormous black leather sofa that took up most of the room. She felt something stick into her back, and pushed her hand behind a cushion. She brought out a dog lead, a pair of handcuffs and a cerise marabou G-string. Reilly crossed his arms in front of him. 'Ain't illegal to have a bit of fun, girl.'

She thought about asking if he intended wearing the knickers, but changed her mind. 'We're here about a murder,' she said instead. 'I'm sure you've heard a young girl was strangled close to this estate.'

'I heard,' Reilly shrugged. 'But it ain't nothing to do with me.'

'Don't insult our intelligence,' Dawes snapped. 'It's common knowledge that you run the street trade around Tidal Lane and Hill Street. The murdered girl was a tom, and we have evidence that she was in the car with the punter who was murdered the night before.'

'I told you, it ain't nothing to do with me.'

'I think we both know it is.' Dawes held Reilly's insolent stare. 'And we both know that lying to the police is a custodial offence.'

Stephanie jumped in again. 'No one is accusing you at the moment,' she said to Reilly. 'For once. We're just asking if you know anything that can help us find the killer. If it's gang rivalry, you might want to drop a hint to us, help us out in a way that would help you too. We haven't come to needle you about your dogs either.'

'For now,' Dawes added.

'We are asking for any help you might want to offer,' Stephanie continued.

'For now, what?' Reilly snapped at Dawes.

'Oh, come on Reilly, you must know your days are numbered,' Dawes snapped back. 'We know who you are, what you do.'

'Can you offer us any help?' Stephanie interrupted. She was beginning to get a headache. She sympathized with Dawes, but she was starting to feel Georgia was right; Dawes was letting his personal agenda get in the way. She wished Georgia was here instead of him; together they might have got somewhere with Reilly. 'A name,' she suggested. 'That's all.'

To her amazement Reilly gave her more than she asked for. 'You could try Mince Delahaye. Word is, he's rounding up a new gang around the Random. Let's say I'm expecting trouble.'

The Random estate was where they had left Lucy. Stephanie stood up. 'Thank you.'

'We'll be in touch,' Dawes said. He held Reilly's gaze just a little too long for Stephanie's comfort.

Alysha was angry. She had to know for sure if Bethany was having sex with Mince, and the only way to find out was to ask the cow. She was on her way over to the Random estate to do just that.

She needed to know if Mince was stringing her along. If he was, it would break her heart. She'd thought he was her friend, the only one she could trust, but now she wasn't so sure. He hadn't told her his plans until she'd got heavy with him. And now he wanted her to lead Yo into the trap. She was to call Yo, tell him she was in trouble and he'd rush out to help her, she'd run off leaving the Block Bois there, and Yo would be surrounded and shanked, and then who knew what would happen. She'd do it anyway; it was time the fat bastard got taken down. But if Mince was lying to her, and hooting Bethany, he'd pay for it big time. No one crossed Alysha Achter.

She'd make a better job than Mince of running the territory, anyway. She already knew Yo's contacts, and with money she could get rid of anyone that got in her way. If Mince was lying to her, he'd regret it.

There was also a question mark over Jade. Why had she gone missing? Was it because she also knew about the take-over? Alysha didn't like that. She needed to get to the bottom of what was going on. The Block Bois were a dangerous crew, and if some of the Brotherhood were going over to them, that would mean real trouble. She had to look after herself.

Approaching the Random estate she noticed a pretty girl, very young, her fair hair tied back in a ponytail, standing on the corner of the road. The girl wore jeans and didn't look like a tom, but if she was soliciting on this territory she either had one hell of a nerve, or an awful lot to learn. No one came looking for trade down here without paying a protection wad to the pimp. The girl was asking for a smack.

She crossed over the road and headed towards the girl. 'Oi,' she shouted. 'What d'you think you're doing?'

Lucy had grown bored sitting in the car, and had got out to stretch her legs and observe the comings and goings. Wouldn't it just be something if she spotted Alice? What a coup, be able to tell the other detectives she had found the missing girl. Dawes and her Mum would be a good half-hour, so she'd

decided to have a look round. When the young black girl with
the long cornrows shouted at her, she was shocked and a bit
scared, but mostly just lost for words.

'This is taken territory,' the girl said.

'Um, sorry,' Lucy answered. 'I didn't realize. I was just
looking for my friend, thought she might be around here.'

'What's her name?' Alysha stood squarely in front of Lucy
and looked her up and down.

'Erm . . .' Lucy wasn't sure which name to use. 'Alice,' she
said quickly.

The girl shook her head. 'Don't know no Alice who hangs
round here. What's she look like?'

'She's tall, with black hair down to her waist with green
and pink streaks and a green nose stud.'

The black girl's mouth dropped open. 'Why you looking
for her?'

Lucy was nervous of saying the wrong thing. She turned
away and began to walk back to the car. 'Her mother asked
me to find her. Thanks for your help.'

The girl followed. 'Where does this Alice live?' she asked,
an urgent note in her voice.

'Not round here.' Lucy clicked the lock on the passenger
door and climbed in, swiftly locking the car from inside.

Alysha stared at the car for a few moments, but the girl didn't
look round. Maybe she should tell Yo-Yo about this; he'd pay
her well for the information. She wasn't going to report back
to Mince; right now she wasn't sure she trusted him any more,
so he wasn't getting nothing from her. She was going to look
out for herself. The rule was the man with the money got the
goods, sex, information, whatever – and for the moment Yo-Yo
still had the money.

She walked away so the girl wouldn't think she was watching
her, then she leaned against a wall from where she could see
but not be seen. As she wrote down the registration number
of the car in lipstick on a bus ticket, the fat female fed came
towards it with another fed, a bloke, who also looked familiar.
Then the pretty young girl opened the car window and spoke
to them.

Alysha stopped writing and watched.

The feds walked off into the Random estate. A few minutes later they were back. They got into the car with the girl in it and drove off.

Hang on a minute, Alysha told herself: the blonde girl had keys for that car. And she'd been looking for Jade. Whatever she called her 'friend', it was definitely Jade. There weren't gonna be two long streaks of nothin' with black hair with pink and green bits in it. So the girl, whoever she was, was looking for Jade for the feds. Why was that, then?

Jeez, Alysha thought. Cops got younger every day.

NINE

Later Tuesday morning

'So what do you think?' Banham asked Georgia.

'About the case?'

'No, about DI Dawes. I get the impression you don't like him very much.'

Georgia kept her eyes on the road and attempted to keep her face expressionless. 'I think he's blinkered,' she said. 'He wants to believe Stuart Reilly is responsible for every crime on the estate.'

'He is, mostly.'

'Mostly.' Georgia reminded herself that Dawes and Banham were old friends. 'But not a hundred per cent. And not necessarily this time.' When Banham didn't answer, she flicked a glance at him, but his face gave nothing away. 'Let's keep our options open, that's all I'm saying.'

Banham bobbed his head slightly to the side, but still made no comment.

'There's an angry wife and a jilted lover,' Georgia pointed out. 'We need to find out how far they'd go.'

'He was castrated. Do you think his wife is capable of that?' Banham asked.

'Hell has no fury like a woman scorned,' she replied. Their eyes met briefly in the mirror. 'Look, I agree it's very much Reilly's style to cut someone's prick off, but maybe someone knows that and has set him up. Even Dawes has pointed out the possibility of gang retaliation. And I'm still wondering if it might be something completely different. A crime of passion, perhaps.'

'DC Peacock ran registration checks of both Jean Eden's and her fiancé's vehicles through the CCTV scanner,' Banham reminded her. 'Neither of them drove into Brixton the night Solden was murdered. Jones was working. OK, he was on his own, but it's unlikely he caught a bus. Even I know that if you leave a bakery for a few hours you won't have the same amount of bread the next day, and all the bakery figures checked out.'

'They both claim they were alone,' Georgia said. 'Without alibis, they're suspects. OK, so they didn't drive their own cars into Brixton, but it doesn't mean they weren't there.'

'The killer would be covered in blood, DI Johnson.'

'No one was around. They could have taken clothes to change into. I've put Peacock on to Oyster records, by the way. The buses run all night.'

'We haven't found any bloodstained clothing.'

'We haven't found the knife either.'

'How far have you widened the search?'

'I've got a small team searching around the Soldens' neighbourhood too, now.'

'Good,' Banham said, rubbing a hand thoughtfully across his mouth.

At last he was taking her seriously. 'We have statements from the Soldens' cleaner and gardener. They both have alibis that check out on the night of Tom Solden's murder.' She paused. 'But they both have said that the family were always arguing, and the daughter hated her father.'

Banham didn't reply. After a beat he said quietly, 'The press know how Tom Solden was murdered.'

'What?' Georgia took her eyes off the road and veered over the centre line. A car hooted a warning, and she swiftly tugged the wheel back to her side of the line. Banham grabbed the edge of his seat.

'Sorry.' She held up her hands. 'I just . . .'

'Keep your hands on the wheel,' he yelled.

'I'm a good driver,' she said defensively. 'I've taken my advanced driving test.'

'So did Alison,' he said. 'I made her take it, and I paid for the lessons. But she failed.'

'Well, I passed,' Georgia said indignantly. 'I'm sorry, but what you just said came as a shock, that's all.' She indicated, and turned into a small side road. 'How did the press find out? We told Kate Solden not to breathe a word to anyone.'

'That's what I'd like to know,' Banham said. Georgia pulled alongside a parking space and started reversing. He looked nervously over his shoulder. 'Just concentrate on parking now,' he said.

If another man had spoken to her like that she would have bitten his head off. As it was, she felt the urge to smile at his nervousness, but contained it. 'I promise you're in good hands,' she said instead.

'Then keep them on the wheel.'

Everyone respected Banham, and his reputation as a detective went before him, yet he was a comically nervous passenger. She couldn't wait to meet Alison Grainger, but made a mental note not to let her drive if they were ever on a job together.

She parked easily and quickly, pulled the handbrake up and turned to face Banham. 'DI Grainger has shot your nerves to pieces,' she said gently. 'I hope you know you can trust me. My driving as well as my discretion.'

Nigel Jones opened the front door, and the smell of frying wafted over Georgia and Banham. Georgia breathed in a lungful of fresh air before stepping inside the tiny cottage, straight into a reception room from which a tiny kitchen was partitioned off by double half-doors like a cowboy saloon.

'We were just having a late breakfast. Can I offer you anything?' Nigel hurried through to the kitchen and lifted a frying pan from the hob. Sizzling bacon slid on to a plate of fried bread.

'Coffee, one sugar,' Banham said.

'Black coffee would be great,' Georgia nodded.

At that moment Jean Eden appeared on the narrow staircase at the side of the room. Her eyes were red and puffy, though covered in heavy black make-up in a failed attempt to disguise the fact. She wore a black velour tracksuit and grubby cream slippers that had seen better days. Last time Georgia had interviewed her she had been dressed up to the nines.

'Before you ask,' she said nervously, 'Nigel knows about me and Tom.'

'That makes things easier,' Georgia said, not really caring whether Jean had told him or not. Jean's adulterous past was important to the case; her feelings about it were immaterial.

'Please have a seat.' Jean pointed at a small two-seater brown sofa in the corner. It dipped slightly in the centre and Georgia's shoulders bumped Banham's as she pulled out a notebook. The overwhelming smell of frying was making her nauseous. She had eaten far too many peppermints earlier at the post-mortem, and now the stink of bacon fat threatened her stomach again. She accepted the mug of black coffee and was about to swallow some of it when her mobile chimed. She read *Stephanie* on the screen. Excusing herself, she stood up and walked toward the door.

Stephanie filled her in on their discovery: Alice Solden was still missing, but it looked probable that she was working as a hooker for Yo-Yo Reilly in the area around the Holster club, calling herself Jade. Banham had followed her outside. Georgia handed him the phone so Stephanie could update him too.

Back in the house, she apologized for having to take the call and swallowed the coffee in a couple of gulps. The news she had just heard made her more sure that Solden's killer might be a lot closer to home than gang retribution or territorial battles.

'We would prefer to talk to each of you on your own,' she told Jean and Nigel. 'It's just procedure, you understand.'

Banham walked back in, giving Georgia a meaningful glance.

'There isn't really anywhere private here,' Jean said. 'The cottage isn't very big. There's a tea shop around the corner. We could . . .'

'No need to go out,' Nigel called from the kitchen, confirming to Georgia that conversation could be heard from anywhere in the house. 'I'll take my breakfast upstairs. When you're finished talking to Jean, give me a shout.' He came out, handed Jean a plate of bacon and fried bread, and made his way upstairs with his own plate.

Georgia turned away and grabbed a lungful of air. 'We're trying to build up a picture of the victim,' she said to Jean. 'You knew him well; perhaps you could tell us what he was like.'

The women's eyes met and Jean quickly dropped her gaze to the maroon patterned carpet. She took a deep breath and glanced at the stairs as if to make sure her partner wasn't within earshot. 'The truth,' she said, fixing her large blue eyes on Georgia, 'was he was a sadistic bastard.'

This was interesting. 'Go on,' Georgia said.

'It started when I came to work as a Saturday girl. I was still at school. Fifteen, I was, and only just. Of course I was flattered when he started paying me attention.' She raised a hand to her face. 'He made me feel like a princess – showered me with presents.' She shook her head regretfully. 'So I went to bed with him.'

'You were fifteen?'

'*Just* fifteen.' She checked the stairs again. 'I knew it was against the law, but I was young and stupid, and I thought we were in love.'

'Did his wife know?' Georgia asked.

Jean nodded and lowered her eyes again. 'She knows everything that goes on. She just turns a blind eye and has another drink.'

'Does she care about him, d'you think?' Banham asked her.

Jean turned her head thoughtfully. 'I hardly know her, but I think she must, although she never shows it. Why would she stay with him otherwise?'

'Same reason you went to bed with him,' Banham said. 'Material assets. She has a nice house and staff to look after it, and she has a daughter.'

'What can you tell us about the daughter?' Georgia asked her.

'Alice?' Jean sighed. 'Alice is a wild one. She was a lovely child, but now she's a bit of a monster.'

'How?'

'She came into the shop, shouting and screaming at him. She does it at Nigel's place too, he told me.' She interlaced her fingers nervously, almost upsetting the untouched plate on her lap. 'Tom dropped me, when I grew up a little.'

Banham leaned forward. 'Go on.'

Jean hesitated, and her head turned to the stairs again. 'All right. He loved it when I was young and naïve. He bought me shoes and clothes, and then expected . . .' She hesitated again. 'He liked doing . . . warped things.'

Banham spoke gently. 'Can you be more specific? This could be very important.'

'He liked me to dress up and hurt him.' The words tumbled out rapidly. 'And he wanted to hurt me. I was a virgin when I met him. I thought it was all normal, just what people did.'

Georgia looked at Banham. He was better at this than she'd expected.

'You need to help us,' he said in the same quiet, coaxing tone. 'I'm sorry, I know it's difficult, but I have to ask. What exactly did he want you to do?'

'He tried to hang me once, and when I cried, he said we were finished. We made up after a week or so. He beat me up for crying sometimes, but then he'd forgive me, and we carried on for a bit longer.'

'Did he beat you often?'

Jean bit her lip and nodded. 'I used to let him, during sex. As I said, at the time, I thought it was normal.'

Georgia pressed her lips together and kept her face blank. 'What else did he ask you to do?' she asked quietly.

Jean opened and closed her mouth, and shook her head.

'It's all right, no one can hear you,' Banham said.

'Except us,' Georgia said gently. 'And we've heard worse.'

'Really?'

Banham and Georgia exchanged glances. 'Really,' she said.

Jean looked at the carpet again. 'He used to call me Alice when we were having sex, and he made me dress like her. I went along with it for a while, but one time I called him a pervert. He went mad, beat me up and really hurt me. Then next day he apologized and opened a bank account in my name with five thousand pounds in it. That was when he finished it for good. He told me I was never to mention any of it to anyone, but I would always have a job and a good salary.' She looked at Georgia. 'He kept his word.' She gave a humourless smile. 'I was about eighteen by then. Too old for him. He'd already told me he could only get a hard on with very young girls.' She paused. 'Mind you, he wasn't expecting Nigel to beat him up at the time.'

Banham's eyes widened, but before either of them could ask another question, Jean continued. 'It happened when Nigel and I first got together. I didn't want us to have secrets, so I told him. He still gets angry if I talk about what Tom did to me. I don't blame him. He loves me, really loves me. Tom just used me, and I was too young to see it.'

'How did Tom react when you started seeing Nigel?' Georgia asked.

'He didn't seem bothered. We'd been finished a while by then.'

'What happened after Nigel hit him?'

'Tom called the police, but he dropped the charges later.' She looked at Georgia. 'He had to, didn't he? He wouldn't want it to come out in court that he was a pervert.'

Banham sat forward. 'Nigel went on working for Tom, though?'

'Yes. Tom gave him a hefty pay rise to keep quiet. We both earn quite a bit more than the other managers.' She shrugged. 'Tom used me, so we used him.'

There was a brief silence.

'Can we move on to Monday morning?' Georgia asked. 'Did you notice anything odd when Nigel came back from the bakery after his night shift?'

Jean frowned. 'He'd never murder Tom, if that's what you're insinuating. Just because he hit him. He worked all night on Sunday, and he came home as usual. I'd been here on my own. I can even tell you what I watched on the box.'

'That's in your previous statement, thank you,' Georgia said. She made a few more notes on her pad, then handed Jean the pen. 'If you wouldn't mind signing this, so we have a record of what you've just told us.'

Jean read the notes and signed her name.

Georgia thanked her and stood up. As she walked towards the stairs there was a scuffling sound, and she glimpsed Nigel Jones's back disappearing on to the landing. He had probably heard everything.

'Mr Jones?'

He turned, looking like a rabbit caught in headlights.

'Best come up here if you want to talk to me,' he muttered. 'Give Jean a bit of space.'

Georgia and Banham followed him up the narrow staircase

and into a small bedroom. There was nowhere to sit but on
the double bed. Banham waited for Georgia to make herself
comfortable, then left a good twelve inches of blue satin
counterpane between them. Nigel Jones leaned against the
wall.

'In your first statement you told us you were at work, baking,
on the night Mr Solden was murdered,' Georgia reminded him.

'I was.'

'But no other staff were there,' Banham asked. 'That's
unusual, surely?'

'Yes, it is.' Nigel scratched his nose. 'Someone had phoned
in sick. Harry Frederick. You can check if you like. I was there
all night. If I'd left the baking unattended, the building might
have burnt down.' There was a pause. 'I told you all this. And
I can't understand why we have to go though all Jean's history.
She certainly isn't capable of killing anyone.'

'Why didn't you mention her involvement with Mr Solden
when you made your original statement?'

'No one asked me.'

Banham leaned forward and Georgia found herself struggling not to topple sideways on the uneven bed.

'You must have realized we'd need to know,' Banham said.
'And that we'd find out.'

Nigel stared at the floor.

Georgia flicked back through her notebook. '*I hardly knew
him. I did my job and he paid me. That's as far as it went,*'
she read. 'That was your reply when you were asked how well
you knew him.'

Nigel shrugged and furrowed his forehead. 'I'm sorry.'

'You're sorry?' Banham said crisply. 'It's withholding vital
evidence in a murder enquiry. It can carry a custodial sentence.'

Nigel looked away. His frame was wiry and his features
dark; Georgia thought if he was an actor he'd make a good
Italian gangster.

Banham pressed him. 'You knew he'd had an affair with
your fiancée, and you'd assaulted him. It must have occurred
to you that you should have told us this? We're investigating
a murder here.'

Nigel became flustered. 'OK, yes, yes I should have told

you.' His head shook like a nervous toy. 'The truth is I'm glad the bastard's dead. He deserved it.' He looked at Banham. 'I'm a baker, not a hit-man. I'm marrying Jean, I love her and she loves me, and we want all that in the past, where it belongs. That's why I didn't mention it. What happened to Jean was quite disgusting. She wasn't to blame, he was. She was underage and innocent and he took advantage. That isn't something you want broadcast. We've put it behind us. We just want to move forward and get on with our lives.'

'Yet you still work for him.'

'We need to earn a living, to buy a house and have children. There's a recession. Jobs are hard to get and he pays us well. We'd be mad to walk away from that.'

'Do any of the other staff know about Jean?' Banham asked.

'Not to my knowledge.' He looked away.

'Do you know if Tom Solden had an affair with any of the other staff?' Banham probed.

He kept his head turned away. 'I've no idea. I don't gossip and I don't listen to it.'

'Did his wife know about Jean, do you know?'

'It's possible. I really couldn't say.' He still hadn't turned back to face them.

Banham caught Georgia's eye: a signal to take over.

'Is the blue Ford outside your only car?' Georgia asked.

'Yes. Why?'

'Just curious.'

Banham stood up to leave and Georgia followed his lead.

They walked down the narrow staircase, and as they headed for the front door Georgia noticed a crash helmet hanging behind it, with a pair of leather driving gloves stuffed inside. She looked at Banham; he had noticed it too.

'Who rides a bike?' Georgia asked Jean.

'Not me.' Jean laughed nervously.

'Nigel then?'

'He used to. It's a bit of a sore point. We're saving for a bigger house, and the bike was one of the things that had to go. He's kept the crash helmet, says it's got sentimental value.'

'When did he sell it?' Banham asked.

'A month or so ago. Quite recently, anyway. I don't bring

the subject up, it caused so many rows.' She reached past Banham to open the door.

'Do you have a receipt for the sale of the bike?' Georgia asked.

'I'm not sure.'

'Did you advertise the sale in the paper? Is there a receipt for that?'

Nigel appeared behind Jean. 'It was a private sale,' he said. 'I sold it to a friend of a friend. I do have a receipt from the bank for the money that went in my account.'

'When was that?'

'Four weeks ago.' He looked nervous. 'Approximately.'

'Good. Can you let us have that by the end of the day?' Georgia handed him a card with a phone number and email address on it. 'And the address of the person that bought it.'

'Yes.' He looked at Jean. 'Of course.'

'And the bike's registration details,' Banham added.

'The motorbike or the bicycle?' Jean asked. 'Oh, no, bicycles don't have registrations, do they?'

Banham and Georgia looked at each other. 'Who rides the bicycle?' she asked.

Now Jean looked nervous. 'We bought it for Nigel when he sold the bike. It's only an old banger.'

'Where is it?'

'In the shed round the back.'

'Do you mind if we take a look at it?'

Nigel sighed and led the way. 'Mind your shoes,' he said as they walked around the side of the house. 'It's muddy out there.'

They examined it carefully. There was no sign of anything out of the ordinary, and no sign that it had been washed recently. The tyres were clean.

Jean walked back to the car with them. As Georgia unlocked it, the other woman touched her arm. 'Will you let me know when Alice turns up?' she asked. 'I do worry for her. She used to be such a nice kid. I hate to see what she's become.'

'What do you mean?' Georgia asked.

Jean turned her head to check Nigel wasn't close by. 'I wouldn't be surprised at anything that pervert did,' she said. 'Even to his own daughter.'

Georgia looked at Banham as Jean continued. 'She grew into a beautiful-looking girl. Nothing would surprise me, especially after what he used to make me do.' She swallowed hard. 'I would have run away too, if I was his daughter.'

Georgia made a mental note to talk to Kate Solden again. Jean seemed to read her mind. 'The mother never said much but, well, you know – the booze. Anyway, you will let me know, won't you?'

'I'll be in touch with you again soon,' Georgia replied.

'One last question,' Banham said. 'Can you bake?'

Jean looked puzzled.

'Bread. Have you learned the trade?'

'Oh, I see.' She smiled. 'Yes, I enjoy baking for a hobby. And I know my way round a bakery. But that's not my job. I just run the shop.'

Banham thanked her and they climbed into the car. As Georgia started the engine and pulled out, she noticed a motorbike parked on the other side of the road.

'Coincidence?' she said, pointing to it.

'Possibly. I'll make a note of the registration, you just watch where you're driving.'

She drove in silence for a few minutes, then he asked, 'What did you make of all that?'

'Am I allowed to talk and drive?'

'As long as you keep your eyes on the road.' She stole a glance at him; his blue eyes were twinkling. So he did have a sense of humour, she thought.

'I think we got enough to show there could be more to this than Yo-Yo Reilly,' she said. 'We need to find Alice. She seems to be the key.'

'Pull in all the CCTV around here.' Banham peered around. 'There's a camera up there. Let's interview the neighbours too. See if we can pick him up riding the bike.'

'We need to re-interview Kate Solden too,' Georgia said.

'But Alice is the priority.'

'I agree.'

'So this was a good idea? There could be more going on than gang retribution?'

'Why don't the two of us keep digging into the family?'

Banham said. 'Dawes can focus on the estate, with Sergeant Green. I know you always work with her, but if young Lucy is going to be involved in any way at all, I want her mother with her. So you've got yourself a new partner for the time being.'

'Fine by me,' Georgia said. 'Can we get a couple of things straight, though? First, my driving doesn't need criticizing. Sir.' He smiled, and crinkly lines appeared round his eyes. 'And I want it on record that I don't like the idea of Lucy being involved.' He didn't react at all to that. Georgia felt a little frustrated. Her driving wasn't important; this was. 'She has no training and no experience. The Aviary has the highest crime figures in London. I can't believe you would agree to let her do more than make the tea.'

'If her mother is OK about it, and we keep her closely monitored, I'm not against it.'

'Give it some more thought. Please.'

'She's doing well. Thanks to her we've found out that Alice hangs around the Holster club. That looks like more than coincidence. You said yourself a large percentage of murders are close to home. Seems Lucy is helping you prove your theory.'

TEN

When Lucy walked into the investigation room Georgia was watching through the glass panel in her office. The team gave her a round of applause, and Hank Peacock congratulated the beaming teenager on her morning's work.

That's quite enough of that, Georgia thought. She strode out across the squad room to where Lucy was holding court, telling the team exactly what had happened. 'Good work, Lucy,' she said crisply. 'Now for the hard graft. Go and sit at the spare desk in my office and write up a detailed report.'

If she put the girl in her own office, Georgia thought, the euphoria might dissipate a bit sooner than if she was surrounded by admiring detectives. That would make it easier to tell her she'd be spending the rest of her work experience here in the station.

She was fuming that Dawes had taken advantage of Lucy's naïvety. That estate was one of the most dangerous places in London; the girl had no idea how much trouble she could have been in. Even Stephanie had gone along with it; was she so obsessed with Dawes, or just turning into becoming a pushy mother? Had the whole department gone mad?

It was partly her own fault, she thought. If she hadn't made that childish bet, Stephanie's eye would have stayed on the ball. As it was, she was going all out to impress Dawes. Dawes was ruthless; he would stop at nothing to get Yo-Yo Reilly, including putting a young girl at risk.

If only Stephanie would get on and bed Dawes, she'd get her brain back in gear and see sense about her daughter. Lucy had had the experience she had coveted, and she'd done the work very well. That wasn't the issue. In time, Lucy would make an excellent detective, but right now, enough was enough.

She followed Lucy into her office and stood by the door as the girl settled herself at the spare desk. 'Every single detail, remember, no matter how trivial you think it is. It might just be a key to catching a killer. You need to get it all down while it's all fresh in your mind.'

She went to the snack machine and bought Lucy a can of coke and a packet of crisps. While Lucy wrote her report, Georgia used the time re-read all the statements from the bakery last night, and add in the new evidence from Jean Eden and Nigel Jones.

So Jean Eden knew her way around a bakery, she thought. That was interesting. As for Nigel – he was clearly given to jealousy, and capable of violence.

And now it appeared that Alice Solden could be working as a tom, around the very street where her father was murdered. Like Banham, Georgia didn't believe in coincidence. Solden had been a pervert and a paedophile. A lot of people might want him dead; could his own daughter be one of them?

Georgia reached for a sheet of paper and wrote the words SUSPECTS at the top. Underneath she listed some names: Kate Solden, Jean Eden, Nigel Jones. She glanced over at Lucy; the girl had her head down, writing furiously. Alice was a couple of years younger than her. Would she be capable of strangling Carly MacIntosh? She had motive if Carly had seen her killer, and if she was Jade, she would probably be known to both Carly and Bethany. There was a team out looking for Bethany. Georgia checked her phone: no messages. Georgia was growing anxious for that girl's safety. Unless Bethany Field was the killer herself? She added Bethany to her list of suspects. Either way, they had to find her.

She looked up, and Lucy caught her eye.

'I'm really loving all this,' Lucy said. 'I'm definitely going into the force. I want to do murder investigations.'

'Good.' Georgia smiled. 'You do need to learn the trade properly, though, and that means starting right at the bottom.' The smile dropped from Lucy's face for a moment, but soon returned. 'You have a lot to live up to,' she said. 'Your mother is a very good detective.' Lucy's face showed both confidence and naïvety. 'Take advantage of this placement and find out everything you can about policing. There's a lot to learn inside the investigation room as well as on the street.'

She had Lucy's full attention.

'I know you want to be out there, but don't try to run before you can walk. Concentrate on learning about the technical side. You have ample opportunity to learn about forensic test results on this case. You'll see how that all works. That will stand you in excellent stead.'

'I want to be hands-on,' Lucy said. 'David Dawes has OK'd me carrying on what I've started.'

'Sorry, carrying on with what? And it's DI Dawes while you're in this department.'

'Yes, sorry. Alice. Carrying on with looking for her. DI Dawes is very concerned for her and wants her found.'

'We all do,' Georgia said sharply.

'That's why he thinks I should carry on. I'm near her age, and I know her. I can go undercover to look for her.'

Georgia had to take several deep breaths. More than anything at that moment she wanted to go in search of Dawes and ask him what he thought he was doing, taking advantage of a young, inexperienced girl without even consulting the SIO. Lucy was a human being, not a resource. When young people came to the police for work experience, senior officers had a duty of care. This smelt of exploitation to her.

But she knew she would have to tread on eggshells if she was to protect Lucy and not turn the girl against her. Stephanie was useless for the time being. She wasn't even sure she had an ally in Banham; she was certain he hadn't taken on board what she had told him about Dawes.

It felt as if she was the only one with Lucy's welfare at heart. She'd been here before, with Alysha, the young black girl on the estate. Georgia had wanted to help her, believing the girl was a lost soul. But Banham had made his feelings plain: Georgia's job was to catch criminals, not mother them.

Then there was Carly MacIntosh. Carly was fifteen, and her body was in the morgue. This killer would stop at nothing. And Lucy saw it all as a game. Georgia had to join in and play her hand very carefully.

'I'll be fine,' Lucy said. 'DI Dawes is talking about me

going undercover as a hooker. Alice knows me; I'm a prefect at her school. She'll trust me.' She looked so pleased with herself, Georgia wanted to cry. 'Dave and Mum would be nearby,' Lucy went on. 'I'll be quite safe.'

'Lucy, it's not his decision,' Georgia said gently. 'I'm senior investigating officer on the case. He should never have said anything to you without running it past me first.'

'But you'll OK it?'

'Absolutely not. I wouldn't bet a halfpenny on Alice trusting you if she's living a double life. Look, you've done really well so far, and the case has moved forward because of what you found out today. But that was luck. You were in the right place at the right time, that's all.'

Lucy's face fell. 'But . . .'

'Look, you need to know something. I'm not nearly as certain as DI Dawes is that Stuart Reilly is our killer. I think we should look much nearer to home.'

'Are you saying you think it might be Alice?'

Georgia thought for a moment. 'Yes, that's a possibility,' she said, 'so all the more reason to be cautious.'

'All the more reason to find her!'

Georgia rubbed the crease between her eyebrows. 'It's not as straightforward as that,' she told her. 'The Aviary is one of the most dangerous places in London. There are drugs, knives, and the place is alive with killer dogs. And that's just for starters.'

'But you've just said you don't think Reilly is the murderer.'

'I said I don't *think* he is.' She paused, and added resignedly, 'Detective Inspector Dawes and DCI Banham disagree. They think it's a possibility. There's no doubting that he's capable of killing. Stabbing people is a hobby for him.'

'Let me help find Alice. Please, Georgia.'

'Lucy, if anyone else in your position spoke to me like this, they'd get their marching orders. As it's you, we'll start again. You're here on a couple of weeks' work experience, and you will do exactly as you are asked.' She raised her eyebrows and pulled a half-smile. 'Have you got that?'

'I won't get much experience running errands and making tea.'

Georgia looked her in the eye. 'I don't like tea.' She smiled. 'I'm sorry, sweetheart, but that's what work experience is. But as it's you . . .' She paused. 'You're getting a lot of leeway *as it's you*, you know. You're going to help TDC Peacock here in the office, running CCTV for cars and checking out a motorbike sale. What you're not going to do is undercover work on the Aviary. For a start you have beautiful skin; anyone could see you're not a drug-user.'

'I don't have to be a drug user. I could say I'm on the game to pay off a gambling debt,' Lucy argued.

Georgia closed her eyes. 'You're really pushing your luck, you know. Let's go and run this past DCI Banham and sort it once and for all.' She ushered Lucy out of the office before she completely lost it and flew at Dawes for causing all this trouble.

In Banham's office Georgia explained what Dawes had suggested and why she was against it. She prayed he had taken on board what she said earlier, and would call a halt before this nightmare went any further.

It seemed a long time before he spoke. Then, 'No,' he said. 'I can't let you do that. DI Johnson is right.'

Lucy didn't argue with the DCI. Georgia was grateful for that.

'While you're here, you're my responsibility,' Banham explained. 'Suppose you actually get offered a punter. How will you get out of that?'

Lucy's face drooped with disappointment.

Banham went on, 'Yo-Yo Reilly makes huge sums selling underage, naïve virgin girls to Turkish drug barons in North London. I couldn't take risks like that with you.'

Lucy brightened. 'He wouldn't make much on me,' she said. 'I'm hardly a virgin. And I'm not naïve either. I've had sex with loads of blokes, and I don't mind doing it to get you the evidence you need.'

Banham's eyes met Georgia's. Lucy carried on talking. 'I'm very ambitious, and I'll happily use my assets to get a result. Sex isn't what it's cracked up to be, you know.' She laughed nervously. 'Sometimes I find it quite boring.'

Banham stared at her, then turned away. To Georgia's relief,

Lucy fell silent. She waited for him to speak. She had to be careful; she needed him in her corner on this one.

In a way she admired Lucy, although she was more than a little shocked; the girl looked so sweet and innocent, but there was clearly more to her than met the eye. She already had a cynicism about her which was way beyond her years. It was good that she was ambitious, and she would make a very good detective one day. But for the moment, tough though she thought she was, Georgia was determined to protect her, from Yo-Yo Reilly, from David Dawes, and if necessary from herself.

She cleared her throat to bring Banham back from wherever he'd drifted off to. He turned to look at Lucy with infinite sadness in his eyes. 'I really hope you don't believe what you just said,' he told her.

Georgia almost handed him a hanky.

'My mum does it with everyone,' Lucy said brightly. 'She thinks it's a laugh. I do too. It wouldn't bother me at all if it helped catch the killer. I really do want to help.'

'You already are helping.' Banham suddenly regained his focus. 'What you found out this morning could be vital. If Alice Solden is working on the estate as a prostitute, you've brought us a very big piece of the jigsaw.'

'That proves I'm capable,' Lucy said.

'No, it proves you had a lucky breakthrough,' Banham told her with a gentle smile. 'A good detective is an experienced one, and that takes years.' He turned to Georgia. 'Have they picked up Bethany Field yet?'

She shook her head. 'A couple of uniforms are waiting at her house,' she told him. 'They'll call when they see her. She'll have to go home at some point: she's got kids. It's just a matter of time. But I'm getting a bit anxious.'

'The press are sniffing around,' he said. 'They can be useful when a kid goes missing, but I don't want them getting hold of this new information about Alice. I want to keep it quiet: just between us three, and Dawes and Green.'

'Yes, sir,' Georgia agreed.

'Yes, sir,' Lucy echoed, obviously pleased to be included.

'I need to go back to the murder scene,' Georgia said. 'I'll take Sergeant Green with me, and we'll keep our eyes wide open for Bethany Field.'

'Can I come?' Lucy asked.

Georgia suppressed a sigh. Hadn't she listened to anything Banham had said? 'No. I want your report finished by the time we get back.'

'Do you think Bethany is in danger?' Lucy asked.

'Any young girl who hangs around that estate is in danger,' Banham answered.

'Bethany's DNA was on the condom found in the car with Tom Solden,' Georgia reminded her. 'If she was in the car with him, and she isn't the killer, she's in serious danger.'

'I've nearly finished my report. What shall I do then?'

'You can keep the team stocked up with coffees and teas,' Banham said with a smile.

'And no flirting with DC Peacock,' Georgia teased.

Lucy pulled a face. 'I'd rather become a nun.'

Half an hour later Stephanie and Georgia were sitting in Georgia's car at the corner of the Random estate. They had knocked repeatedly on Bethany's door to no avail, and the neighbours claimed they'd never heard of her. They decided to keep a watching brief. Tidal Lane was less than half a mile up the road, as was the dark alley where Carly MacIntosh was murdered. It was cordoned off with tape, and uniformed officers guarded the scene while scenes of crime officers combed the area.

Stephanie was sucking an ice lolly, and sticky juice dripped on to her hand.

'I thought you'd be back on the bubblegum today,' Georgia said lightly. Stephanie crunched ice and shook her head.

'I've noted that you haven't asked me for the fifty pounds.'

Stephanie swallowed the ice. 'We had a call-out, if you remember.' She grinned. 'He's coming round tonight with pizza and wine.'

'Looks like tonight's the night then.' Georgia tried not to show her distaste as another blob of lolly fell from the stick. Stephanie licked the ice and grimaced as it hit her gums.

'So why the lolly and not the gum? You're confusing me.'

Stephanie swallowed and breathed out. 'Ice lollies are calorie free.'

'That's a new one on me!'

'He's great with Lucy,' Steph said thoughtfully.

'Just be careful he isn't using her.' It came out before Georgia could stop herself.

Stephanie laid the empty lolly stick carefully on the dashboard. 'I'm the one doing the using,' she said. 'I just want some good sex.'

'And Dawes just wants Reilly.' Georgia paused. 'Seems to me he'll go to any lengths to get him. I think we're all being used. I don't know what Banham's playing at. It's not as if we can't manage without him.'

'Because he knows everything about gang crime, especially on this estate.'

'He's obsessed. His judgement isn't sound.'

'He's a good detective.'

'You're a good detective. And Lucy is going to make a blindingly good one. She's ambitious and confident – so don't let her run before she can walk. And don't let Dawes use her.'

Stephanie turned to face Georgia, obviously not pleased. 'She's done well so far,' she said calmly. 'If she wants to do more, and it's OK with you it's fine with me.'

Georgia opened her mouth to reply that it was far from OK with her or Banham, but Bethany Field chose that moment to appear, along with a tall, oriental-looking boy with bleached blond hair. He held a dog on a gilded chain. It looked like a very angry Rottweiler.

Georgia pulled her keys from the ignition and jumped out of the car. 'That's Winston "Scrap" Mitchell with her. He's one of Reilly's lieutenants.'

Georgia held up her ID as she walked toward Bethany. The girl looked at Scrap Mitchell; he did an about turn and started running. Stephanie ran after him. 'Stop. Police,' she shouted. 'It's not about your dog. We only want to ask you a few questions.'

Scrap stopped and turned to face Stephanie.

Georgia left her to it. 'Bethany, we need to talk to you,' she called as the girl turned toward her flat.

'What about?'

'You know what about. Tom Solden and Carly MacIntosh.'

'Fuck off,' Bethany shouted.

Georgia sighed. 'OK, we'll do it the hard way if you prefer. Bethany Field, I'm arresting you on suspicion of involvement in the murders of . . .' She reeled off the familiar words, as she took a firm hold on the girl's arm and hustled her into the back of the car. 'You do know who Tom Solden is, don't you?' she asked, climbing into the front seat.

Bethany nodded resignedly. 'The punter who got his nuts shanked, ain't it?'

'What do you know about him?'

She shrugged. 'Nothing. Look, is this gonna take long? I got kids.'

'Up to you.' Georgia tapped her fingers on the steering wheel. 'But you might want to ask your babysitter not to run off.'

'Your dog doesn't bite, does it?' Stephanie asked, trying to keep the atmosphere light. Mitchell's pupils were huge; he was clearly off his head. 'What do you know about this punter, the one who was murdered in Tidal Lane?'

He scratched the back of his head. His jeans hung so low on his hips, she wondered if they might fall off. His shirt gaped open, and she spotted a knife tattoo of a twisted BB on his stomach.

'You wanna ask Yo-Yo Reilly,' he answered. 'I don't know nothing.'

'Come on, Scrap. You're part of the Brotherhood inner circle. You've got the tattoos to prove it.'

Scrap gave her a blank stare.

'What did the punter do wrong?'

Scrap shrugged. 'Things move on around here, innit.'

'In what way?'

'I don't know nothing about Brotherhood stuff no more.'

'Oh, come on,' Stephanie scoffed. 'You're a lieutenant, *innit*?'

The sarcasm fell on deaf ears. He shrugged again.

Stephanie sighed. 'OK, let's try something else. What do you know about the girl who got strangled last night?'

'Look,' he said fiercely, 'I ain't heard nothing, and I don't talk to the feds. I ain't saying nothing, cos I've nothing to say. If you want answers, try Yo-Yo. Got it?'

'Not really, no. What about Carly? Did you know her?'

'Who?'

'Don't play games, or you'll end up at the station.'

'Oh, yeah? What's the charge, then?'

'Obstructing a murder enquiry.'

'How can I obstruct what I don't know?'

'Just answer the question, Winston. Tell me about Carly MacIntosh. She worked for Yo-Yo, didn't she?'

'I don't know no one called Carly, right? Have you finished? Or are you gonna arrest me?'

She threw him a contemptuous look. 'Don't go too far,' she said. 'We'll be back.'

Georgia drove back to the station in silence. They checked Bethany into the custody suite and set off for the squad room.

Georgia had a sudden thought. 'Look, after this morning, Lucy could well be on CCTV in the Holster; we'd better make sure Bethany doesn't see her in here.' She held Stephanie's eyes. 'We're not taking any risks with Lucy's safety.'

Stephanie nodded. 'Of course not. She's my baby. And she'll be going back out there.'

'She's not going back out there.' Georgia shook her head. 'I've forbidden it.'

ELEVEN

Tuesday, late afternoon

Georgia was rapidly losing patience with Bethany Field. The girl was slumped in her chair, fiddling with the ends of her curly black nylon hairpiece. It clung precariously to her own short hair with the aid of three large hairpins, and she had attempted to disguise the join with a long paisley-patterned scarf. The hairpins stuck out, and the whole lot was an untidy mess. Georgia suppressed the urge to lean over and push the pins securely into place.

Bethany wore a short khaki gilet over a tight lime-green top, cut low enough to reveal the edge of a tiger-print bra. She seemed to be wearing more shiny lipstick than jeans, the denim was so full of frayed holes. A pair of scuffed, grubby red stilettos completed the unsightly outfit.

She had refused a solicitor, repeating endlessly that she didn't have time for all this.

'I gotta get back,' she said. 'I left the baby wiv my little boy – gawd knows what he's up to.'

Georgia stared at her in disbelief. 'You've left your nineteen-month-old baby with your six-year-old son?'

'I only went down the road for a bottle of milk and a loaf.'

'So where are they?'

'My kids?'

Georgia rolled her eyes. 'No. The loaf of bread and the bottle of milk.'

Bethany bit her lip. Her teeth were custardy-yellow, and there were dark red lipstick stains on the front ones. She rubbed her nose vigorously with the back of her hand, but didn't answer.

'You took a punter, didn't you?' Stephanie said.

Bethany still said nothing.

Stephanie spoke again. 'That's neglect. We could have your kids taken away.'

Bethany leaned across the table and hissed into Stephanie's face, 'I'm a good mum for your fucking information, and I do not neglect my kids. I'm just trying to provide for them. If you know that I should be with them, then let me go and be bloody with them.' She twitched her shoulders and rubbed her nose again.

'We've sent a uniformed officer around to your kids,' Georgia told her. 'They'll probably have called social services by now.'

'Jesus.' Bethany stopped rubbing and sat up straight. 'Tell me you're kidding.' Her legs began to jiggle.

'You're in big trouble, young lady,' said Georgia. 'You need to start talking to us.'

'I ain't done nothing,' she protested, terror in her eyes.

'Your DNA was on the condom we picked up from the car when Tom Solden was killed,' Georgia said. 'That puts you at the scene of the murder. You were in the car with him just before he died.'

'No, I weren't. I swear to you I weren't in the car. I've never done him. He came round Tidal a lot, but not for me. He liked Carly.' She put her hands on the table. 'I'm not his type. I'm too old for him.'

Georgia knew that was true. Enough people had said the same. 'Your DNA is on the condom,' she pointed out.

'Ain't on him though, is it?' Bethany looked triumphant. 'Cos I never bloody done him. He was Carly's punter.'

Georgia leaned forward. 'Are you saying Carly murdered him?'

''Course not. Carly was a daft cow, a bit green, but she was a good kid. She was me mate, she'd never kill nobody.'

'Your DNA is on the condom that was used?'

'Was it cherry cheesecake flavoured?'

'Yes.'

'Just before he come up Tidal Lane, Carly was horsing around. It was fucking freezing.' She hesitated. 'Carly lit us a joint, just to keep warm. She dropped her bag when she was looking for matches, and I helped her pick up her stuff. She had loads of johnnies, all funny flavours. One was fucking cherry cheesecake flavour.' She blinked a tear away. 'I opened it and licked it to see if it tasted of cherry cheesecake.'

Georgia leaned back in her chair, but kept her eyes pinned on the girl. Forensics had found a wrapper as well as a used condom; it was cherry cheesecake flavour. The team had a good laugh about that. Perhaps Bethany was telling the truth. 'She was so untogether, was Carly. She had no idea how to pull a punter.' She gave a wide grin, and Georgia noticed one of her side teeth was missing. 'Always willing to share a joint though.' She blinked nervously, but continued when neither Georgia nor Stephanie reacted. 'That punter came specially for her. I seen the car before. I don't know nothing about cars, not really, but it was big and flash. He always stopped by Carly.' She closed her eyes and a tear rolled down the side of her nose. 'Carly got in the car and that's the last I saw of her. She didn't deserve that.'

Bethany's knees started jiggling again.

'Where did you go when Carly got into the car?' Georgia asked.

'I finished the joint, then I got a punter. I got him to drive over to Marsden Close. He's a bit of a perve, that one – likes to wank in stiletto-heeled shoes. All you do is lend him your shoes and tell him what he wants to hear.' Neither Georgia nor Stephanie batted an eyelid. Bethany went on, 'I dunno why he don't just buy himself a cheap pair and spray 'em wiv perfume. That'd cost 'im less than me sayin' *'oo's a clever boy, then?*. P'raps he thinks I'm a budgie.'

'What's his name?' Georgia asked.

Bethany shrugged.

'What car does he drive?'

'I told you I don't know cars. It's got electric windows and it's big and black. Like his dick.'

Georgia flicked a bored glance at Stephanie.

'What did you do after that?' Stephanie asked.

'I walked back to Tidal and I met Jade . . .'

Stephanie and Georgia looked at each other. 'Jade? Jade was there on Sunday?' Georgia asked.

'Yeah, she'd just done a punter. I hadn't seen her for a bit. Scrap was supposed to be minding us but he'd gone off somewhere, so Jade and I decided to call it a night.'

'Where did she go to?'

'I dunno. Home, I suppose. I know she don't live round our way, but I ain't never asked where she lives.'

'Have you seen her today?'

Bethany scratched at the base of the ponytail. One of the hairpins fell on the table in front of her. Stephanie reached over and picked it up. 'I'll give it to you when you leave,' she said to her.

'When did you last see Jade?' Georgia asked again.

'I ain't seen 'er since then.'

'Did you see anyone else that night,' Georgia asked. 'Anyone at all?'

'No. Look, I told you all I know. Can I go now? I need to get 'ome to me kids.'

The girl's attention was clearly wavering. 'Not yet,' Georgia snapped. She placed the photo of Alice on the table. 'Is this Jade?'

Bethany studied it for a moment, then looked at Georgia. 'Yeah, that's her. Was it her then? Did she do that to that punter?'

'That's definitely Jade?' Georgia asked again.

Bethany nodded. 'I said. Yeah. Look, can I get back to my kids now? Please?'

'We're concerned for your safety.'

'And I'm concerned for me kids. Look, I weren't in the car. An' I told you that's Jade in the picture. Why can't I go?'

Georgia looked at her but didn't answer.

'I ain't working, if that's what you're worried about. I'm staying off the street till this is sorted. So I ain't in any danger.'

Georgia shrugged. 'I'm glad to hear it. But if any of my officers see you soliciting, they have orders to lock you up. For your own safety.'

She sniffed again. 'Fair enough. So can I go now?' She wriggled and rubbed her nose. Georgia steepled her fingers.

After a few uncomfortable seconds Georgia unclasped her hands. 'Yes, all right. You're free to go. For now. But don't go far.' She handed her a card. 'And call me as soon as you see Jade. We need to talk to her.'

Stephanie handed the hairpin back. 'We're looking out for her safety too.'

'Yeah, like you looked out for Carly's.' Bethany snatched the hairpin and stood up to leave.

The last meeting of the day couldn't come soon enough for Georgia. She had been up since half past four, and was absolutely exhausted. The team had already assembled when she walked in. Banham and Dawes were at the front by the whiteboard. Lucy sat at the back again, beside Hank Peacock. Georgia smiled and winked at her as she passed.

She took her place beside Banham and David Dawes and addressed the team.

'Firstly, we owe a big thank you to our work experience student. Lucy went into the Holster club undercover this morning, then she picked up an invaluable lead on the Aviary estate. She found out that Alice Solden is working as a prostitute under the name of Jade. I've just had confirmation of this from another source.'

Lucy blushed but looked pleased with herself. Hank nudged her and started clapping. All the other detectives joined in. Stephanie beamed with pride too, Georgia was glad to see. She wasn't in her friend's best books after pulling rank on her and calling a halt on Lucy's further activities.

Georgia was more angry with Dawes than with Stephanie. She could see through him, and it was obvious Stephanie couldn't. Well, she'd had enough. He'd met his match now.

He was looking at her, waiting to see if she had anything else to say. She had plenty.

'DCI Banham has drawn a line under any more undercover work for Lucy, but that doesn't diminish what she achieved. She has done exceedingly well for us.' She turned to the whiteboard and pointed to the picture of Yo-Yo Reilly. 'We know Stuart Reilly runs the prostitution racket around the estate, so it's highly likely Alice is working for him. One of his other toms, Bethany Field, has just told us Alice, or Jade, was working on Sunday night, at the time her father was murdered. A coincidence?' She shook her head. 'I don't believe in coincidences.' She looked at Dawes and raised one eyebrow. 'There's also Jean Eden.' She tapped the picture of Tom Solden's ex-mistress that was pinned to the bottom of the board. A red marker pen had arrowed it to the picture of Tom Solden. 'Ms Eden told us Solden was a pervert and a paedophile. That opens this investigation even wider. We need to ask ourselves why his fifteen-year-old daughter is on the game. Hardly for the money. And did Solden sexually abuse her? Jean Eden implied that he did.'

Dawes was shaking his head. She ignored him. 'Finding Alice now is our top priority,' she said. 'She is our key witness, and she could be in great danger. We have issued her photo to all the uniformed officers around the estate. Bethany Field has also said she'd call if she sees her.'

The noise level began to rise, but Georgia put her hand up for hush. 'Kate Solden told us her daughter was in the house with her when Tom Solden was killed, but we now have a witness who says she was in fact down in Tidal Lane. That leaves Kate Solden without an alibi, and she is someone else with a strong motive. We'll be talking to her again.'

She added the photo of Kate to the row of suspects at the top of the board, then moved Jean Eden, Nigel Jones and Alice Solden up there too. 'So the wife, daughter, ex-mistress and her fiancé all have strong motives and no solid alibis. DC Peacock?'

Hank Peacock rose smartly to his feet. 'Ma'am.'

'Do we have anything back yet on the bike Nigel Jones told us he sold yet?'

'Yes, ma'am. He faxed us a receipt with the name and address of the purchaser, dated three weeks ago. We ran the registration through the system. That vehicle didn't enter Brixton that night.'

'Good, thank you.' Georgia looked at Banham.

'Check out the name and address anyway,' Banham said to Peacock. 'We'll follow it through.'

Dawes interrupted. 'Remember nothing happens on that estate without the knowledge of Stuart Reilly,' he said. 'If this is about a family feud, Reilly would have known. It's possible Reilly put Alice up to it. There's still no doubt in my mind that he was behind this.'

'Not necessarily,' Stephanie argued. 'Gang warfare is brewing on that estate. It's possible this is the work of another gang, not Reilly's at all.'

'Let's you and I go and pay Alysha Achter another visit tonight,' Georgia said to Stephanie. 'She knows everything that goes on around there. I would bet she knows Alice. She knows all the street girls.'

DCI Banham spoke up. 'OK, let's look at what we've got. The first murder took place on Brotherhood territory. Either Yo-Yo Reilly was involved, or he's hell-bent on finding out what went down.' He gave Georgia a warning glance. 'Let's suppose for a moment that Carly MacIntosh killed Solden. In that case, it's odds on Reilly having her killed, for seeing off one of his regular punters.' He turned and nodded to Stephanie. 'And gang warfare could well be brewing down there.' Now he looked at Dawes. 'Somewhere along the way Reilly will be involved. He always is. So we maintain a presence on the Aviary. But we also follow up every lead we have on the family.'

Result! Georgia thought. 'We need to talk to Reilly again,' she said calmly. 'Stephanie and I will do that tonight, after we visit Alysha Achter. We'll pay Michael Delahaye a visit too.' One of the newer detectives raised a querying finger. 'He's an ex-Brotherhood member. Reilly stabbed him a little while back,' she explained. 'There's a possibility he's heading up the gang who plan to challenge the Brotherhood.'

'I'll come with you,' Dawes said quickly.

Time to show him who's running this show, Georgia thought. He might be the same rank as she was, but she was SIO. 'No,' she said firmly. 'I want you to go and interview Kate Solden. She said Alice was with her on Sunday evening – ask her why she lied.' Dawes opened his mouth to argue but she didn't give him a chance. 'Try to get a handle on her too – is she capable of killing her husband? My feeling is she's unstable enough, and God knows she has motive.'

Dawes opened his mouth again, but this time it was Banham who cut in. 'Take Lucy with you.' He looked round the room until he spotted her. 'Would Mrs Solden know you as a school friend of Alice's?'

Lucy looked doubtful. 'We're not even in the same year. She's quite a bit younger than I am.'

'OK, then.' Banham rubbed his mouth. 'Tell her you know

Alice, that you are at the same school, that you're helping us look for her and that your mum is a detective sergeant working on the case.' He smiled. 'That'll keep you occupied,' he added.

'What happened about Bethany Field?' one of the team asked. 'Wasn't there DNA evidence?'

'Because the condom was one of those flavoured ones, she licked it to see what it tasted of,' Georgia explained. 'We have nothing to prove otherwise, so we had to let her go.'

'She was around at the time of the murder,' Stephanie said. 'I'm concerned for her safety too.'

'If she's in danger, couldn't we have made her stay here?' This was DC Peacock.

'She wanted to get home to her children,' Georgia told him. 'She said she wouldn't be working until the murderer is found. She's not stupid.'

'Uniform are keeping a close eye on her,' Stephanie added. 'They'll arrest her if she starts soliciting.'

'Have we dismissed her as a suspect?' Peacock asked.

'No,' Georgia told him. 'We're not dismissing anyone, but there are plenty with strong motive. Bethany Field has none that we yet know of.'

'We're still linking the crimes,' Banham reminded them. 'Despite the different MOs.'

Georgia nodded agreement. 'Yes. And we all agree Carly would have seen the killer – unless it was herself. According to Bethany Field, Solden was one of her regular punters, so she knew him.'

'Let's go back to the other line of enquiry for a minute,' Banham said, looking at Georgia. 'What's your thinking? Solden abused his daughter, and she turned to prostitution and found a way to kill him?'

Dawes shook his head. Georgia ignored him.

'That's one possibility,' she said. 'Or it could be the mother. And neither Jean Eden nor Nigel Jones has a cast-iron alibi. They were both alone all evening, Jean at home and Nigel at work. Or so they claim. And Jones has a bicycle. No licence plates for the scanner to pick up.'

'How long does bread take to bake?' Banham asked.

'Not long enough to cycle to Brixton, commit murder and cycle home again,' Dawes said sourly.

Georgia ignored him. 'DC Peacock? Can you chase up the copy of Solden's will, and his bank and phone records?'

'For Chrissake.' Dawes suddenly raised his voice. 'Solden had his dick cut off and left in full view. That's got Reilly written all over it.'

'Carly MacIntosh was strangled,' Georgia pointed out calmly. 'That's not his style.'

'He'll be behind that too, mark my words.'

Georgia took a deep breath. It had been a long day. 'OK. So we're following that line too,' she said.

Banham put his hands in the air. 'Arguing is a waste of time,' he said. 'We've already agreed to follow every lead we have. Alice Solden is still out there. Let's make that priority.'

Lucy put her hand in the air. 'Georgia? I mean, ma'am – sorry. Please can I come with you? If we see Alice, I might be able to talk to her.'

Georgia exhaled loudly and closed her eyes. 'We've had this conversation. DCI Banham has said no. You'll be a lot more help with DI Dawes.'

Dawes jumped in. 'DCI Banham said no to Lucy going to the estate alone. If she was with her mother and me she'd be quite safe. Let's do it that way round – you go and interview Kate Solden.' He looked at Banham. 'Don't you agree?'

Georgia's temper began to rise. He really was pushing his luck.

Banham shook his head. 'No, I don't. Lucy, I'm sorry. I don't want you going back to the Aviary. If Alice doesn't show up in the next twenty-four hours, perhaps I'll reconsider, but for the moment . . .' He flicked a glance at Georgia. 'Tonight you go with DI Dawes, please. To interview Kate Solden,' he added firmly, as Dawes opened his mouth to argue again.

Georgia nodded her thanks. 'Right, let's get on with it,' she said, picking up her jacket from Stephanie's desk.

The team began to disperse. Lucy joined Dawes at the front of the room. 'I'll run you home after we go to Kate Solden's,' he said to her, making sure he was in earshot of Stephanie.

Georgia looked at Stephanie, but her eyes were on Dawes.

'I'll bring home a takeaway,' she said. 'We can do some catching up.'

'OK, I'll pick up some good wine,' Dawes answered.

Georgia left them to it. Clearly Stephanie was on a promise. Well, hooray for that; the sooner she went to bed with him the better for all of them. Stephanie always went off a man after she had bedded him, and tomorrow she would see him for the pain in the arse that he truly was. Why, oh why, had she made that stupid bet?

TWELVE

Tuesday evening

Alysha was seething. She was perched on the edge of the arm of Mince's sofa, arms folded tensely across her chest, glaring at Mince as he walked a tearful Bethany to the front door.

Scrap Mitchell slumped in the armchair opposite, his long legs stretched lazily in front of him. His peroxide-yellow hair stood on end, displaying an inch of black roots.

'She's just doing all this larkey to get Mince's attention,' Alysha said to Scrap. 'I ain't never known nothin' frighten the bitch before.'

Scrap's mouth widened into a smile. 'It's working, then. Cos what I hear is, she's getting more than just his attention, innit.'

Alysha opened her mouth to tell him to shut the fuck up, but Mince walked back in the room so she kept it buttoned.

'She ain't in a good way,' Mince said, shaking his head. 'She's really scared. We need to keep an eye on her. And we need to get things moving down here.'

'Ah, diddums,' Alysha snapped. 'She's got you running round after her, ain't she?'

'She needs a bit of care and attention, that's all. She's one of us now – she's left the Brotherhood. Here we look out for each other, we are a tribe and a family, and that's what we do for each other, right?' Mince fixed his eyes on her.

Alysha was about to spit more venom, but he spoke again. 'First things first. We have to sort Yo-Yo Riley. That's our top bit of business.'

'So you're gonna do for all of us what you doing for her then, are you?' Alysha persisted, unable to hide her jealousy.

Mince flung his arms in the air. "How many more times? The feds picked her up. They frightened her, telling her she's in danger big time an' all. She's got every right to be frightened, and we gotta be there for her. She needs to make brass and she can't work. She's got kids to feed.'

'As well as a habit,' Alysha sniped.

Mince's patience was wearing thin. 'The feds know she was there when that punter got his nuts done. For Chrissake, Lysha, she's scared witless. She could be next.' He looked across at Scrap. As usual, he was only half listening. 'You get it, don't you, bro? It stands to reason Beth ain't safe out there, and the feds ain't doin' nothing, so we gotta come through for her. She's one of the Block Bois now.'

'What about that Jade?' Scrap said. 'She ain't wiv Block Bois. She works for Yo, and she's gone missing. I don't trust that bitch one little bit. I reckon we oughta find her.'

'Perhaps she's been done in an' all,' Alysha said absently. She couldn't get bloody Bethany out of her mind: the tender way Mince had put his arm around her, telling her he was there for her, and his new tribe wouldn't let her down. Yo-Yo was getting what was coming to him, he'd said, and there'd be big changes around here. A whole new army of Block Bois were gonna look out for the girls.

Alysha wanted to spit. It was down to her that Mince would be able to get to Yo, but he never gave her any of that soft stuff. She had to look out for herself – and she would too. In the end that's what it was about around here: every man for himself.

Mince had always said he would wait for her, yet here he was, in front of her nose, sucking up to that bitch Bethany. She had risked her own skin when Yo-Yo stabbed him: she stood up to Yo and got Mince to hospital. She saved his life, and this was how he repaid her. If this was looking out for each other he could stuff it. All his sweet talk about showing her honey, but waiting for her to be the right age first – what a load of tosh. All he wanted her for was for her to set Yo-Yo up so he could have the estate for himself. Well, he was about to learn who he was playing with, because she was going to outsmart both him and Yo.

He looked at her expectantly, and she realized he had asked her something.

'What?' she said.

'Jade. D'you think we should go and find her?'

Alysha curled her lip.

'She ain't one of us,' Scrap pointed out. 'She only comes over to make money to pay for her stuff. She's Yo-Yo's property, she might blab to him.'

'She was there when the punter got done,' Mince reminded him.

'She ain't our problem,' Scrap insisted. 'Once this takeover is sorted any girls who stay with Yo will be off our patch. So she can't give us no grief.'

'OK, my new lieutenants of the Block Bois,' Mince said, 'here's what's going down. Alysha will be in Water's Lane. She'll call Yo from her phone, tell him she's been set on by a punter. Alysha? You listening?'

She looked at him coldly. 'I know what I'm gonna do.'

'You're gonna say a punter's hurt you really bad and you need Yo to come and sort it. Yeah?'

'Yeah.'

'Make it sound good. Say you know that you shouldn't have pulled him, but there weren't no one else there and he offered you double, like. You can cry and do all that girl's stuff, just say he's got to come quick, that you're hurt. You got that, babe?'

Alysha gave a quick nod.

'You have to tell him no one's around, not Scrap, not no one, and you're scared and in a bad way. That's sure to get him out. He's to meet you in Water's Lane alley. Lysha, have you got all that?'

Alysha screwed her face and tutted. 'Yeah, yeah, I got the shit,' she said irritably.

Scrap pushed his boot into her leg and nudged her spitefully. 'Listen up, girl, and show some respect. The new boss is talking, innit.'

Mince continued. 'We'll be there, round the back with the Bois. You lie face-down on the pavement like you're unconscious. When he gets out of his car, we'll surprise him and stick him real bad. All you gotta do is run.' His face creased into a satisfied smile. 'Then him and me will be even.'

'Sorted,' Scrap said, grinning back. 'Night after tomorrow, right?'

'Thursday,' Mince agreed. Alysha said nothing. 'Lysha, babe? Have you got it?'

'You ain't half a liar!'

Mince stared at her. 'Whassup wiv you, babe?'

'You said before that all you want is a quiet life. No trouble, sell a little weed here and there. No honey wiv me cos I'm underage.' Her voice rose. 'Now you've got a crew of seventy-odd, and you're planning to take Yo out and take over the Brotherhood.' She was shouting now. 'You can fucking do all that, but you can't go to bed wiv me, cos it's fucking illegal. That is what's up wiv me, babe.'

He raised his hands placatingly. 'Hey, darling, calm down.'

'You fucking calm down. You lied to me.'

Mince closed his eyes. 'Listen, babe, listen good. Yo-Yo Reilly is a bad person. You know it's right that we take him down. He hurts his own. He raped you for your virginity, and nearly killed me cos I respected you. He don't deserve to live.'

'He's right,' Scrap agreed. 'He treats us like we're his dogs.'

'I thought you were with us on this,' Mince said. 'What is it, babe?'

'You're doing Bethany,' Alysha said angrily.

'That ain't no crime,' Mince said.

'It is, cos you promised *me*.' She poked her own chest with her long nail extensions and raised her voice again. 'You even said you loved me.' Tears of anger sprang to her eyes.

'Shut your noise, will ya,' Scrap said.

Mince touched her shoulder and she shrugged him off.

'I'm respecting you, babe,' Mince told her. 'That's more than Yo's ever done for you. That should tell you how much I truly care for you.' He fixed his eyes on her. 'Love you, if you like, cos I do. I honestly, truly do.'

She held his stare, but her eyes were angry.

He carried on. 'Like I said, when you're sixteen, I'll be twenty-two and then we'll see how it is between us. If it's still the same feelings, then I will show you real honey.'

'Bethany will probably have your babies by then,' she snapped, unable to stop her jealousy spilling out. 'I've set all this up for you wiv Yo an all, and you've turned me over real good. You've used me. You're sleeping wiv Beth.' Again her voice rose to a shout. 'And you lied to me. How's that for family that trust and looking out for each other?'

Scrap suddenly sat up. 'Christ, you ain't gonna fuck this up for us, are you?'

'I ain't gonna be used.' She turned and stomped towards the door.

'Wait.' Mince stepped in front of her.

She pushed past him into the hallway. 'I ain't grassing you up, but I'm still thinking whether I'll do the set-up stuff. Why should I let you get Yo's territory so Bethany can fucking lord it? I fucking hate her.'

Her high heels clacked along the hallway, and the front door slammed.

Scrap jumped up to follow her, his knife in his hand. Mince blocked his way.

'Leave her,' he said. 'She'd never grass on us. She saved my life, remember. And we don't hurt one of ours. Family, that's what we are now. I'll sort Alysha.'

The estate was still busy when Stephanie and Georgia walked in from a few streets away. Police cars and uniformed officers were still patrolling the area, so for once it should have been safe to park nearby, but Georgia wouldn't risk it on this estate.

Stephanie had been quiet on the drive over. Georgia was disappointed she had reacted so badly to her decision about Lucy, but she wasn't going to back down.

'I hope tonight's the night for you and DI Dawes,' she said lightly as they crossed into the outskirts of the Aviary.

'Don't worry, I don't intend to lose the bet.'

'Good.' Georgia paused, choosing her words carefully. 'It's just, you seem a bit distant at the moment. I'm hoping that once you've had him in your bed, you'll be able to focus clearly on the case again. You know how much I need you.'

Stephanie stopped and turned to look at Georgia. 'Excuse me,' she said indignantly. 'There's nothing wrong with my focus. Sex helps my concentration. I'm in serious need of a large portion, that's all.'

'Delighted to hear it. This fifty pounds is weighing my wallet down.'

Stephanie lightened up. 'I'm not just doing it for the bet, you know. He's got a dinky little body, don't you think?'

'Not really, no.'

'Well, I do, and I fancy it rotten.'

They set off again.

'If you really want to know, I think he's a gigantic pain in the arse,' Georgia said. 'Not to mention a grade-one trouble-maker. I truly sympathize over the death of his sister, but it's taken him over. He's obsessed with Stuart Reilly. I really think Banham made the wrong decision, bringing him in.' She cast a glance at Stephanie. 'Don't get me wrong, I want Reilly behind bars as much as anyone else – but I don't want another killer to go free because we've put him there. Dawes doesn't care who's really responsible. He won't look further than Reilly. I'm amazed you can't see it.'

'That's because he believes Reilly's guilty.' Stephanie's eyes made it plain that she thought Georgia was the one who couldn't see. 'He studies London gangs. He knows how they work and how they think. And I agree with him. I believe that this is a gang killing.'

Georgia stared at her. 'I totally disagree,' she said quietly.

'You don't think either of the killings are gang-related?' Stephanie asked, a little surprised.

'I'm pretty sure the victim's family are involved.' Georgia picked up the pace, and Stephanie almost broke into a trot to keep up. 'That's why finding Alice is a priority, for all our sakes. I'm seriously concerned for her safety.'

'Lucy could have been a real help there,' Stephanie said. 'Can't you . . . ?'

'That's not up for negotiation,' Georgia cut in. 'Her safety is my responsibility.'

They walked in silence for a few minutes. Suddenly Stephanie grabbed Georgia and pulled her to the side of the pavement. 'Mind that dog shit,' she warned.

'Why can't the owners just pick it up?' Georgia screwed

her face. 'I'm going to send a memo to the residents' association, and get the PCSOs to come down heavy on owners that don't clear up their animals' shit.'

'Like Yo-Yo Reilly?' Stephanie giggled. 'Like he'll take any notice, or anyone on this estate for that matter. Get real, will you?' She pursed her lips. 'You know, I think a night of good sex would do you the world of good too.'

'Excuse me.' Georgia pretended to be indignant. 'I'm your senior officer and you make remarks like that?' She pulled her mouth into a small smile. 'For your information, I get my fair share.'

'Doesn't seem like it. Or else it's not really good. Good sex helps you chill, and clears your mind.'

'That's what it does for you.'

'What about DCI Banham?' Stephanie suggested. 'He's not married and he's quite a hunk.'

'Oh, please,' Georgia shook her head emphatically. 'He's a wimp. He never stops bleating on about his pet DI, Alison Grainger. The man's in lurve.'

'All the better. No strings. You probably both need a good session. I'm not asking you to marry him, just chill with him, and have a shag.'

'I'd rather chill in a mortuary container.'

'See what I mean.'

They both snapped back into work mode as a teenage boy with bleached hair and a dog on a lead turned the corner and walked towards them.

'Scrap Mitchell,' Georgia said.

'Mitchell!' Stephanie shouted. 'We want a word.'

He stopped, tugging at the dog's lead. 'Oh, yeah? What word's that, then?'

Georgia moved towards him, keeping her distance from the dog. Several other youths nearby began to move in, and a patrol car slowed to a halt beside Stephanie.

'We want to ask you some more questions,' Georgia told Scrap. 'Do we take you to the station without that animal, or do we have a chat in your flat? You choose.'

He said nothing for a couple of seconds. The patrol car driver revved the engine. 'Second floor, Wren block,' he said, turning away. 'Number 146. My mum's place.'

The door was open as they followed him up the stairway and into his mother's flat. His mother looked half Chinese and half Indian. 'Now what's 'e done?' she asked as they flashed their warrant cards.

'That's what we're here to find out,' Stephanie said.

They waited in the narrow hallway while Mitchell shut the dog in the back room, then followed him into the lounge. Georgia pulled a packet of tissues from her pocket and held one over her nose, pretending to blow it. The smell, a mixture of mouse droppings, dog excrement and curry, was overpowering. Stephanie seemed to find it amusing. She glared at her.

She took out the photo of Alice Solden and held it in front of Scrap. The look on his face told them he recognized her.

'You'll know her as Jade,' Georgia said. 'When did you last see her?'

'I ain't done nothing. I don't know where that tart is.'

'If she's a tart, you should know her. Isn't it your job to mind the tarts?' Georgia said coldly.

'I don't know where she is and I ain't done nothing wrong.'

'You're beginning to sound like a broken record,' Georgia said flatly. 'Here's a clue. The girls were on the streets on Sunday. You were supposed to be minding them. We don't care about that at the moment. We're more interested in the punter that got murdered. The girls working were Carly MacIntosh, Bethany Field and Jade. I'm sure that rings a bell.' She raised her voice. 'Now don't fuck us about, tell us what happened the night the punter got murdered.'

His mother appeared in the doorway. 'Can I offer you tea?' she asked.

'No, thank you,' Georgia answered, a little too quickly. Her stomach heaved at the thought of the cups and the kitchen.

Scrap had his hand over his eyes. 'What happened on Sunday night?' Stephanie repeated.

He lowered his hands. 'OK. I was around there, but I don't know what happened cos the lane was quiet and I went off to have a smoke. When I got back, Beth and Jade weren't there. Carly was standing against the railing, sort of shaking. She said she wanted to go home. I said fine.' He looked at his fingernails. 'I thought she was ill or something. She didn't say nothin', and I weren't interested. I'd had a drink, I was a bit out of it.'

That meant drugs. 'Go on,' Georgia said.

Scrap picked at his dirty nails. 'I came home after Carly went. Ask my mum. Then next morning I heard that the punter had been done.' He grimaced. 'It's Yo-Yo you should be talking to. He's Mr bloody Fix-it around here.'

'We have spoken to him, and to a little bird, who tells us you're having a fallout,' Stephanie said. 'Is that right? The Brotherhood are in for a takeover?'

He shrugged. 'I don't get involved in all that.'

His nervous blink didn't go unnoticed.

'Clean as a whistle, are you?' Georgia said sarcastically. 'Where do you get your gear?'

He looked blank.

'That little smoke you had, and the rest of the stuff. Where do you get that from?'

He sat bolt upright. 'I don't know his name. He hangs around near the Holster club. Only a bit of smoke an' that. I don't do no bad shit.'

'Reilly runs the protection at the Holster club,' Stephanie said.

'Wouldn't know.'

'Wouldn't you?' Georgia snapped. 'For someone with a Brotherhood of Blades tattoo on his belly, you don't know much.' She leaned in close to his face. 'Well, here's something you should know. A man called Tom Solden was castrated in his car in the alley behind these flats, and the hooker he was with has been strangled. We are going to find out who was responsible. And if I find out you've been withholding evidence and obstructing our enquiry, you'll be going back inside for a very long stretch. So I'll ask you once again, is there anything that might have slipped your mind?' She sat back and held her breath for a few seconds to let the smell of him subside.

'I ain't done nothing.'

Georgia stood up and dropped a card on to his lap. 'If you catch sight of Jade, call us,' she said. 'You'll be doing yourself a big favour.' He returned her stare and she lifted her chin.

'You need to remember that I don't make threats that I don't carry out,' she told him.

Scrap's mother followed her to the front door, a baby held in the crook of her arm. 'I've got seven children and no husband,' she told them. 'He's just young, and a bit wild. It's hard to keep him in check.'

'Try harder,' Stephanie said sarcastically. 'Other women manage without a man.'

They walked down the graffiti-clad stairway. 'Did I actually hear you say that?' Georgia asked.

Stephanie made no reply.

They reached the bottom of the stairs. 'When have you ever got through a week without needing a man?'

'Only for shagging. It's good for the heart.' Stephanie's face broke into a wide grin. 'Remind me to stop for condoms on the way home.'

There was a half-empty bottle of gin and a used glass on the table beside Kate Solden's chair. Dawes and Lucy had been shown into the large Victorian-style sitting room, where she waved them into seats before settling herself into a comfortable armchair. 'Drink?' she asked, lifting the bottle.

'Coffee would be good,' Dawes said. 'For all of us, I think.'

She put the bottle down and stood up unsteadily. Dawes and Lucy followed her into the kitchen.

'This is Lucy,' he said as Kate filled the kettle, splashing water on to her clothes. 'She knows Alice. They go to the same school.'

Kate dumped the kettle on the worktop and switched it on.

'Her mother is a sergeant in our team,' Dawes went on. 'Lucy is helping us look for Alice.'

'I'll do the coffee,' Lucy suggested. 'Where do you keep it?'

Kate opened a cupboard and handed her a packet of individual coffee filters. 'I know who you are,' she said. 'Your mother is Sergeant Green. She gives talks at the school sometimes.'

'That's right,' Lucy said brightly.

'Has Alice ever run off like this before?' Dawes asked her.

Kate nodded, a little embarrassed. 'I didn't want to say much before . . .' She rubbed her forefinger round and round a spot on her forehead. 'My husband was an ogre. Alice hated him. She stayed out a lot when he was around. I often wished I could go with her.'

'Do you know where she goes?'

'Friends. She stays with friends.'

Dawes was pleased she had been drinking; it meant she was speaking freely. 'Who?' he asked. 'Do you know their names?'

'I've told your colleagues all this,' she snapped. 'I told them, I don't know. They've interviewed all her school friends.' She dropped her gaze. 'I know I probably shouldn't give her so much freedom.'

The kettle boiled and Lucy poured water on the coffee. She handed the first one to Kate. 'Milk?'

Kate shook her head. 'Alice is different from other girls her age,' she said. 'I didn't want to drive her away.' Tears rolled down her face and she wiped them on the sleeve of her cream tracksuit. Black eye make-up smudged the velour, but she didn't seem to notice.

'How is she different?' Dawes asked.

Kate blinked, and wiped mascara from under her eyelid with a finger. She began twisting her wedding ring. 'He should have been locked up years ago,' she said in a low voice. 'He interfered with her, you know.'

Lucy handed Dawes his coffee. His face was expressionless.

'I didn't believe her,' Kate said after a brief pause. 'Well, what woman wants to believe that of her husband?' She took a sip of coffee, winced and held the mug under the cold tap for a moment. Her hand shook, and water splashed the draining board. 'That's when she started staying out for nights on end.' She carefully put the coffee down on the granite worktop. 'I didn't tell her off. I didn't want to lose her.'

'You should have gone to the police,' Lucy said.

Dawes flicked an angry glance at her.

'What would you know?' Kate snapped. 'You're only a kid yourself.'

Lucy began to protest, but subsided when Dawes looked at her warningly.

'Why did you tell us Alice was in her room on Sunday, when you knew she wasn't here at all?' he asked Kate.

'I thought she *was* in her room.' The penny dropped. 'Oh. Now I have no alibi.'

'Can anyone else confirm that you were here? Dawes went on. 'Did you get a takeaway or anything?'

She shook her head. 'No, but I downed a lot of gin. I'm afraid I was too drunk to go out and kill him. The empty bottles are somewhere. Would that help?' She looked at the coffee as if it disgusted her, and emptied the mug into the sink.

'You said you and husband had a normal sex life,' Dawes said. 'That's not true, is it?'

She gave a humourless bark of laughter. 'Oh, I'm well past my sell-by.' She picked up a glass from the draining board, filled it with water and downed most of it in one go. 'Not that I would have let him near me. God knows who he'd been with.' She opened the dishwasher and put the glass in, but didn't bother to close the door.

'That must have hurt. You must have really hated him.'

'Oh, I did. But I didn't kill him.' She looked at Lucy. 'Do you think Alice did?'

'We need to talk to her,' Lucy replied, with half an eye on Dawes.

'Then get out there and find her. I don't know where she is.'

'Do you know a woman called Jean Eden?' Dawes asked. 'She works for your hus . . .'

'That tramp!' Kate picked up the used coffee filters Lucy had put beside the sink, and threw them at the waste bin. They missed, and landed on the tiled floor. Lucy put them in the bin, then picked up a J-cloth and wiped up the mess.

'Go on?' Dawes pushed.

'She got fat, and he got bored.' Kate picked up another glass and looked around the kitchen – for her bottle of gin, Dawes thought. 'Fat women. Something else Tom didn't like.' She looked at Lucy. 'Mustn't say that in front of your mother, though, must we?'

Lucy gasped, but Dawes ignored the remark. 'If Alice comes home, or gets in touch, you must phone us right away,' he told Kate. 'We're as concerned as you are for her safety.' Probably more, he thought.

'Alice can look out for herself,' she said with a dismissive wave. 'She's very grown-up for her age.'

'I'm sure she's worried about you,' Lucy said.

Kate gave another snort of laughter. 'If she did kill him, she'll know I don't give a duck's fart. I hope he rots on hell.' She paused, and when neither Dawes nor Lucy reacted, carried on, 'She cared for him though. Well, I think she did. Who knows?' She lifted her empty glass as if in a toast. 'What does it matter? He's dead. No one cares now, do they?'

'We do,' Dawes told her. 'And we will find who's responsible and we'll bring them to justice. And my advice to you is to go easy on the gin.'

The uniformed sergeant sifting through the upended rubbish bin looked as if he hadn't slept for days.

'Any luck finding the weapon?' Stephanie asked him.

'Take your pick. A hammer, seventeen knives, at least a dozen screwdrivers, a machete and two hatchets. They've all gone to forensics. None of them match that description of yours though. We may still strike lucky, who knows. DCI Banham wants us to widen the search.'

'I'm delighted to hear it,' Georgia commented. 'But sorry for you having to sift through that lot.'

The sergeant stood up and rolled his shoulders. 'Plays havoc with your back, this job. You should try it sometime.'

'Oh, I've done my share. Listen, I don't suppose you've seen Alysha Achter tonight?' Stephanie asked. 'Thirteen going on thirty, lives on the thirteenth floor, cornrows, always over-dressed?'

''Course I know Alysha. Is there anyone around here who doesn't?' He gave a wry smile. 'She went into Stuart Reilly's gaff not twenty minutes ago, and if she's come out I haven't noticed.'

'Thanks,' said Georgia. 'What about Alice Solden?'

'The girl in the photo? People round here shake their heads before they look at it.'

'I have a bad feeling about her.'

'We'll keep on it,' the sergeant assured her.

It was four full minutes before Yo-Yo answered the banging on his front door. He must have hoped they'd go away, Georgia thought, shouting over the barking of his dogs. Finally he appeared, barefoot, wearing grubby tracksuit bottoms, his sweatshirt inside out. Alysha stood in the hallway behind him.

'I need to ask you some questions,' Georgia said briskly.

Yo-Yo opened the door wide to allow them to enter. 'Fucking harassment,' he said. He kicked a door off the hall. 'Shut the fuck up!' he yelled at the dogs behind it. 'What is it this time?'

'Are you here on your own with a minor?' Stephanie asked him.

'She's my neighbour, for fuck's sake,' Yo-Yo snapped. 'She dropped something in. Don't start making accusations, or I won't answer nothing without my legal representative.'

'How are you, Alysha?' Georgia asked pleasantly.

'I'm a bit nervous cos of what's happened,' Alysha said. 'A letter for Yo got delivered to me by mistake, so I popped in with it and Yo said to come in for a minute. Me dad's out, you see.'

The stink of stale smoke mixed with dog excrement turned Georgia's stomach over.

'Come on, what's this about?' Yo-Yo demanded. 'I got stuff to do.'

'Carly MacIntosh,' Georgia said. 'Did you know her well, Alysha? She was about your age, wasn't she?'

'She lives around here,' Alysha said a little too pointedly. 'Yeah, I knew her. Not well, though.' She flicked a nervous look at Reilly.

'Actually, it was you we wanted to see,' Georgia said to him.

Yo-Yo pushed open the lounge door and waved a hand at the leather seats. Georgia and Stephanie followed him into the room, but remained standing. Yo-Yo lowered himself into a chair and folded his arms.

'What can I do for you?' he asked.

Georgia handed him the photo of Alice. 'We're looking for this girl. Do you know who she is?'

He held the picture out to Alysha and they exchanged a look. Yo-Yo shook his head. 'Never seen her before,' he said. Alysha shook her head. 'No idea. Sorry.'

'She was last seen near this estate,' Stephanie said. 'We're concerned for her safety.'

Yo-Yo scratched his crotch. 'Why don't you have a television appeal?'

'Oh, why didn't we think of that?' Georgia said sarcastically.

'Is she a witness or something?' Alysha asked.

'She's missing,' Georgia answered. 'Her family are worried about her.' She looked at Yo-Yo. 'She's underage, you see. And since underage girls are a speciality of yours . . .'

'Is that an accusation?' Yo-Yo said, sitting bolt upright. 'That's libel, that is.'

'Just answer the questions,' Stephanie jumped in. 'Have you ever seen this girl?'

'No, I fucking ain't,' he answered, mimicking her sing-song tone.

'You see, I heard she hung out around the Holster bar,' Stephanie pushed.

Yo-Yo's hands lifted defensively. 'Wouldn't know.'

'You have the protection contract around the Holster bar. Hence you'd know people that hang out there. You're not denying that, are you?'

'Not me. Something else you've got wrong.'

Georgia held his eyes, and her temper. She reached into her pocket and threw a card at him. 'If you do see her, it'll be very much to your credit if you would let us know,' she said, turning toward the door.

'Thanks for that.' He picked up the card. 'I'd run out of bog paper.'

'Where is your father?' Stephanie asked Alysha.

'He's out working.'

'In that case, since you're so nervous, quite understandably, Inspector Johnson and I will walk back to your flat with you.'

'She'll be fine,' Yo-Yo said. 'The place is swarming with feds, didn't you know? Safest place in London at the moment.'

'We'll walk you to your flat door,' Stephanie repeated.

'Hey, why don't I come too?' Yo-Yo smirked. 'I was just gonna give the dogs a walk when you knocked.'

'Not tonight,' Georgia snapped. 'Neither my sergeant or I are keen on dogs.'

Yo-Yo grinned maliciously. 'Oh, Inspector, you do surprise me. There's enough of you in the force.'

THIRTEEN

Tuesday, ten p.m.

'What time will your father be back?' Georgia asked. They had walked around the block and stood at the foot of the thirteen flights of stairs to Alysha's flat. 'Don't know. Soon, I expect.'

Georgia and Stephanie looked at each other, but neither commented. They followed Alysha as she took the stairs two at a time. Stephanie was huffing by the sixth flight and paused for a rest. Alysha carried on, and Georgia followed.

When they reached the walkway Georgia opened her mouth to speak, but almost collided with a washing line overladen with underwear and T-shirts. She ducked under it and found Alysha digging in her shoulder bag for her key.

'Being on your own with Stuart Reilly is asking for trouble,' Georgia said, following the girl inside.

Alysha turned her big brown eyes on Georgia. 'People have been murdered, right by this block,' she said. 'I'm scared. Yo-Yo just asked if I was OK.' She shook her cornrows. 'He looks out for people, you know.'

She was about to close the front door when Stephanie appeared, breathing hard. She followed them in.

'He's not all bad,' Alysha said.

Stephanie opened her mouth to argue but Georgia shook her head. They were here to find Alice Solden, and Alysha was the best contact they had. Lecturing her about Reilly's criminal activities could wait.

The place smelt of mould. Georgia closed her eyes; she could hardly wait to get home to her own flat, with its fresh lemon fragrance, gleaming white bathroom and power shower.

'I wasn't there long, anyway.' Alysha flicked the light on. 'He just asked if I was OK and if I needed anything.'

'Just don't let him befriend you,' Georgia said.

'Better than making an enemy of him. Anyway, it's nice to see you.'

'We're looking for the girl in this photo.' Stephanie passed her the photo again. 'Are you sure you haven't seen her?' As Alysha took it, she added, 'You should be careful, you know. Reilly grooms underage girls for prostitution.'

'I heard he won't be here much longer,' Alysha said casually. She handed the photo back. 'Well, won't be running the place.'

Stephanie and Georgia looked at each other. 'Who's taking over?' Georgia asked quickly.

'Don't know.' The beads on Alysha's cornrows rattled. 'I don't ask questions. Don't wanna get involved.'

'Who did you hear from?' Stephanie asked.

Georgia watched the girl smooth her fingers through her hair. This girl was streetwise, but she was also young, and perfect picking for Yo-Yo Reilly. He probably had her lined up already. Normally Georgia left the personal stuff with Stephanie, but she felt an affinity with Alysha; the girl reminded her of herself when she was young. Alysha brought out maternal instincts she thought she didn't possess. Georgia hoped she hadn't been sexually abused.

'Come on, Alysha. Talk to us,' she coaxed.

'I heard talking,' Alysha said, scratching her head. 'I listen, and I speak when I'm spoke to, but that's all. Someone was talking, that's all.'

Georgia smiled. 'Best way. Keep in with everyone, even the police.' She met Alysha's eyes. 'The uniformed officers are looking out for you too. If you're in any trouble, just shout.' She held up the photo of Alice Solden again. 'You have seen this girl, haven't you?

Alysha shook her head.

'Are you sure?'

'I have seen her around,' Alysha said flippantly, 'but not since the punter got done. No one hangs around since what happened to Carly.'

'So she hung around the streets?'

Alysha shrugged. 'I seen her there, but not for a while.'

Georgia said nothing. Alysha shifted uncomfortably.

'How well did you know Carly MacIntosh?' Stephanie asked after a few moments.

'Hardly at all.'

'She lived on this estate. You said yourself you know everyone on it. You were a similar age. You must have spoken to her.'

Alysha turned out her bottom lip. 'It's a big estate. Lots of people live here. I've seen her, that's all.'

'OK.' Georgia paused and flicked some lint off the knee of her jeans. 'Alysha, if you had to venture a guess at who might try to take over the Brotherhood territory, who would it be?'

Alysha dropped her gaze.

Georgia pushed on. 'It's in your interest. We want to protect the residents from people like Reilly.'

'It's probably just talk,' Alysha said. 'I'm surprised anyone would dare.'

'Michael Delahaye might dare? There's no love lost between him and Reilly since the stabbing. I bet he'd like to see Reilly ousted.'

Alysha tugged at the hem of her blue denim micro-skirt. 'No. He's had enough trouble. Wouldn't want no more.'

'You still see Delahaye, don't you? Sorry, he's Mince to his friends, isn't he?'

'I don't see him loads. I just bump into him, that's all. He's moved on.'

Georgia smiled. 'You used to be sweet on him, didn't you?'

Alysha shrugged.

'That's why I'm surprised you think Reilly is being kind to you. After what he did to Mince. You saved his life.'

Alysha met Georgia's eyes. 'I don't want to fall out with no one,' she said. 'Best not to do that round here.'

'Has Reilly ever made any sexual advances to you?' Georgia asked her.

'No.'

'You see, if he had,' Stephanie put in, 'we could put him away. That would save Michael Delahaye, or whoever was thinking of taking Reilly out, from getting done for attempted murder.'

'Underage sex counts as rape, you see,' Georgia added. 'All

it would take is a statement from you, and Reilly would go to prison for a very long time.'

'I'm not frightened of him, and I ain't had sex with him. I told you, I don't want to fall out with no one,' Alysha said.

Georgia nodded. 'As long as no one is frightening you.'

'If Mince was caught with weapons,' Stephanie added, 'he'd go to prison, what with his previous record of carrying and using.'

'This place is buzzing with uniformed officers,' Georgia continued. 'If anyone is carrying, they will very likely get caught. Those officers are going to be around for quite a while.'

Alysha scratched her cheek with her long mauve nail extensions. Georgia and Stephanie looked at each other; were they hitting home?

'But we could stop it all, and protect Mince from going to prison, if we knew he was thinking of taking over the territory,' Stephanie said again.

Alysha slowly shook her head. 'Not Mince. You're wrong there. He wants an easy life. He got a real bad scar from that shanking.'

Georgia realized she wasn't going to get much out of Alysha on that front. She lifted the photo of Alice up again. 'OK. Let's think about this girl,' she said. 'She could be in danger.'

'What kind of danger?'

'She might have been in the vicinity on Sunday, the night of the first murder.'

Alysha's eyes bulged. 'You mean you think she done the punter?'

'I didn't say that. We do need to talk to her, though. Please, Alysha – think. Did you see her on Sunday?'

Alysha shook her head. 'No, I don't think I did.'

Georgia tried another tack. 'What about Bethany Field? How well do you know her?'

Alysha's eyes narrowed. 'A bit,' she said cautiously. 'She's got two kids. I babysit for her sometimes.'

'You know her quite well then,' Stephanie said.

'She gets about a lot,' Alysha said sarcastically.

'We know she's on the game. We're not here to arrest anyone for soliciting,' Georgia assured her. 'We're here to find out

who killed Tom Solden and Carly MacIntosh. We spoke to
Bethany earlier. She couldn't tell us anything.'
   'Why d'you think I can, then? I don't work the streets.'
   Georgia dug in her bag and pulled out a twenty-pound note.
She laid it on the table in front of Alysha. 'If she says anything
to you, about Alice, or Carly, or anything at all that might
help us, I want you to let me know. Will you do that?'
   Alysha stared at the money but didn't answer.
   'We are trying to protect you. All of you. Bethany is vulner-
able too.'
   'She don't talk much to me,' Alysha said. 'I'm just a kid.
Anyway, she could be the killer. She works round there.'
   'Alysha, I'll be honest with you. We need help catching this
killer. You know what goes on around here.'
   Alysha picked up the twenty pounds. 'Only some of what
goes on. I don't know much.'
   'We need to find Alice.' Georgia placed another twenty
pounds on the table. 'We think she is known around here as
Jade.'
   'Did you try the Holster bar?' Alysha took the second note
and smoothed them both out on her lap.
   'Some officers have been there, yes. Is that where she hangs
out?'
   Alysha's eyes flicked quickly from Georgia to Stephanie.
'Plain clothes, like you?'
   'No, they're in uniform,' Georgia said quickly.
   'I'll ask around, OK?'
   'And I really need to know who is going to try and take
this territory from Yo-Yo Reilly.'
   'Yeah.' Alysha nodded. 'If I hear anything.'
   'And find out if Carly . . .'
   'Yeah, yeah, what I hear, I'll tell you,' Alysha said impa-
tiently. 'Ask me, you should arrest Bethany. I wouldn't trust
her. Her and Carly were always fighting.'
   'Do you know something about her?' Stephanie asked.
   Alysha shook her head. 'But I'll see what I can find out.
Don't you let on it's me, though.'
   'Of course not.' Georgia stood up and placed another of her
cards on the table. 'It's really important that we talk to Alice.

You will call me as soon as you hear something, won't you? No matter how insignificant it seems.' She walked towards the door, then turned to look at Alysha. 'We meant what we said about Reilly. We can get him put away for a very long time. All we need is someone to speak up, so we can charge him with having sex with a minor. Anyone brave enough to do that would do this estate a very good turn.'

'Seems to me everyone's doing illegal stuff,' Alysha said.

'What do you mean?'

She shrugged innocently, but her eyes looked very wise. 'Well, isn't it illegal for the feds to interview someone of my age without an adult? And offer bribes?'

'We weren't interviewing you,' she said quickly. 'This was an off the record chat. And bribes?' She looked at Stephanie. 'What bribes?'

'I was only asking,' Alysha said. 'I'd never drop you in it or nothing. I wouldn't want to do nothing illegal, that's all.'

'Say hello to your father from us,' Stephanie said sarcastically as she followed Georgia out the door.

'Do you think she'll help us?' Stephanie asked a few minutes later as they fastened their seat belts.

'She has in the past,' Georgia said.

'She's a clever, calculating street cat.'

'She's a survivor, that's all.' Georgia pulled out into the traffic. 'And I'm glad she is. If anyone can help us find Alice, she can.'

'Let's hope.' Stephanie called the station on her mobile and spoke to DC Peacock. She clicked her phone shut. 'They're going through Solden's mobile records. He used a few numbers regularly. One of them was Jean Eden's.'

'She still runs a shop for him,' Georgia said. 'Anyone else?'

'A couple of unregistered pay-as-you-go mobiles. Could be his connection to his underage prozzies. Peacock's getting them checked out.'

'Good. What about the bread thing? I asked him to find out whether Nigel Jones could have left the bakery on Sunday night.'

'The longest window would have been fifty to sixty minutes. And they had the normal amount of bread on Monday morning.'

'So Jones's alibi sticks,' Georgia said thoughtfully.

'There's more.' Stephanie sounded almost excited. 'Solden's will. The bulk of the estate goes equally to Alice and Kate – but there's a rather interesting legacy. Jean Eden gets half a million pounds, on condition that she carries on running the business.'

'That is interesting,' Georgia said. 'I wonder if Jean Eden knew.'

'She was home alone on Sunday night.'

'So she says.'

'I think we need to talk to Ms Eden again, Detective Inspector.'

'I think you're right, Detective Sergeant.' Georgia smiled. It looked as if Stephanie was over her strop. 'But not till tomorrow. Why don't you phone lover boy, make sure he's with Lucy, then put some lippy on and I'll drop you home?'

Georgia couldn't resist a quick glance at Stephanie's smiling face as she chatted to Lucy. She and Dawes were obviously waiting for her at home. Georgia was rarely lonely, but something tugged at her as she thought of her own empty flat, and Alysha, all alone in hers.

Stephanie clicked her phone shut, still smiling. 'I needn't bother with a takeaway. David is cooking spaghetti bolognese, and he's laying the table as we speak.'

'Obviously in a laying mood,' Georgia teased. 'What did Lucy say about Kate Solden?'

'She was half-cut. Swore she didn't know Alice wasn't home in bed on Sunday night, but she'd had a lot to drink. Dawes didn't think she would be capable of cutting a slice of bread, let alone driving over here and bobbitting her old man.'

'That's what Dawes wants to believe,' Georgia said. 'Kate Solden is still high on my list of suspects.'

Stephanie didn't disagree. As they approached her house, Georgia noticed her flip the sun visor down and use the mirror to freshen her lipstick. Her mobile chimed: Peacock again. She put him on speaker while she finished brushing her hair.

Kate Solden's car had just popped up on the Brixton registration scanner.

'Get an urgent trace on that car,' Georgia shouted to him. 'Ask TIU to trace her phone as well as Alice's. Alert patrol cars in the area, tell them the driver is most likely over the limit and we need to know who she is. She should be stopped on sight, breathalyzed and arrested. Call me on my mobile the minute there's any news.'

Alysha wriggled out of her tight skirt and threw it on the bed. Her green lurex T-shirt followed. She pulled on black leggings, a black hooded sweatshirt and a dark anorak, pushed black gloves into her pocket and bunched her cornrow plaits into a woollen beret. She closed the front door quietly and walked quickly but cautiously down the thirteen flights of stairs.

There were feds all over the place. If she was recognized she was inviting trouble. She needed to make sure she stayed out of Yo-Yo's way too; he took those vicious dogs out at all hours, and he was the last person she could afford to bump into right now. She pulled out her phone and quickly sent Jade a text, just in case.

Georgia could still smell the Aviary estate: stale urine, dog shit and rotting food clung around her like yesterday's clothes. She couldn't wait to peel everything off and stand under a hot shower. That place always got to her: the dirt under Stuart Reilly's fingernails, the smell of his vile dogs, and on top of that Scrap's mother's flat. She wanted to scratch herself all the time she was there.

She was seething about Reilly. She suspected he was grooming Alysha for sex. Even if he hadn't murdered Solden, and Georgia didn't believe that he had, with a bit of luck she could get him for statutory rape. Alysha had told her months ago that Reilly had raped her, then lost her nerve and denied it. Georgia knew from her own experience rape made the victim feel guilty; you felt you must have somehow invited it. She hoped that hadn't happened with Alysha.

She turned the shower on, peeled her clothes off and threw them in the wash basket. Why had Alysha gone to Yo-Yo's flat tonight? It didn't add up. If she was scared because two people had been murdered, why hadn't she gone to Michael Delahaye? Alysha had said he was going straight, but Georgia didn't believe that; he was about as straight as a go-kart circuit. So was Alysha lying? Or was she just taken in? Perhaps Reilly really had seen her passing, and asked if she was OK. She was just vulnerable enough to think he cared for her welfare. Georgia wanted to ask uniform to keep a closer eye on her, but if they did, the girl wouldn't have enough freedom to pursue Alice. Georgia had to hope she had convinced her she could trust the police if she needed help. If she kept her as an informant, and paid her regularly, Alysha could be a great asset. If Alice was on the Aviary, there was no doubt Alysha could find her.

Then again Alysha might feel the gangs offered better protection than the police, and start playing Georgia around. She had studied Alysha closely tonight; the girl's eyes were bright and her skin clear. She hadn't been steered on to the drug route yet.

She wrapped herself in a clean towel and checked the temperature of the water. It needed to be hot enough to kill off any germs she'd picked up from that disgusting estate. She turned the power up to full and stepped into the shower. It was burning hot and felt good. She enjoyed the sting as the scalding water landed on her skin.

They hadn't considered Michael Delahaye till tonight. Was it possible Kate Solden had paid him to kill her husband? Or some other low-life? Dawes had suggested that Solden might have been caught in the crossfire of a gang battle. That didn't ring true. Emotions were running too high in the Solden family. Tom Solden was a perverted paedophile, and his wife, daughter, ex-mistress and her fiancé all hated him. But Alice working the streets down there meant there had to be a connection; according to Bethany Alice had been around on Sunday. Alice had to be found; she was the lynchpin.

Georgia stepped out of the shower into a fluffy white towelling robe and white towelling flip-flops. When she'd dried herself she used up nearly a full bottle of citrus-scented body lotion.

In the kitchen she filled the kettle, then took a notepad and pencil from a drawer, drew a line down the page and headed the columns TOM SOLDEN and CARLY MACINTOSH.

The two murders were quite different, but they had to be linked. Was it possible Kate Solden paid someone to kill her husband, then had Carly disposed of because she knew the killer? And why was Kate's car in Brixton tonight? Georgia's instinct told her Reilly wasn't the killer. Why would he kill a punter who put money in his pocket? If Kate Solden had been paying, top of the list would be the gang leader planning to take over Reilly's territory. Was that Michael Delahaye, or was there someone else – someone even David Dawes didn't know about? Someone clever enough to send out warning messages and at the same time make it look like a Brotherhood killing. When Reilly cut or stabbed someone, it was usually personal. He hurt Michael Delahaye because Delahaye disobeyed him.

She picked up the pencil again, flipped over a page of the notebook and wrote: *Gang warfare. Who wants Reilly's empire?* Then: *Retaliation – Alice, Kate, Nigel, Jean.*

The kettle boiled. She laid the pencil down and tipped a packet of powdered soup into a mug. She poured boiling water over the powder, picked up her pencil again and crossed out Nigel Jones's name. She checked her mobile; no one had called while she was in the shower. She put the phone on a tray along with the mug of soup and carried it into the bedroom. She half hoped she wouldn't be called out again tonight; she had been up since four thirty and needed to sleep. But she needed to know when there was an update on Kate's car, or if Alysha called with news of Alice.

She sat on the side of the bed and sipped her soup. Her mind began to switch off. She slipped into bed and as her head hit the pillow she was asleep.

Stephanie hung her coat on the back of the door, and left her shoes nearby. She walked up the stairs to the first floor of her maisonette.

Dawes was in the kitchen chopping vegetables. A pan sizzled on the hob; she could smell garlic, and as she walked through the door, the vegetables went into the pan.

Lucy was sitting at the table drinking hot blackcurrant from the large mug that Georgia had given Stephanie as a gift last

Christmas. It was engraved with the words *I love chocolate.*
'Smells good.'
'Lucy said you liked pasta,' Dawes said. 'Any news?' He
stirred the vegetables, filling the air with a delicious aroma.
'Kate Solden's car registration came up on the Brixton
scanner. We've got an all-car alert on her.' There was a bottle
of Valpolicella on the table: her favourite. 'Better not drink
too much of this,' she said. 'We might get called out.'
'Kate Solden shouldn't be behind a wheel,' Lucy said.
'I think that might be my fault,' Dawes said uncomfortably.
'I told her Alice had been seen hanging around the Aviary.'
'Jesus!'
'Could someone else be driving her car?' Lucy asked. 'What
about Alice?'
'She's not old enough to drive,' Stephanie said.
'She's not old enough to have sex, but that hasn't stopped
her.' Lucy set her mug down on the table. 'Did you go to the
Holster bar tonight?'
'No, but uniform are there, and they've been given photos
of Alice. Funny you should say that: Alysha Achter asked
the same thing.'
'I think Alice goes there a lot,' Lucy said. 'The guy I spoke
to knew exactly who I meant when I described her.'
'Oh, leave it to someone else for the moment,' Stephanie
said. 'Let's have some supper and get an early night.'
Lucy gave her mother a knowing look.
Stephanie ignored her. 'Someone is helping Alice lie low,'
she said to Dawes. 'We'd have had a sighting otherwise. What
I'd really like is to get the estate searched flat by flat, but
manpower aside, that would start another riot.'
Dawes flicked a glance at Stephanie. 'Maybe we should
send Lucy back to the Holster club tomorrow,' he said. 'You
told them you were what, fifteen?'
'Yes,' Lucy answered.
'Perfect for underage grooming. Play the game, act dumb.
See what they say. We'd be only yards away.' He lifted his
eyebrows at Stephanie. 'What d'you think?'
'Let's see if anyone picks Kate Solden's car up tonight,'
Stephanie said noncommittally. Georgia would be furious, and

she wasn't over the moon about putting Lucy in danger herself. Then again, if Lucy did well, the job she coveted in CID after university was a dead cert.

Dawes put a piled plate in front of her. 'Smells terrific,' she said.

After supper Lucy excused herself and went off to her room. She was already wearing jeans; she slipped on another jumper and thermal boots, checked her phone was in her pocket, then sat anxiously by her bedroom door listening and waiting.

Before long Stephanie and Dawes climbed the stairs to the upper floor and closed the door behind them. Lucy gave them a quarter of an hour, then picked up her scarf, gloves and hat and crept out of the front door.

The night bus from the end of the road would take her all the way into Brixton. Alice would almost certainly be somewhere around the Holster bar. Alice would listen to her. Lucy had been on her side over the tattoo, and they got on quite well, even though Alice was a couple of years younger. Lucy would get her talking, take her off somewhere quiet, then call for back-up on her mobile. The investigation team was going to think she was brave and brilliant. She certainly wouldn't be making the tea tomorrow.

FOURTEEN

The small hours of Wednesday morning

One thirty was early for a night bird like Bethany. She was always wide awake at this time; tonight she was twitchy. She had snorted a line of the good coke Yo-Yo had given her earlier, and now she was dancing around the room swinging her head from side to side in time with a Lady Gaga CD. She'd offered to share the coke with Mince, sure he would have been delighted to snort Yo-Yo's handouts, but Mince had turned it down, sent her home, told her things were too dangerous right now, it wasn't safe to spend a whole night with her. Once Yo-Yo was finished, he said everything would be very different around here, but until then no one could be sure who was on which side and who was telling the truth; best to keep everything low profile. If any of the loyal Brotherhood saw them together, they just might go making calls and putting Beth in danger. The estate was a pretty dangerous place right now, what with Carly being murdered; that really gave her the willy-jibbles, and that was why she needed the coke.

It hadn't given her the same high as usual, nor calmed the fear that had gnawed at her since the feds picked her up. She'd been careful to tell them nothing, just make it sound like she was shocked like everyone, and knew nothing about the punter. There was the other pack of lies too – the stuff she'd fed to Yo-Yo. It was all giving her serious brain-ache.

Yo-Yo had given her the third degree: who had she seen hanging around on Sunday, who was minding the girls in the adjoining territories, which girls had been working round there, a whole load of shit. She tied herself in bloody knots thinking about it. The more she remembered, the more he rewarded her with free gear, so she lied through her teeth about the girls, and he handed it out like fucking candy.

He wasn't letting her work again either, not till he gave her the OK. So she needn't have lied anyway, she'd got what she wanted. She told him the feds had said the same, it was too dangerous to work. At the moment she was well suited. She could be a lazy cow and still get as much stuff as she wanted. But she was still edgy, and scared witless. She didn't like that new bird, Jade; posh cow didn't even live near the estate, just came and went as she pleased. So Beth had well dropped her in it. Last week, not for the first time, Jade had come over and nicked Carly's punter. Carly was Beth's mate, so as a last salute to her, Beth had told Yo that Jade sneaked off that night the punter got done. She told him Jade was putting out to the customers at the Holster club too; Scott, the manager, was well fed up with her undercutting his prices by offering her services for a line or two. She reckoned Jade would get a good beating for that. She hoped so; it would be a pay-back for stealing Carly's punter.

She'd been careful not to say much about Scrap. She wouldn't make trouble for him; he'd gone over to Mince's new gang. Talk about bloody nerve-racking! At least she didn't have to go out on the streets in the freezing cold and suck stinking dicks.

Next time Yo asked her what she'd seen, she'd tell him about the grey car that was always driving up the road; the driver yelling that they were skanks, telling them to find God and clean the streets up. She'd seen a motorbike too, parked around the corner. They'd laid bets on how long it would be before someone nicked it, then when she came back from doing a punter it was gone. That should keep Yo busy for the next couple of days. After that he wouldn't be worrying about nothing cos Mince would be running the estate. She couldn't bloody wait. Mince would be great to work for, and now she was his girl he wouldn't make her work the streets. She'd get plenty of corn just for doing his special customers. Life was going to get one hell of a lot easier.

Not for poor Carly, though. She wondered what had happened to little Oscar, and a picture of him, hungry and crying for his mum, flashed into her mind. She stopped swaying to the music and sat down with a bump. Suddenly she felt alone, and very afraid.

This so-called upmarket gear was doing no good at all. She picked up her tobacco tin and her Rizla papers and started to roll a joint. She didn't know who she could trust, so she'd kept what she really knew to herself. She hadn't even told Carly that she knew who that punter was. Some things didn't add up, though. What scared her most was why Carly had been done in. She was a silly cow, but they'd been mates. Now the poor kid was lying on a mortuary slab, and all because of – what? *What?*

Bethany clicked the remote and the music died. This was supposed to be a night off. She'd given the kids half a valium in their bedtime drink so they wouldn't wake when she went out to see Mince, and they were out for the count. The night was hers. She was going to smoke this grass and chill out. She didn't have to economize; Yo was giving her all the gear she wanted, and Mince was passing stuff her way too. So why wasn't she happy? She flicked the lighter and the spliff caught. She inhaled deeply. It was good grass, warm in her throat.

Yo-Yo hadn't exactly helped her mood. It looked like someone was targeting his toms, he'd told her; he'd moved his other girls from their usual patch and put them next to the Block Bois territory. He obviously suspected something was brewing, and was putting the girls out as bait. She shivered. Yo-Yo wasn't stupid; something must have wised him up. Still, she was pretty sure Carly's murder and the punter's were nothing to do with the gang stuff. If it was, she'd have known.

So who did kill Carly? Mince wouldn't, surely? She dragged on the spliff, and another shiver ran through her. Mince had hurt a lot of people before Yo had stabbed him, and he was well capable of killing. He was planning to kill Yo in a couple of days. But Carly? Would he kill her? And why?

She took another drag. No one was sorry he was going to get rid of Yo-Yo, the perverted bastard. Life would be one hell of a lot sweeter without him. But something else was going on that she couldn't get a handle on. She put the spliff in the ashtray and flicked the CD on again. She managed a little bit of a dance, but she started thinking again about Carly's kid again. Christ, what *was* going to pick her up tonight? She picked up a half-full bottle of vodka Mince had given her and took a few glugs. She was going to get off her face, whatever it took. The kids were sound asleep and she bloody needed it.

The knock on the door was so soft she thought she'd imagined it. Had Mince changed his mind? Couldn't he get enough of her? She grinned at the thought of that, and went to open the door.

The knife was in her stomach before she saw it coming. She doubled over with the pain, and her hand flew to the second pumping wound in her groin. She pulled her hand away and glanced in horror as warm and sticky liquid dripped between her fingers. Christ, it really hurt.

She missed seeing the knife as it came at her again. This time it knocked her off balance. She toppled on to her knees, looked up, opened her mouth to scream, but everything felt so far away. She was vaguely aware of a strange high-pitched mewling sound.

Then she felt the knife in her neck. Her hand was too slow to halt the tear it made as it slid along the side of her long, skinny brown skin. She slowly brought her hand to touch the area and felt skin flapping loosely against her palm as mucus and blood soaked her fingers. The carpet moved in front of her face. She lifted her bleary eyes to look into the face of her attacker, willing her mouth to open, to beg for the lives of her babies, but she fell forward, face to the ground in front of her. Her two children were the last pictures her mind was able to form before her world went into darkness.

Lucy stepped off the night bus and headed up the road toward the Holster bar. She didn't want to invite trouble, so she carried no handbag. Her mobile and Oyster card were zipped safely into the inside pocket of her jacket. She had a little money with her; ten pounds would be enough for an eighth of grass. If she did get mugged, she'd have a tenner to offer, which could save her face from being slashed.

She couldn't wait to see her mother's proud face when she brought Alice in and announced it at the morning meeting. It was two thirty a.m.; the Holster was in full swing. She could already hear music and she was still some way down the street.

The queue spilled back from the door, but it was moving quickly. She joined it, and was nearly at the entrance when a bouncer stepped out in front of her. He was as broad as he was tall, with a gold tooth and a yellow bow tie, and he smelt of peppermint. He looked her quickly up and down and shook his head. 'Sorry, love, no chance. No way are you eighteen.'

That was ironic, Lucy thought. Alice was two years younger, but nearly six feet tall; no one ever questioned her age. Lucy's was queried all the time; she was blonde, slightly built, and wore hardly any make-up. She looked younger than her years on a good day.

Being turned away at the door wasn't in her plan. Her brain worked quickly. 'Is the manager in?' she asked.

'No.' The bouncer still blocked her way.

She cocked her head flirtatiously. 'Oh, that's a shame. I met him yesterday. He offered me work, told me to come back any time, and I'm looking for a job. I'm looking for my friend too – is she here, d'you know?'

The bouncer laughed. 'We see a lot of girls.'

'You'd remember her,' Lucy said. 'She's very tall, with long black hair, pink and green streaks. Her name's Jade.'

He smiled, displaying the gold tooth again. 'And a butterfly tattoo in a *private* place? Oh, I know Jade. Quite a few people are looking for her. Hang on, I might have been wrong about Scott. Let me check if he's here.'

Scott was out within seconds. His face relaxed when he recognized Lucy.

'Well, hello again.' He jerked his head at the bouncer, who moved away. 'Looking for work, are you?'

Lucy was suddenly nervous. 'I'm still looking for my friend Jade too. Have you seen her tonight?'

Scott narrowed his dark eyes. 'Matter of fact she's here, in the back office. Come through.'

Lucy followed him through the crowd on the dance floor. The music pounded, dancing bodies obscured her path, and the flashing lights made her dizzy. At the far end of the room Scott ushered her through a door and signalled that she was to climb the stairs on the other side. Her heart began to hammer in her chest. How was she going to handle this? Alice would know exactly who she was.

She wondered if she had done the right thing, but there was no turning back now. Scott was right behind her, phone held to his ear; she realized he was describing her to whoever he had called. She turned swiftly. 'You're talking about me? What's going on?'

'You said you wanted to earn money.'

'I said . . . I might think about it.'

'Well, someone's on his way to help you decide. Be nice to him. He's a powerful man. You could make a lot of money, enough to buy all the wraps your heart desires.'

Wraps? That was hard drugs. Yesterday it was grass; now he was talking serious dealing. Apprehension morphed into excitement. The drugs squad would give her a thumbs-up for this. 'Look, I need to talk to Jade first,' she said.

'You and half the world.' He led the way to a door at the end of a dark passageway. Lucy took a deep breath and followed him.

Alice, or Jade, was in the room behind the door. She was tied to a chair, hands bound behind her, long black hair flowing loose behind her. Lucy managed a tiny head shake as a warning not to drop her in it.

'Jade has been a very naughty girl,' Scott said. His charm had vanished; his face was hard and mean. 'We thought you should see what happens to naughty girls before you start working, then you'll know to behave yourself. That way your pretty face will stay intact. Not sure Jade'll have hers for much longer.'

'What's she done?' Lucy asked nervously.

'Broken all the rules, and upset a lot of people. Why don't you girls catch up? I'll be back in a mo.' He turned and left the room, and Lucy heard a key turn in the door.

The second he was gone her finger flew to her lips. 'He could be out there listening,' she whispered.

'What on earth are you doing here?' Alice hissed.

'I've come to find you. Your mother's worried sick, and everyone's looking for you. What's going on?'

'It's none of your fed-nosing business.'

'Please keep it down,' Lucy begged. 'If someone hears you say that we're both in big trouble. I'm on your side here.'

'Oh, yeah?'

'Listen, I've put my neck on the line to find you and help you. I'm gonna be in deep shit.'

'With who?'

'With the force, with my mum, and with your mum. These people are very, very dangerous. We have to get you away. Personally I don't care what you've done. I care that you are safe.'

Alice turned away.

Lucy dropped on her haunches beside the chair. 'Alice, your mother's beside herself. You do know your dad has been murdered?'

''Course I do. I'm surprised my mother's noticed I'm not there. She's usually too drunk to know I'm alive.'

There wasn't time for sympathy and reassurance. Lucy stood up. 'Let me try and untie you.' She moved round the chair and began to fiddle with the knots. 'What's going on? Who have you upset?'

'Yo-Yo Reilly. He's looking for me, to punish me. It'll be a quick beating, that's all. I'm not that scared. It's still better than being at home.'

'What happened to you at home?'

'My father happened to me. He was a fucking pervert.'

'I'm so sorry.' Lucy was at a loss. What else did you say to a kid who had been sexually abused?

'Anyway, I'm not going back,' Alice said defiantly. 'I can make easy money around here. I can help you to get started if you want.'

Lucy shook her head, unsure how to play this. 'Let's get you away from here, then we talk more.'

'The first punter is hard, but it gets easier. You get immune to it, and gear's so easy to come by, you can get off your head, then you hardly know you're doing it. Anything's better than being at home.'

'What have you done that's upset Yo-Yo Reilly so much?'

Alice shook her head.

Lucy was trying to untie the knots that dug into her wrists. 'Please try and keep still.'

Alice wriggled her hands defiantly. 'Leave it. You'll get hurt too, if you interfere.'

Lucy stood up and took a pace back. 'Do you know who killed your father?'

'No, but I'm glad he's dead. He came looking for me.'

'Your mother's looking for you too. I think she's here in Brixton.'

'Oh my God!'

Lucy dropped down beside the chair again. 'Please let me help you. These knots aren't impossible. If I loosen them you can pull your hands free.'

'OK, but be quick.' Alice squirmed, growing agitated.

'Do you think your mother killed your father?'

'Is that what the feds . . .'

The door flew open at that moment and Scott strode in, followed by Stuart Reilly and two other men. Lucy jumped to her feet and faced him.

She had seen pictures of Reilly on the board in the CID room, but in the flesh he was even more grotesque: larger, more blubbery, his head out of proportion to his body. The short spiky hair made him look like a cockerel. She had an urge to laugh, but the look in his eyes told her not to mess with him.

'So you're looking to earn some money,' he said.

Things weren't going well for Stephanie. Dawes had happily agreed to stay the night, and offered to sleep on the couch. Stephanie had given him one of her alluring looks, and suggested that her bed was much comfier and had enough room for two. He followed her up the stairs and headed into the bathroom. Stephanie took the opportunity to run around tidying up, and was in bed totally starkers by the time she heard the loo flush.

She was used to doing most of the chasing with men, but once a man was in her bed she expected him to be willing, preferably eager. Dawes merely climbed into bed in his shirt and Union Jack underpants, and turned over to go to sleep.

Stephanie had no intention of going into work the next day and telling Georgia to keep the fifty quid because Dawes had snored the night away. Besides, she was randy.

Normally she had no trouble keeping a man awake. She knew exactly what turned them on; she had made it her business to learn every trick in the book. But tonight she began to wonder if she had lost her touch. Then finally he turned toward her, and let out a sexy breath. Halle-bloody-lujah! By now she was nearly out of her mind with desire, but she managed not to act on it. Climbing on top of him wasn't an option; last time she had done that, the bloke begged her to get off as he couldn't breathe, and feared he was going to suffocate under the weight. She was thirteen and a half stone, so maybe he had a point. Dawes was quite slightly built; she would crush his crown jewels. It had taken her long enough to perk them up, and she wasn't about to waste all that effort.

Neither of them had drunk much in case they were called out. Dawes was probably inhibited, maybe even a little shy. Sweet. She decided to take it slowly. They had all night, and she was determined to give him a good time. She might even come back for seconds. He really was quite cute.

Her phone rang first. It was a rap song Ben had downloaded for her; she hated it, but hadn't worked out how to change it. They both jumped as the drumbeat boomed out, and Dawes's erection tickled her leg as it shrivelled. She nearly cried out with disappointment. Then, as she reached for the bedside light, church bells chimed out from Dawes's mobile.

A neighbour had noticed blood seeping under Bethany's front door. The police had broken in and found the children drugged and Bethany stabbed to death.

Georgia arrived on the scene within minutes of the call.

There are hand prints on the door,' Phoebe Aston told her. 'Let's hope they belong to the killer, and not the neighbour.'

'How long has she been dead? Could you take a guess?'

'Not long. The blood's still sticky.'

Georgia's mobile bleeped. Stephanie's name came up on the screen.

'Where the hell are you?' she snapped.

'It's Lucy. She's not here.'

Georgia closed her eyes. This was the last thing she needed.

'Does Ben know where she's gone?'

'No. He came in late and hasn't seen her all evening.'

This was Dawes's fault, Georgia thought. 'Stephanie, I'm at the Aviary, standing by the third murder victim in three days. Please don't tell me she's decided to go looking for Alice on her own.'

She hardly listened as Stephanie told her Lucy wasn't stupid, and it was completely out of character.

Georgia wondered exactly how much Stephanie knew about her daughter's character, especially since Dawes had filled her head with his tunnel vision about Yo-Yo Reilly. Dawes didn't give a damn who he used to achieve his goal, and Stephanie was too besotted to see it. This was the last straw; Dawes was off the case, and she didn't care who hated her for it.

But right now there was work to do. 'I'm putting her description out to all units, from Wandsworth down to Brixton,' she told Stephanie. 'Alice Solden is hard to miss, but nobody's seen her. Let's hope it's easier to find Lucy.'

Alysha had been on her way to Michael's when her mobile rang. Yo-Yo had found Jade, and there was another girl too, young, pretty, naïve, and she wanted to earn. She was perfect for the private parties with the perverts. Alysha examined her new nail extensions as he rabbited about how he wouldn't try the new girl himself, seeing that Lysha was his only girl. She nearly laughed out loud.

She was outside Mince's flat now. Yo-Yo was still rabbiting: him and Lysha were like salt and pepper, or fish and chips, or some load of tosh. Silly fucker. Didn't he realize she had him eating out of her hand?

Michael wasn't in her best books either. She had saved his life and he had betrayed her with Bethany. She had decided she would set Yo up for Michael, and stand back and let the fuckers rip each other's skin off. She looked over to Michael's window. She hated him. From now on she was looking out for number one.

Yo was still whining on. Something made her start listening: he was on his way to her flat with Jade, who was going to get a beating for taking him for a mug, and this new girl, who was going to be locked in a room overnight with Boot and

Scrap, for them to do what they wanted with her. After that, she'd be used for the pervert parties. She was fair-haired and blue-eyed, like Carly; she'd do well for him.

'Better take care, Yo,' Alysha said, trying to sound as if she cared. 'Feds are everywhere. Better take the long route – come up to the roof on the fire escape, then down a flight.'

'I'll do that. Thanks.'

Thanks! Yo-Yo Reilly never thanked no one. Stupid bastard. Up till recently he had made her do whatever his rich West End clients wanted. He had taken a fat fee, and given her a small slice of it, then driven her home without giving a flying fuck what kind of shape she was in. She had played the game, done what the punters wanted of her, then told Yo-Yo he was the one – that she really only liked doing it with him. He had fallen for all that, stopped her doing the punters, and come over all possessive. It suited her. He still gave her all the money she wanted. The fat bastard even told her she could run the street girls and take a cut of the money. Well, soon he'd be dead, and so would Mince. All the corn from dealing and girls would be hers then. She would be queen bee, running the territory. And no one, but no one, would dare to disrespect her.

FIFTEEN

Very early Wednesday morning

Dawes and Stephanie signed in at the murder scene and were handed their forensic oversuits. Stephanie struggled one-handed to drag hers over her clothes; the other hand clamped her mobile to her ear.

'Still not answering,' she said to Dawes. 'Where can she have gone? She's the sensible one.'

Dawes slipped plastic overshoes over his feet, unconcerned. 'Maybe she's got a fella.'

Georgia was kneeling just inside the open front door studying the blood spatter over the floor and walls. She was listening but made no comment. Her temper was at boiling point.

'She probably knew we were *occupied*, and nipped off to have a bit herself,' Dawes said loudly. 'She said yesterday that she thought sleeping around was no big deal.'

The exhibits officer squatted beside Georgia with a whirring video camera, filming the bloodstains. He winked knowingly at Stephanie. She ignored him.

'Then why is her phone switched off?' Georgia asked, glaring at Dawes. 'Yes, she is sensible and bright, but she's also naïve and too keen to impress.' She flicked another glance at Dawes. 'And desperately inexperienced.'

Dawes ignored her. He knelt beside Bethany Field's corpse and moved the head gently for a closer look at the neck wound. He looked up at Stephanie. 'Make sure all available uniform in this area have got full descriptions of Lucy, and Alice and Kate Solden.'

Stephanie nodded.

Georgia stood up and followed Stephanie as she headed down the path. She waited till they were out of hearing. 'Are you fit to work?' she asked quietly. 'Wouldn't you rather go home, in case Lucy turns up?'

'I'm fit,' Stephanie assured her, pulling her blue forensic cap off her uncombed hair. 'I'm going nowhere.'

'Good.' Georgia tried to smile. 'In that case, I'm putting you in charge of the search for Lucy. Alice and Kate Solden too.' She raised her eyebrows. 'Oh, and I give the orders, not Dawes. But this isn't an order, it's a piece of advice. Now you've had him, stay away from him. He's bad news.'

Stephanie was hardly listening. 'I can't believe she's turned her phone off,' she said. 'She never does that.' Her face was taut with anxiety. 'I hope nothing's happened to her.'

'Listen to me,' Georgia said. 'Lucy's a sharp little fox. She'll know we can trace her if her phone is on, and for whatever reason, she doesn't want to be traced at the moment. If she was in trouble, she'd turn it on.'

Dawes was standing by the door with a tape measure. Georgia raised her voice to ensure he heard. 'DI Dawes has filled her head with rubbish. He'll be hearing from DCI Banham about that.'

His shoulders tensed. Good, she thought; I've got him worried.

'It's my fault too,' Stephanie said wearily. 'She wanted to help, and I thought it would be good for her. I had no idea she'd be so stupid.'

Georgia pressed her lips together. This wasn't the time to remind her friend that lust had a way of clouding her judgement. 'I've already spoken to the uniforms at the Holster bar,' she said. 'They've interviewed the staff and some of the punters. No one has seen her there. That was my first thought.'

Dawes had moved towards them. 'No one at that place would admit to anything,' he said. 'It is like the Aviary estate. You'd do better to put those uniforms on the streets, searching for the women themselves.'

Georgia's eyes flared but she bit her tongue. 'Every spare patrol car is searching,' she said calmly. Turning to Stephanie, she added, 'There are three around the Holster bar. If Lucy is in there, she won't come out unnoticed.'

Dawes flicked his wrist and checked the time. 'It's too early to get on to TIU,' he said crisply to Stephanie, 'but as soon

as there's someone in there, chase them. We've given them
Alice's mobile, haven't we? And Kate Solden's?'
   'They've been given all the mobile numbers,' Stephanie
said. Her cheeks started to mottle and glow red. 'They've
been monitoring for Alice and Kate all night, and they've
begun to look for Lucy's phone even though it's four in the
morning.'
   Georgia had seen Stephanie blushing like that many times
before. It happened when she fancied someone. She looked
quickly around at the forensic team, then the penny dropped.
If Georgia hadn't been feeling so angry with Dawes, she would
have hugged Stephanie.
   'You used to know someone *very well* in TIU,' she said.
'Ken Wright. Did you ring him at home?' Georgia was remembering a recent case during which they had worked closely
with TIU to find an Iranian woman on the run from her
husband. Stephanie had had one of her brief affairs with Ken
Wright during that investigation.
   'I still see Ken sometimes,' she said, still glowing like a
Belisha beacon. 'I gave him a call and got him out of bed. I
gave him all the numbers, told him it was an emergency. He's
on it. He's already been back to me. None of their phones are
switched on. But as soon as they are, he'll trace their whereabouts and get straight back to us.'
   'Well done, Sergeant!' Georgia caught Stephanie's eye.
'Right, you go on supervising the search. Dawes and I will
carry on here.'
   Phoebe Aston was heaving herself to her feet. She rubbed
her back and winced, pointing to the wound on Bethany's neck.
   'Someone's been careless,' she said. 'We've taken a hair
off that wound that isn't dark enough to be the victim's. We've
got that hand print by the door too. You could just be in luck
here.'
   'This is very much Reilly's style,' Dawes said.
   Georgia turned her back on him.

Alysha needed to get home to change and hide these clothes
before Yo-Yo arrived. He mustn't know she had been out. She
was lucky she knew the estate better than the feds, and was

small enough to get around via the kids' play tunnels, and climb like a baby monkey up the back of the broken lift machinery.

The feds were stopping and searching everyone right now. She couldn't let that happen; she had strapped the small handgun Yo-Yo had given her inside her knickers. It was loaded too, though she wouldn't use it unless she had to, not with all these feds about.

She was back in the flat in no time. She undressed, washed herself down, then rang Yo-Yo and told him which way to come to avoid the feds. She left the front door open for them.

When they arrived she got the shock of her life. The new girl was the one she had spoken to in the street yesterday, the one who'd asked her about her friend Alice, better known around here as Jade. Alysha had seen this supposed new girl with her own eyes, climbing into the back of an unmarked fed car.

She only looked about fifteen – but she had to be older, the cow was an undercover fed.

Alysha had to make a split-second decision: did she let on, or keep shtum?

She had big things planned, and nothing could get in the way of all that. Michael believed she was setting up Yo-Yo for him, but Alysha had decided to let Yo in on that so he could bring his own boys; they'd kill Michael after he had stabbed Yo-Yo, and if they didn't, she would. She'd kill Yo too, if Mince couldn't manage it. It was time for both of them to get their comeuppance. This was going to be her territory.

She made a quick decision to use this girl too. If she kept the feds thinking she was on their side she wouldn't be suspected of anything or any shanking. She could go on looking the little innocent. She looked the girl up and down, held her eyes for a second, just long enough to make the bitch nervous, then she crossed her arms and nodded. 'She'll do.'

Stephanie's phone rang. She listened for a few moments, then looked across at Georgia. 'Remember the motorbike

Bethany Field saw? Parked in the street the night of Tom Solden's murder? She gave us the first three digits of the registration.'

Georgia nodded. 'Go on.'

'They're only the same three digits as the one Nigel Jones says he sold. He showed us a receipt, remember?'

'Have they got the name and address of the purchaser?'

'Someone who lives in Tulse Hill.'

'Not far, then. What about CCTV?'

'That's the bad news. It hasn't come up as entering Brixton any time that evening.'

'Could have been there a while, there are no parking restrictions on that street.'

'A bike like that? It would have been nicked within the hour, surely? And if it hadn't been there long, why was it there then?'

'Get on to Peacock,' Georgia told her, 'Tell him to bring Nigel Jones in again.'

'Ma'am.' Stephanie saluted smartly.

Georgia had another thought. 'Jean Eden too. And find out if she has a motorbike licence.'

'What d'you say your name was?' Yo-Yo said.

'I didn't,' Lucy answered sullenly.

Yo-Yo smacked her hard in the face. She shrieked. He grabbed her ponytail and twisted her head so that their faces were an inch apart. 'First thing you learn is you don't fucking smart answer me,' he spat. 'Got that?'

Her hand flew to her stinging cheek. 'Yes.'

'Say you're sorry.'

'Sorry.'

'I give the orders. Number one, you do as you're told. Got that?'

'Yes, I've got that. I'm sorry.' She fought back tears. 'Please don't hurt me.'

He burst out laughing. 'Oh, you're gonna get a lot more than a slap when you work my punters.' He reached into his pocket with his free hand. 'I hear you like a bit of good stuff.' He took out a small polythene wrap of crystal meth and wiggled it under her nose. 'On the house,' he said, folding it into her hand.

Alysha watched carefully. This girl was terrified, and out of her depth. She was trying not to cry, and staring at the crystal meth like she'd never seen it before. Maybe she hadn't. Jade spoke up. 'She's not a hard user. And she doesn't really want to do punters. She's only come here to find me. She's an old mate and she's worried about me.'

Lucy's expression grew even more desperate.

So Jade knew the girl was a fed, Alysha thought. This was getting better by the minute.

The silly cow didn't know when to shut up. 'You know the punter that got murdered?' she went on. 'That was my dad.'

Alysha's jaw dropped. Yo-Yo let go of Lucy and turned to look at Jade.

'Your . . . dad?' he said slowly.

'Is that why you killed 'im?'

That shut her up. Jade looked at the floor.

Yo-Yo laughed. 'Good on you, girl. Bastard deserved all he got. He liked hurting girls, didn't he, Lysha?'

'Yeah. He beat me up real bad.'

'Liked to knock 'em about. So no one's cross wiv ya for killing the bastard.' Yo-Yo took a step towards her and peered into her face. 'But Carly? That was different, Carly never deserved to die. She was a big earner. What did she do? Saw you kill him, did she?'

Jade shook her head adamantly. 'No. I didn't kill anyone. I ran away because I was frightened. Bethany's scared too.' Her voice rose. 'We all are. There's a murderer on the loose, for Chrissake.'

Alysha was looking at Lucy. 'I saw you on the Random yesterday,' she said to her, deciding to change the mood. 'You were asking for Jade. Alice, you said. You called her Alice. D'you remember?'

'Yeah,' Lucy nodded, but her voice had a wobble in it. 'Of course I remember. I came looking for her when I heard her dad had been murdered.'

Alysha held her eyes. 'What made you come looking down here?'

Lucy grew flustered. 'I . . . know her mother. And the . . . the girls at school said she hung around down here.'

'What are you about?' Yo-Yo said, narrowing his eyes at her. 'You said you wanted to earn.'

All eyes were on her. 'I said I might.' She shrugged nervously. 'I wanted to score some grass yesterday, so I went to the Holster bar. Scott told me I could make some money to pay for it.' She swallowed. 'Everyone knows you can get good stuff at the Holster.'

'Who told you that?' Yo-Yo quizzed. 'Who said you could get good grass there?'

A flush spread over her face. 'Just someone I met. Look, I'm not sure I wanna work the streets. I just didn't want to go home. I wanted to find Jade, and have a bit of fun. I heard this was a good place to hang out.'

The girl was rambling. Alysha could tell she was lying. Time to let her see who ran things around here. 'You don't get to choose,' Alysha told her. 'We decide for you. Some of the boys try you out, then they'll tell us if you're a good fuck, and if you're good at doing what you're asked. If you are, then we give you a trial.' She was enjoying watching the fed girl squirm. But she wasn't going to give her away, not yet.

Yo-Yo turned to Jade. 'If you didn't kill that punter, where were you when he got done in?'

'I was doing another punter, then I came back and saw my dad's car. I thought he'd come looking for me, so I ran off.' She saw Boot and Scrap exchange glances, and took a step towards Scrap. 'You were there,' she shouted. 'Was it you? Did you kill my dad?'

'Hey,' Alysha intervened. 'Chill out. We all thought you done it, and that's why you was lying low.'

Jade started to cry. Lucy put out a hand to comfort her, but Yo-Yo tugged her back. She resisted, and he hit her hard, across the back of the head.

Lucy shrieked.

'Cut that out!' Alysha shouted.

'She does as she's told.' Yo-Yo raised his voice.

Alysha would have liked nothing better than to see Yo give the fed girl a good beating; she'd even stick a few punches in herself. But if she let him start smashing Lucy about, she could be done for accessory. She needed the feds on her side, which meant not letting Lucy get beaten – shame, but it would look good for her when Lucy told them Alysha had helped her. It might be a good idea to tell the feds about the stake-out between the two gangs, turn the whole lot of them in. She'd come out of it smelling of roses, and she'd have the territory as well. Maybe not, though; if they got bail, they'd all come after her. She'd be better off letting Yo and Michael kill each other. That would be the end of them both.

'No.' Alysha shook her head as Yo went to belt the fed girl again.

'A lump on the back of her head, that's all,' he said to Alysha. 'No punter'll mind that.'

Alysha had no choice if she was to save herself. The girl's cover had to be blown. She shook her head and let out a sigh. 'She's working with the feds,' she said.

Everyone in the room looked at Lucy.

'Ask her,' Alysha urged.

Lucy shook her head vigorously. 'No, no, I'm not.' She looked petrified. Alysha wanted to laugh. 'Jade and I go to school together,' Lucy bleated on. 'Her mum told me her dad had been murdered and she'd gone missing, so I came to find her. That's all, I swear.'

The doorbell rang, followed by urgent knocking.

'That'll be the police,' Lucy said. 'You'll have to give it up now.'

Yo-Yo grabbed her arm and twisted it up her back. 'Get in the other room,' he told Jade. 'Out of sight.'

Georgia's mobile bleeped again. It was Sergeant Sidney East's number on the screen: the uniformed sergeant working with Stephanie Green and running the weapon search, and heading up the unit looking for Kate, Alice and Lucy Green. Georgia was convinced Lucy was around here playing at being a hero; now she was worried sick that she would end up a dead one.

'Something happening?' she asked.

Sidney told her they had found Kate Solden's car, parked a few streets away; it was locked up, and no sign of the driver.

Georgia rang Stephanie. 'They've found Kate Solden's car,' she told her, peeling off her forensic suit as she walked toward the car. 'I'll meet you there.'

She was halfway to her own car when she heard someone running behind her. 'Wait,' Dawes shouted. Without waiting to be invited, he opened the passenger door and jumped in beside her.

'It can't have been here for long,' Stephanie said a few minutes later, as they peered through the windows of the dark four-by-four. 'There's all sorts of stuff in the back – blankets and boxes. Nothing stays put very long in cars around here.'

'Lots of police around,' Dawes pointed out.

Georgia put a hand on the bonnet. 'Cold. It's been here a while.'

'I can't believe she drove in that state,' Dawes said.

Stephanie looked through her notes and pressed Kate's number into her mobile. It went to voicemail right away.

'She's obviously come looking for Alice,' Dawes said. 'She has no idea how dangerous this place is.'

Georgia couldn't resist. 'Another one then.'

Stephanie pressed another key. 'Lucy's still not answering.'

Georgia put a hand on her arm. 'She's not stupid. She can look after herself.' But even Georgia didn't believe what she was saying.

Stephanie stabbed another set of numbers into her phone. Another phone started to ring. They all looked at each other. It was coming from inside the parked car.

'Who are you ringing?' Georgia asked.

'Alice.'

Dawes raised a hand to a uniformed constable keeping watch. 'We need an enforcer here.'

'Sir.' There was a patrol car parked across the road; the constable ran towards it and opened the boot.

Within seconds Dawes had rammed the bright red battering tool through the window of Kate Solden's car and opened the driver's door. The phone was in the pocket by the seat. He started to scroll down her call history.

'Incoming recent calls,' he said. 'Mum, Scott, Bethany, Alysha.' He looked up. 'And us.'

He checked the messages. Kate had left no message. Someone called Scott had invited Alice over to his place, saying he had something she might want, and Bethany had called at around eleven o'clock, asking her to come round, and she would tell her what happened at the police station. Alysha was asking where she was, and said everyone was looking for her. There was a text from Alysha too, saying the same.

'How come her phone is in her mother's car?' Stephanie said. 'It hasn't been there long, judging by those calls.'

'Perhaps Lucy was right.' Georgia looked at Stephanie. 'Maybe Alice took the car.' She turned to Dawes. 'You said yourself Kate was drunk when you interviewed her.'

'So she could still be at home,' Stephanie said.

'Get uniform over to the house and tell them to keep knocking. If she doesn't answer, I'll ring a magistrate for permission to break in. She's a strong suspect.'

'We've only circumstantial on that,' Dawes reminded her.

Georgia took Alice's mobile from Stephanie's gloved hand and slipped it into an evidence bag. 'I know you're convinced Yo-Yo Reilly killed them all,' she said. 'I'm not. I'm covering all possibilities.'

'If Reilly didn't want those women dead they would still all be alive,' Dawes said sharply. 'Tom Solden too. Trust me.'

'Jesus,' Georgia shook her head and turned away from him to Stephanie. 'I'm calling in helicopter Indie 999,' she told her. 'Three women are now missing and there's a murderer on the loose. I'll need to wake DCI Banham up, bring him up to speed, and get him to request the helicopter.' She was suddenly aware that Stephanie had lost all the colour from her usual ruddy complexion. 'Lucy has got a lot of sense and she will use it,' she added.

'I wish I was convinced,' Stephanie said, looking at Dawes who for the first time seemed uneasy.

'What time is it?' Georgia asked Dawes.

'A quarter past five.'

'We'll go and wake Alysha Achter. She has her ear to the ground. Stephanie, can you send three uniforms to interview Yo-Yo Reilly? We need him to account for every second of last night. The slightest problem, tell them to arrest him and bring him in. Oh, and warn them about the dogs.'

'I'll go with them,' Dawes said.

Alysha opened her front door and came face-to-face with a furious Mince. 'What d'you want?' she said in a low voice. 'Yo's here,' she warned.

Mince kicked the door back, pushed her out of the way and stormed into the flat.

If Yo-Yo was surprised it didn't show. 'Michael, my friend,' he greeted him. 'How's it goin', old son?'

Boot and Scrap both stood up quickly, but neither spoke.

'Bethany's been shanked,' Michael shouted. 'She's dead.'

Yo-Yo pushed Lucy away, but made no reply. He flicked a glance down at his ankle. Alysha followed his eyes. There was a bulge in his sock. He was strapped. He had a knife in there, or was it a pistol?

'What you know about it?' Michael shouted.

'I've just told you to fuck off,' Yo-Yo said.

'Have you killed my girl?'

Yo-Yo clicked his fingers at Boot. 'Get him out of here.'

Boot didn't move.

Alysha was furious. Mince had just referred to Bethany as his girl. She had the gun, that Yo-Yo had given her a while back, strapped in her knickers. She felt like shooting Mince herself.

Yo-Yo faced Michael. 'Are you asking to be shanked again? I'll happily oblige.' He kept his eyes on Michael as, quick as a whip-crack, he bent down and pulled a knife from his sock. There was a small bloodstain on it.

'Go ahead and try,' Michael said, looking from the knife to Yo-Yo. 'The odds ain't in your favour, loser.' He pulled a knife from his own waistband. 'There's three against one here,' he added, pulling his mouth into an ugly curve.

Yo-Yo looked across at Boot and Scrap. They both took a step, and stood beside Michael.

'Are you turning toerags?' His voice rose. 'Are you moving over to that scumbag? What? You ain't my bros no more? Is that it? You fucking toerags, both of you.'

Boot drew his knife. Yo-Yo grabbed Lucy again. He held the shaking girl in front of him, and pushed his razor-sharp knife against her throat.

Boot took a step towards Yo-Yo.

Alysha stepped in quickly. 'She's a fed,' she shouted. 'If you shank her, you'll never see daylight.'

Boot pulled his knife back.

Michael looked at Alysha. 'That right?'

'Yeah, that's right.'

Yo-Yo was dragging Lucy toward the door. 'Get out of my way,' he said to Boot and Scrap.

Michael stood to block their way.

'Don't,' Alysha urged Michael. 'Let them go,'

Suddenly Jade leapt at Yo-Yo. 'Let her go,' she said, hanging on to his arm. 'Don't hurt her, she's not part of all this.'

Yo-Yo tried to flick her off, but she clung on.

Quick as a flash he sank the knife into the top of her arm. She screamed and jumped back as blood welled out and ran down her arm.

'I'll kill her,' Yo-Yo warned, digging the knife against Lucy's throat again. 'Come on, Lysha, we're getting out of here. But I'll be back to even the score.'

'Do it,' Alysha shouted to Jade, throwing her a cushion to stop the bleeding.

Alysha looked from Mince to Yo-Yo.

'You ain't going with him?' Michael told her.

'Lysha!' Yo-Yo shouted as he got to the door. 'Come on. No one will dare take us on with her.'

Alysha stood still.

Yo-Yo tightened his grip on Lucy's neck. Lucy was gasping and her eyes were starting to close. Her head lolled to the side.

Alysha took a couple of steps towards Yo-Yo. 'Don't break her neck, stupid. You don't know your own strength.' She spat at Michael. 'That's for breaking my heart.'

Then she snatched up her mobile and followed Yo-Yo through the front door.

'Did you kill Bethany?' she asked him, checking over the wall for feds.

'Fuck off.'

She opened the fire escape to let them through, and ran ahead to keep a lookout over the side walls. Once she was sure they were safe, she turned to face him. 'You've got blood on your sock. Did you shank Bethany?'

'No,' he said to her. 'How many more times?'

Lucy was struggling. 'Please, you're hurting me.'

'Shut your fucking noise.'

'If I scream the whole of the Met will be here. Just let me go, and I won't say anything.'

Yo-Yo scraped the knife across her forearm. It drew a fine line of blood, like a raindrop running down a windscreen. She winced and a tear ran down the side of her nose.

'That's just a warning,' he growled. 'Fucking behave, will ya. I'll really hurt you if you don't. And we don't wanna hurt you, cos you're our ticket out of here, see. So we can't let you go.'

'My mum will get you for this.'

'I'm wetting me knickers, darling.'

'Did you kill that punter?' Alysha asked him again.

When he didn't answer she asked again, 'Who strangled Carly? I have to know, Yo, was it you?'

'You know full well it weren't.'

The temperature had dropped to near freezing, and as usual the lift wasn't working. Stephanie and Georgia set off up the thirteen flights to Alysha's flat. They had left Dawes with the uniformed officers outside Reilly's door. The dogs had barked and growled, but no one had answered their knocking.

There were lights but no sounds in Alysha's flat. Georgia knocked on the door. No one answered. She rapped harder. 'Police,' she shouted. 'Alysha, open up.'

It took nearly a minute before the chain rattled behind the door. Michael Delahaye opened it.

'Where's Alysha?' Georgia asked him.

'Don't know.'

'Is her father there?'

'No, he ain't.'

'Why are you here?'

'Her friend's been murdered. I came to see she was OK.'

'So, where is she?'

'She's gone out for a bit.'

'Gone out where?'

Delahaye shrugged.

Georgia took a deep breath. 'Can we come in and wait?'

'Have you got a warrant?'

'Do we need one?'

'No. Just asking.'

'No, we haven't.'

'Then you can't come in.' He closed the door in their faces.

Georgia turned to Stephanie. She was furious. 'What's going on there?'

Stephanie banged on the door. 'Lucy? Lucy, are you in there?'

No one answered.

'Could we have him for underage sex?' Georgia wondered.

'Alysha's not there.'

'So he says. But she might be. Something's going on. Indie 999 is on its way. That helicopter will see everything around the estate. If Lucy's with Jade or Alysha, they'll spot her. And if they don't, that means she's likely in one of the flats.' She paused thoughtfully. 'Make the call. Request a warrant. We need to get in there.'

'On what grounds?'

'Suspected underage sex.' Georgia stared at her. 'For Chrissake, Stephanie, who gives a shit on what grounds? Lucy could be in trouble in there.' She banged on the door and shouted again, 'Lucy, Lucy are you in there?'

There was only silence.

Stephanie pulled her phone from her pocket and started stabbing in numbers.

Georgia had a sudden urge to kill Dawes. If anything happened to Lucy, she promised herself she would. She pulled herself together; two of them in bits wouldn't help.

'Get a team of uniform standing by, outside this door,' she told Stephanie. 'Anyone that comes out, get them searched, and tell the team to go in if there is the slightest opportunity, and turn the place upside down.'

Georgia's mobile rang. It was DC Peacock telling her Wandsworth police were at Kate Solden's house, and the woman was completely inebriated. She had no idea her car was even missing, let alone how it had got to Brixton. In her current state, the woman couldn't have driven two yards. 'Lucy was right,' Georgia said. 'It's looking likely that Alice has driven her mother's car here. Apparently she's been learning on their private land.'

Stephanie was talking on her phone, arranging a warrant. Georgia had never seen her look so worried.

'That's Kate accounted for,' Georgia told her. 'So one down, and two to find.'

'Three,' Stephanie said. 'The killer, who has just claimed another victim, and is somewhere around here.' She flicked frightened eyes at Georgia. 'Like my daughter.'

SIXTEEN

Wednesday morning

'When did you use your shank?' Alysha asked. Yo-Yo was walking backward, dragging Lucy as quickly as his twenty-stone bulk could manage in the narrow space. He had one hand over her mouth; the other twisted her arm painfully up her back.

'Yo, when did you use your shank?' Alysha asked again.

He still didn't answer.

Alysha stopped. 'There's blood on your sock,' she said.

He turned his head. 'For fuck's sake, move it,' he said urgently. 'We need to get out of here.'

'Are you strapped?'

'Yeah. Now stop asking questions and move, will ya?'

Lucy started to struggle. Yo-Yo tightened his grip on her face, but quickly pulled his hand back as her teeth made contact with it. He smashed his fist into her mouth.

'Fucking pack it in!' he spat.

A loud rumble sounded overhead.

'It's a fucking copter,' Yo Yo growled. 'We've got to get to the car before that fucker spots us.'

'They're looking for her,' Alysha said. 'Let her go. That'll buy us time.'

'Bollocks. My car's in the road.' He jerked his head at the locked gate only a few yards away. 'Climb over. The bolt's on the other side. We'll make a dash for it.'

'Let her go first,' Alysha said defiantly. 'Then I will.'

'What's got into you? We'll let her go a mile down the road.'

'You killed Bethany, didn't you?'

'For fuck's sake!'

'Why?'

He let out an angry breath. 'I didn't. I fucking didn't, OK? Now shift for Chrissake, that copter's circling.'

Lucy jerked her head and pulled her mouth free, but she wasn't quick enough to scream. Yo-Yo's hand clamped back over her mouth, jarring her neck against him. He brought his knee up and landed it hard in her back. 'Don't rile my temper,' he shouted, shaking her like a rag doll.

She gagged.

'Puke on me and you'll fucking regret it! He wrenched her arm further up her back.

'Go easy, Yo,' Alysha urged him. She needed Lucy to tell the feds that she had tried to help.

Helicopter Indie 999 was co-piloted by Malcolm Hill. He used a telescope to scan the estate as they circled.

'Lots of activity down there,' he said to Norman, the pilot. 'Keep circling, but drop as low as we can.' He moved the telescope around. 'I can pick out heavy police presence, but no sign of girls.'

'They could be together, or alone,' Norman offered. 'The CID's daughter is slight and blonde apparently, and the other one is tall, dark hair with green and pink in it. Not that we'll see that from here, but they'll stand out if they're together.'

'So far I can only make out silhouetted figures, so get as low as you can.'

'It's a bastard of an estate,' Norman reminded him. 'Orders are not to drop too low – someone could be armed.'

'Yo, ease up on her,' Alysha said, using the situation to gain Lucy's confidence. The feds would thank her when Lucy told them she'd helped her get free of Yo-Yo.

She moved ahead and was about to climb the gate when she heard Lucy yell for help. She must have wriggled free again. The girl had guts, Alysha had to give her points for that. Yo-Yo's hand was over her mouth again, and he was kicking her hard in the legs. Her body started to buckle and slip but he held her by the face. Her eyes looked terrified.

'Yo, careful,' Alysha shouted. 'And you – keep quiet, for your own sake,' she barked at Lucy.

But Lucy wasn't listening. She lifted her knee in an attempt to fight back. But it was a futile fight. Blood dripped from her nose and lip, and Yo-Yo's other hand was on her throat. 'I'll take you unconscious, or dead if I have to,' he said. His temper had started to boil over. 'Now fucking shut your noise.'

'Go easy, for Chrissake,' Alysha called to him.

'Just climb the gate and let's get out of here.'

Alysha hoisted herself up and peeped over the top. The road was clear.

'Car's at the end of Tidal Lane,' Yo-Yo said.

'There's a couple of fed cars out there,' she lied, jumping down. 'Better move back against the wall, in case they come this way.'

She had this last card to play, then this territory would be hers. Yo and Mince would both rot in jail. 'I'm going out there,' she told him. 'I'll tell them I just saw Lucy over at the other block, so they'll drive off to find her. Then I'll open the gate, and we can make a run for it.'

She scrambled up the gate and swung her leg over. Sitting astride it, she looked down and said, 'You did kill Beth, Yo. That's new blood on your sock. You just killed her. Why d'you do that?'

Lucy's eyes cleared for a moment.

'She saw,' Yo-Yo said.

'Saw what? Saw you do the punter?' Alysha asked calmly.

'Yeah.'

A cold shiver ran down Alysha's spine. Lucy was listening to this. 'Why did ya do the punter, then?' she asked.

'He hurt you. I gave you to him, a while back. He beat you shitless, marked your face with his fists, remember?'

'And you killed him for that?'

'Yeah.'

'You must really love me then.'

'Yeah. Go and get rid of them feds,' he said impatiently. 'We need to get out of here.'

'You cut his dick off cos he hurt me?'

'I'll kill anyone who touches you.'

She wondered where else she had seen cold, calculating dark eyes like his, and realized it was in her own mirror.

'You got your gun on you?' she asked.

Yo-Yo nodded. She didn't tell him that hers was still safely tucked in her knickers. 'Carly saw you too, did she?'

He nodded. 'I weren't taking no chances.'

'Were you gonna kill Jade too?'

'Yes, I reckon I was.'

She looked at him for a moment. 'OK. Stay there. Don't come near the alley or you'll be seen. I'll get rid of these feds then I'll be back.'

She swung her leg over the gate and jumped down. Checking her gun was still in place, she broke into a sprint.

She ran flat out to the run-down garages a hundred yards or so down the road, then squatted, panting, and took out her phone.

She swiftly stabbed Georgia's number into it. Engaged. 'Shit,' she whispered desperately. There was so little time. Any second Yo would suss her, then she was dead meat.

She tried again. Still engaged!

It was dark, but she could text in any light. She speedily tapped a message with nervous fingers, added Stephanie Green's number, then pressed Send.

The message said Michael had taken over her flat and was holding Alice hostage, that he'd had tried to have sex with both her and Alice. Let him try and get out of that. Jade would back her up, especially if she promised to take her into the new gang as a high soldier.

Georgia's phone rang on her next attempt. Alysha was good at sounding like she was crying. 'Yo-Yo's got Lucy,' she said. 'He killed the punter. Bethany and Carly too, he's admitted it, and now he says he's going to kill Lucy. I'm by the old garages. Please hurry.'

'We're on our way.'

'Mince is in my flat. He's got Jade. Alice. He tried to rape me. I managed to text Stephanie. He's . . .'

She clicked off, and just managed to stop herself laughing. She stood up. No one was around. She had about a minute before all hell broke loose.

Reilly's flat wasn't far from the old garages. Dawes was still outside when his mobile rang. Georgia brought him up to speed, and he turned and started running toward the garages.

Georgia sped along the walkway with Stephanie right behind her. About thirty uniformed police clumped past them carrying the red enforcer. They had orders to break down the door of Alysha's flat, arrest Michael Delahaye and save Alice Solden from being raped.

Indie 999 sounded like a low thunderclap as it descended. Alysha looked up at it, then ran back towards the gate before it reached the ground. She slipped the bolt and joined Yo-Yo in the alley.

'What kept you?' he said, looking up as the helicopter was starting to descend.

'The feds,' she said breathlessly.

He started to drag the terrified Lucy toward the gate. 'Let's go,' he urged.

The other side of the gate he came face-to-face with David Dawes. They all stopped dead.

'Help us,' Alysha pleaded to Dawes, summoning up more artificial tears. 'He's going to make off in his car and take Lucy. He killed Carly and Beth and that punter.'

Yo-Yo looked at Alysha, and the penny dropped. He stared at her, pure astonishment on his face.

Dawes had his radio to his mouth. 'All units Tidal Lane, go, go, go. Lucy Green is hostage to Yo-Yo Reilly.'

He stepped in front of Yo-Yo. 'Game's up,' he said. 'A hundred police are heading this way. Let her go.'

Yo-Yo's eyes were on Alysha.

Dawes raised his voice. 'Let her go. Now.'

Yo-Yo was still looking at Alysha. 'You? A fucking fed licker? I never thought I'd see that day.' He bent and reached for the pistol in his sock, shouting at Dawes, 'And you can fuck off. I'm leaving and she's coming with me.'

The helicopter landed in the middle of the road, blocking his path. He started to drag Lucy. 'Keep out of my way,' he shouted loudly. 'Anyone comes near me, I'll shoot the bitch.'

*   *   *

'Did you get that?' Georgia turned back to Stephanie. 'Dawes is with Lucy. Step on it, for Chrissake, Steph. Run!'

For the first time in her life Stephanie sprinted. She overtook Georgia, down the stairs, and headed for the old garages.

Patrol cars screeched from all directions and pulled up sharply in Tidal Lane.

Keeping his eyes pinned on Dawes, Reilly bent Lucy at a painful angle and pulled his gun from its ankle strap. He pushed the barrel into the side of her head.

'Yo, don't!' Alysha shouted.

'Tell that fucking copter to move,' Reilly said to Dawes. 'I don't make threats I don't see through. I will kill her.'

Malcolm Hill had seen Reilly pull the gun. He was on the radio to CO19 for armed back-up.

More sirens wailed as patrol cars screeched up the road and blocked it, waiting for further orders.

'Let her go,' Dawes said.

Yo-Yo's gun was still aimed at Lucy's temple. He reached into his pocket and pulled out a knife. 'One step nearer,' he warned Dawes, 'and I'll take you both.'

Alysha stepped towards Yo-Yo.

'Stay back,' Dawes warned.

'Reilly, you're surrounded,' Dawes said calmly. 'Drop the gun, and let Lucy go.'

'Tell the flying mosquito to move,' came the reply. 'I'm going to my car. Anyone attempts to stop me, I'll slice your pretty young fed's face. And that's just for starters.'

Alysha was delighted that her plan was going so well. Yo-Yo would go down for three life sentences minimum after this, and Lucy would say that Alysha tried to help her. She had sorted Mince Delahaye too. The two-timing bastard would be done for kidnap of underage girls, and attempted rape. That carried a long sentence too. She would come out of all this smelling of roses, and she would be rich and powerful.

'Don't, Yo, please,' she said, pretending to cry. 'You've already killed the other girls. Don't hurt Lucy, I'm begging you.'

She edged a bit nearer. Yo-Yo turned the gun in her direction.

'Alysha, for Chrissake step away!' Dawes's tone verged on hysterical.

'I ain't killed no one,' Yo-Yo shouted toward Alysha. 'Are you trying to grass me up or something?'

'Lucy heard you,' Alysha shouted back, ignoring the danger. 'You said you shanked Beth, strangled Carly, and you done the punter. She heard you, Lucy heard you say it.'

'I ain't killed no one!' He cocked the gun.

Dawes grabbed Alysha and pushed her behind him. Uniformed officers jumped out of their cars and stood ready.

'You son of a fucking bitch,' Dawes shouted at Yo-Yo. 'You're going nowhere. Let her go.'

Yo pulled Lucy in front of his body as a shield, and started edging sideways toward his car. 'Get the fucking mosquito out of my way,' he ordered.

Georgia and Stephanie ran up the road toward them, with thirty-plus officers in pursuit. Alysha dropped her hand down into her knickers and pulled her own gun out.

She lifted it and aimed at Yo-Yo's head. 'Let Lucy go, or I swear I'll shoot you,' she shouted.

Yo-Yo slowed and turned to face her, still holding Lucy as a shield.

'You ain't got the bottle,' he taunted, swaying Lucy in front of him. 'Go on then, kill the fed and get yourself locked up for life.'

'Alysha, drop that gun,' Dawes shouted. 'Now.'

She cocked the gun and took aim.

'Alysha!' Georgia screamed.

Dawes took a step towards her. 'Don't!' he shouted.

Yo-Yo fired. The bullet hit Dawes in the shoulder and he tumbled to the ground.

Alysha didn't waste the chance. She fired off a round of bullets.

'Luceeeeeee!' Stephanie shrieked, struggling against the arms that held her back.

But Yo-Yo had taught Alysha well. She knew exactly how to aim and hit her target. Her first bullet hit his shoulder. The next entered his head, the third his heart, then his spleen, his stomach, and finally his eye.

Dawes had managed to scramble clear. Lucy somehow found the strength to run to her mother's waiting arms.

Yo-Yo lay on the ground, blood pooling around him like an overflowing drain. Bubbles leaked from his mouth, and his own gun lay limply in his hand.

Alysha stood over him. 'I warned you not to mess with me,' she said. His hand twitched, then became still, and his remaining eye closed.

Lucy sobbed as Stephanie hugged her close. Dawes was helped to his feet by two uniformed officers, while a third called for an ambulance. Georgia walked over to Alysha and held her hand out for the gun. Alysha handed it to her.

And CO19 roared up the road, minutes too late.

Georgia began to read Alysha her rights.

'You are joking,' the girl cut in. 'I deserve a medal. I just saved Lucy's life.'

Lucy half-turned towards them. 'She did. She saved my life. She helped me, Georgia.'

'We'll see about that.' Georgia completed the caution. 'Get in the car,' she said flatly to Alysha.

'I told you about Mince Delahaye, too,' Alysha protested. 'He had Alice. You did get him, didn't you?'

'Yes, we've got him too,' Georgia told her. 'But you're still under arrest. You were in possession of a firearm, and you've just shot a man in cold blood.'

She clicked handcuffs on Alysha.

'In self-defence,' Alysha and Lucy said in unison.

SEVENTEEN

Ten days later

T he case was almost finished. When the last of the witness statements emerged from the copying machine, all Georgia had to do was incorporate them into her report and present them to the CPS for their decision.

All the forensic reports were back. The hand print on Bethany Field's door was a match for Yo-Yo Reilly; so was the hair on her neck wound. A fibre on her cheek matched the hooded sweatshirt Reilly was wearing that night too. There was no doubt he had killed her. Lucy's statement said she had heard him admit to Alysha Achter that he murdered not only Bethany, but Carly MacIntosh and Tom Solden too, and that he also threatened to kill Alice, and herself. Alysha Achter's statement said the same.

Since Reilly was dead, the CPS's main decision would be what to charge Alysha Achter with. They had taken a statement from both Alysha and Jade who were accusing Michael Delahaye of attempting underage sex with them, two minors, and he would be sure to go down for a long stretch. Lucy was adamant that Alysha was innocent, and had acted in self-defence. Alysha had told them Yo-Yo bullied her into hiding a gun for him. She kept it in her knickers because nowhere in her flat was safe, and she had only taken it out and fired it when she thought he might shoot Lucy – and hadn't she been lucky not to hit anybody else? Georgia thought that would probably keep her out of prison, but they still had to await the CPS's decision. She really hoped that Alysha would get off lightly. She felt the girl was one of life's victims.

Raucous wolf-whistles made her turn her head. Stephanie had just walked in, giving the whistlers the finger. Georgia blinked. Stephanie was wearing a vivid violet shirt over green corduroy trousers. Around her neck was paisley scarf in electric pink, yellow and mauve, tied in a large bow. Her usually lank hair swung around her shoulders, brushed and shiny. The look was finished with full make-up including too much shiny strawberry-pink lip-gloss, and a pair of flowered earrings any pub landlady would kill for. Georgia fought a smile as Steph headed towards her.

Georgia dug into her shoulder bag for the crumpled fifty-pound note she had stowed there until her bet with Stephanie was won. She handed it over and lowered her voice. 'I hope the wait was worth it.'

Stephanie took the note and shook her head. 'No,' she said, stony-faced. 'Not even taking into account the shoulder wound.' She checked no one else could hear, then added, 'The earth did not move. Hardly even a tremor.'

Georgia tried not to laugh. Same old, same old, she thought. Stephanie's conquests followed an inevitable pattern. This time she was relieved. Dawes was finally out of her sergeant's head. Yo-Yo Reilly was dead, so he could move on. He had patronized and pressurized Georgia throughout the investigation, and the worst of it was he was right. But Dawes put every crime on that estate down to Reilly; for once it had paid off.

It was his manner that enraged Georgia. She had been appointed senior investigating officer on the case, and he had shown not an ounce of respect for her. She was sorry he got shot, but she had little sympathy; if he had followed orders and waited for armed back-up it would never have happened.

His secondment was over, thankfully, and she wouldn't have to work with him again. Stephanie had slept with him, so Dawes was about to be history.

Stephanie put the fifty pounds in her purse and popped a piece of bubblegum in her mouth. Diet time again. What was that about, Georgia wondered, and why had she come to work dressed up to the nines?

Georgia picked up the last of the witness statements from the tray. It was Nigel Jones's, explaining the series of coincidences that led to the motorbike being parked overnight only yards from where the murders happened. The man who bought the bike from him had made everything clear; his girlfriend lived in Tidal Lane, and he spent more nights with her than in his own Tulse Hill flat. Coincidences do happen all the time, but this one had sent Georgia looking completely the wrong way in a triple murder case.

Dawes had ignored all the information coming in about the bike and the Solden family, and had focused solely on Reilly. Normally Georgia would have commended someone in her team for sticking to their instincts, especially when they turned out to be right, but no way was she going to congratulate Dawes. He had been responsible for putting ideas into young Lucy's head, ideas that put her young life at risk.

Once Stephanie had recovered from the shock, she said it was the best training Lucy could ask for; if that hadn't put her off going into the force, nothing would. But Lucy could have been killed; Georgia knew that and Stephanie knew it too, and that was her way of justifying it to herself. She had a feeling Steph had only gone on pursuing Dawes to prove a point – and possibly to win the fifty quid.

The good news was that Lucy still wanted to join CID after university. No one was more delighted than Georgia.

She had made an official complaint to DCI Banham about Dawes, and hoped he would take it further. She doubted he would; Dawes and Banham went back too far. She might have to console herself with the fact Dawes was going back to his own station, his mission to get even with Reilly for the death of his sister accomplished.

She put Nigel Jones's statement in the file, and studied the one from Alysha Achter. The girl could be charged with possession of a firearm, and possibly even manslaughter. Both crimes could put her in a Young Offenders Institution, but Alysha had no previous convictions, and Lucy would speak up for her in court; Georgia was confident she would get off with a suspended sentence or probation. Alysha needed parental guidance, not prison.

She put the statement back in the file, and reminded herself for the umpteenth time that Alysha wasn't her problem.

Stephanie was still good-naturedly fielding jibes from members of the team. 'How is his shoulder, by the way?' she asked her.

Stephanie shrugged. 'He won't be able go boxing for a few months, and he'll be on desk duty for a while, but no serious harm.' She laughed raucously. 'The shagging didn't do it a lot of good,' she said. 'About as much as it did for me.'

Georgia was still trying to work out why Stephanie was dressed up and on the chewing gum. There had to be someone else, she thought: someone in the department. She opened her mouth to ask, but Steph spoke first.

'Lucy's putting in her application for a full-time post this morning,' she said.

Georgia beamed. 'She'll make a great detective. And I'll write her a brilliant reference.'

'Thanks, I appreciate that.'

'My pleasure.' There was a pause, and then Georgia said, 'So, not great in bed then?'

'Who?'

'Oh, come on. It was only last night.'

'Yes, it was,' Steph laughed. 'But I got a lot of sleep, so it could have been a year ago.'

'Unmemorable then?'

'Very. No great technique, and terrible timing.'

Georgia laughed and then paused. 'So why are you so dressed up?' she asked, lowering her voice.

'I've got my eye on someone,' Steph winked. 'If you must know.'

'Yes, I must,' Georgia said. She liked to keep in touch with the station gossip, even though she never got involved. 'Obviously someone in the station?'

'Correct.' Stephanie nodded.

'So, who?'

Steph lowered her voice. 'Banham.'

Georgia blinked. 'You are kidding?'

'Why not? He's a widower, isn't he?'

Georgia nodded. 'Yes, but he's totally besotted with that DI Alison Grainger. He talked about her all the time when he came out with me on a couple of interviews.'

'A bit of competition's healthy,' Stephanie shrugged. 'Did he mention his wife?

'No.' That wasn't exactly true; Banham had told her his wife had been murdered many years ago, along with his eleven-month-old baby girl. But Georgia wouldn't break a confidence, even to Stephanie. 'I won't put fifty pounds on that one, if it's all the same to you,' she said.

'I need coffee,' Steph said, heading for the new machine. 'And you need a chocolate muffin.'

A few minutes later Banham appeared in the doorway. 'Johnson and Green, a word.'

Georgia stood up. 'Guv,' she nodded, and raised a hand to Stephanie, who was hurrying back armed with coffee and goodies. She handed Georgia a cardboard cup of latte and a blueberry muffin and they made their way to the end of the corridor.

David Dawes, his arm in a sling, was in the chair next to Banham's. The DCI gestured for the women to sit down.

Georgia pulled up a chair, half an eye on Stephanie. She and Dawes were avoiding each other's eyes.

'As you know,' Banham began, 'Detective Inspector Dawes was seconded here to lend us his expertise, and to help solve the murder of Tom Solden. The case could easily have dragged on. DI Johnson and I were looking in totally the wrong direction.'

Georgia's eyes flared angrily. She flicked a glance at Stephanie; she obviously felt the same. 'Sir, I was following . . .' she started.

Banham put his hand up and continued. 'We are indebted to David for his help in bringing the case to a rightful and speedy close.'

Georgia was furious. She had done her job properly, gathering information and examining all possibilities. Ninety per cent of murders were committed by someone the victim knew; that was an elementary lesson of murder investigations, and as it turned out Alice Solden was closely involved. OK, so Dawes had been right, but more by luck than judgement. Banham hadn't even mentioned the way he had put the life of an inexperienced work-placement trainee in grave danger.

She caught Dawes's patronizing look and returned it with an icy stare.

'I think DI Johnson did an excellent job as SIO,' Stephanie said, looking Banham in the eye. 'And in my opinion, Detective Inspector Dawes was completely blinkered. He didn't look at the evidence, and he didn't take any new information into account. All he did was follow Stuart Reilly's movements right through the investigation.'

'That's because Reilly was behind everything that happened on that estate.' Dawes spoke slowly, as if she was five years old. He turned back to Banham, as if he was dismissing Stephanie. 'Reilly was the worst of his kind. Possibly the worst we've had to deal with since gang warfare started.'

'It's poor policing . . .' Georgia began.

Banham raised his hand. 'Nevertheless,' he said, 'Dawes was right. Reilly was our murderer, and now he has been stopped. His reign of terror is over.'

'Someone else will take over his territory,' Dawes said in the same know-all tone.

'That won't be your problem,' Stephanie snapped. 'It'll be ours.'

'Which brings us to why I called you all in here,' Banham said.

Georgia and Stephanie fell silent.

'As you know, for a while . . .' Banham paused; his throat seemed to close up. He coughed to clear it, and started again. 'As you know, DI Alison Grainger has been away on compassionate leave, and we've been a DI down for some time.'

Georgia caught Stephanie's eye and held her breath.

'DI Dawes has put in a written application for that position.'

Georgia was speechless. Stephanie's ruddy complexion paled.

Banham watched them. 'I wanted to call you all in together. I know, like me, you would both like to welcome David to the team.'

Neither woman said a word.

'David and I go back many years,' Banham continued. 'His father was my commanding officer when I first started in the force. Speaking personally, I would be honoured to work alongside him.'

Georgia and Stephanie remained stone-faced.

'However,' Banham continued, 'I am sorry to say that won't be happening.'

Georgia noticed Stephanie sit up straight. She had recently passed her DI exam and the board; the post could be on the cards for her. She was a great detective, although since she hadn't been a sergeant long, it would be surprising if she did get it. Still, Georgia was hoping.

They all waited for Banham to go on.

He looked from one to the other and then his face broke into a wide smile. 'Detective Inspector Grainger is coming back,' he announced.

Stephanie sank into her chair. A double blow for her ego; she would need cheering up Georgia thought. She would take her to the eat-all-you-can pizza restaurant for lunch. Stephanie would certainly eat all she could, now DCI Banham was out of bounds.

So the future wouldn't be so bad. Dawes was leaving, and Banham would be happy again. OK, DI Grainger would get all the best cases, but Georgia would get a lot more freedom. Stephanie would be OK too. Georgia knew only too well it wouldn't be long before her sights were set on someone else.

Georgia's mind wandered to Alysha Achter. What did the future hold for her? How would the thirteen-year-old fare if she got off with a suspended sentence and a new gang formed on the estate? There was a big drug business around there and a lot of gang leaders would go to war over it. Alysha would still be at risk.

Georgia decided to keep a discreet eye on her. If she could make a friend of her, not only would it fill her own maternal void, but she could also keep up to date with what was happening on the Aviary estate: a big bonus for the murder unit, and one in the eye for David Dawes. She would probably be competing with Dawes in a year or two, when the next DCI post came up; when that happened she'd show him exactly what she was made of. She was Georgia Johnson, a broken girl who rebuilt her life after a horrendous rape, and became stronger. She had vowed when she was fifteen that no man would ever get the better of her again, and she sure as hell was going to keep that promise to herself.

Disappointment was written all over Dawes's face. Hers broke into a smile. He hadn't got one up on her, and she'd make sure that it stayed that way. Sorry as she was for Stephanie, she was delighted Alison Grainger was coming back.

ACKNOWLEDGEMENTS

There are always so many people that a book would never happen without, so thank you to every person that has been a part of the dotting of an i that I forgot to dot, or given technical advice that I had to find out to make the story credible – I am deeply grateful to you all, because I know the book wouldn't have been as good without your help.

I would, very sincerely, like to thank everyone at Severn House, including the editors, the admin, the designers, and the publicity, and everyone else there for your support and individual talent.

I would also like to go on my knees and salute the kindness of the many, many, police people (some don't mind being named, and others do), and with that in mind I have kept you all undercover! You know who you are, and I truly appreciate your wisdom and time. THANK YOU for keeping this book up to date and my police procedural correct. Any mistakes are my own doing.

A big thank you to the Boater Brigade, for, as ever, keeping me going, with food and fun and frolics when I hit the low points.

Finally, and as always, I want to thank my wonderful husband for making very good cups of tea, and taking our little dog Millie out for her walks, dressed in her trendy, woolly pink coat, when I didn't have the time to do it. You are simply THE BEST!